the guilt of arthur finchley

the guilt of arthur finchley

Richard McCarthy

Copyright © 2015 Timothy R. Moore

All rights reserved. This book or any portion thereof may not be reproduced or used in any manner whatsoever without the express written permission of the publisher except for the use of brief quotations in a book review or scholarly journal.

First Printing: 2015
with CreateSpace

ISBN-13:978-1508644088
ISBN-10:150864408X

Made in Sheffield

www.rchrdmccrthy.com

For Sarah

one

The landscape drifted quickly past in the grey dawn light, the fence posts a stuttering blur. The sound of the car echoed back from them as a pulse; whispering.

—Don't you know? Louise had said from the bed. Her skull showed through the stretched thin skin, webbed with veins, haloed with the faint remains of hair.

—What? He had said, stood holding the tray, distracted, the shirt over his arm.

The road entered woodland. Tall, dark conifers shrouded out the bleak morning sky. He should have walked away. Shut the door on her. Not listened.

—I thought you knew. I've fucked a lot of men behind your back.

Below the roar of the tyres he could still hear her voice, cracked, persistent, churning out names and times, the betrayal dribbling painfully forth.

Even Bob Krigelow? He thought. Even him? After she took such fucking joy in getting him to resign? Him?

—Of course. Her voice whispered in his ear. —Why wouldn't I? If I could fuck an ugly shit like you, why not Bob as well?

The road burst out into open fields again. Looking out across them, he knew that he could just twitch the wheel and be through the fence and into the mud, a rolling, rutted ocean, a November sea, where wars had been fought and bodies buried. He wanted to plunge the car into it, sink deep beneath its surface, never finding the bottom.

The tyres thudded over the lane dividers. He flinched, jerking the car left, then correcting, swaying and snaking, oncoming headlights bright and quick. His veins stung, his heart thumped. He allowed himself to exhale. A cold trickle of sweat crawled down his side.

—You're a useless idiot. She whispered.

He focused on the road and tried to breathe steadily. Glancing in the mirror, he saw Ben, smiling from the back seat, rolling a cigarette.

Peter shook his head. —You knew this was coming, didn't you?

But the back seat was empty: Ben long dead. Peter sighed.

At the next turning, he followed the road between thick fir trees to a square of four seven-story Neo-Georgian buildings around a squat, central hub. Beyond the trees was a retail park: the warehouse-sized shops and restaurants blank and uniform, bright logos standing out against the grey. The office complex had originally housed several different companies, but over time they had been swallowed up by the Midlands' office of The Safe Atoll Insurance and Investment Company. —Keeping your money safe; your future sunny! Peter drove around the central building, sunlight glinting from its tall windows, and parked on the far side.

When he turned off the engine, the silence swamped over him, filling the air with faint voices and accusations. He sat there, staring into nothing for a while, waiting for everything to settle, all the shards that were floating around him, glittering in the thin air of autumn.

Keep busy, keep your mind off it. He told himself. Work. Do a good job. Think about the appointment later on.

Getting out, he smelt the sweet mix of pine resin and car fumes, swirling together in the drizzle. He pulled on his waterproof jacket and picked up the heavy laptop case from the back seat. When he slammed the door, it echoed round the buildings, returning faintly, mournfully.

Where's my card? He thought, walking quickly over to the central building. Where's my fucking card? His hands fluttered over his coat and jacket pockets, reaching in, fingers searching. Oh shit! No, I haven't, have I? Shit! He stopped. I can't go back for it: too far, all the way back there, with her upstairs, listening, waiting.

He got to the glass door and peered in, looking for the receptionist. Shit! She's not there. Shit. Shit! Shit!

The wind flicked a spray of drizzle into his face, making him blink. He pulled out his phone and stared at it. Who might be in at seven-thirty? Telephony?

He rehearsed the conversation, explaining what had happened, hearing the laughter already.

—You always fuck things up, don't you? Said Louise. —You always find a way. Go on! Lose your temper! Kick the door in, you know you want to!

He scrolled hurriedly through names. I need someone discreet, he thought. Someone who can keep a secret.

In the white light of the screen, he noticed something glint between his coat and his suit.

Oh, for fuck's sake…

He yanked the card up to the sensor, the lanyard hurting his neck. There was a beep and a click, and Peter barged through the door, hands clenching and twitching.

Ahead of him, at the end of the short corridor, were the doors to the canteen, their two round, unblinking windows looking back at him. A shape darkened the glass and a red-haired woman pulled open the doors, holding a paper bag and coffee. The wine-coloured paper poppy pinned to her jumper had curled and creased. She smiled at him, her mouth spread wide and curled. But as she passed him, he caught her face relaxing, falling.

—I've deceived you too. Said Louise, lying in bed.

There was a clash of metal from inside the canteen.

—I've lied to you so much, I can't remember what's true anymore.

Peter stopped at the doors. There was another loud crash and someone laughed.

He turned, went down the branching corridor a few feet, and pushed open the toilet door, wafting out the smell of stale urine.

I need to keep busy today, he thought, checking for shoes and ankles under the cubicle doors. Keep my mind off things, concentrate on work, get through the day.

And at three PM? What should I do then?

He straightened with a grunt, went into the left-hand cubicle, and slid across the rattling lock.

But now, he thought, I need to start by getting the On-Boarding quarterly figures off the R-Drive.

Staring straight ahead, he unzipped.

I'll get the data sample from them. Then I can build the spreadsheet up, slowly reading and copying data over, assigning reasons, etcetera.

He stared down into the toilet.

Just the thing for today: get me through to three without having to think too much.

He stood still, nothing happening, staring at the pipe leading down from the cistern above him.

What's likely to come up? Broker error, I'll bet. Maybe a fair bit to do with On-Boarding as well. Jane won't like that, me saying her team are making mistakes.

He thought about his own pipes, deep inside him, relaxing, opening, the water flowing down through him in a warm rush, pouring to the outside.

Urine tinkled into the pan below.

I'll have to word it carefully, so as to not cause offence.

Point out it's not so bad. Always have to tip-toe around these things, as though you're walking on a thin crust of lava: stamp too hard and you'll get burned. He imagined the conference table being thumped, angry voices and pointing. His veins ached with adrenaline.

He shook and zipped up. Leaning forward, he pushed the flush button and stared down at the instant whirlpool.

No. If I want this to work, I have to keep Jane on my side. Makes things so much easier. He pictured Jane smiling at him, her short hair revealing the smooth skin of her neck, her jumper tight around her bust and belly.

He clicked open the door and strode to the sinks, in front of the wall-width mirror. Looking up, he tried to see Jane stood next to him, her hand in his. He clenched the case handle tighter. He saw the bend of his nose, the asymmetry of his skull. His right eye sat solid and unmoving in its socket. And behind him, peeking round his shoulder, blinked Louise, her face grinning, lips pulled back from teeth. He shook his head and set the laptop down, turning on the hot tap.

He scrubbed his hands in the tepid water.

Shame, really. Every time I've thought about Jane, her warm flesh, her stomach under that jumper, the small of her back... I've always felt guilty. He laughed. Ridiculous.

And there was Sarah, her back to me, typing, bra straps showing through her blouse. And the guilt, just from looking? I could have slept with her, with Jane, with most of the women in the office and not felt guilty. What was I actually guilty of? What did I have to agonise about? I would go home and barely be able to speak for the guilt. And there she was, fucking half the men she met, never losing sleep!

He leant on the sides of the sink, staring down into the running water, feeling nauseas. His mouth was wet with saliva. He spat into the basin and watched the stringy spit swirl round and down into the plughole.

Didn't even brush my teeth this morning. Just dressed

and left. He pushed a finger into his mouth and rubbed it vigorously over his teeth. It came away tinged with blood. He stared at it, then sighed and rinsed his finger. Forty years old, he thought, everything's falling apart.

Looking in the mirror, he could see his father staring back at him. Tilting his head to one side and half closing his eyes, he mimicked his earliest memory of him, imagining the tubes coming out of his nose and mouth, concentrating only on the eyes.

—Petey? Love? Come give mummy a cuddle!

He had been four years old when the call came. He got up from his toys on the living room carpet and went through to the kitchen.

—That was the shipping company... They're... they're bringing your daddy home. Yes they are. They left Chile last week, and that's... a long way away, Petey. Do you remember when we showed you on the map? His tiny little ship has to sail over the big, wide, blue Atlantic? But... they're working hard to get him home. Really hard. So don't you worry yourself, eh, love?

And she kissed him on the forehead and smoothed down his hair.

Over the next two weeks, Peter and his mother played at 'Daddy Coming Home' and imagined a speedboat coming crashing over the waves. Peter would run around the house and the backyard, or his mother would carry him and he would have to lie as still as he could while she whirled him through the air. Their games would end when his mother would collapse onto a chair and breath noisily, her face in her hands.

On the morning his father was due, Peter and his mother were at the harbour in the bright early sunshine. The immense scale of everything terrified him. He remembered the boats towering above him, the ropes bigger and thicker than he was. A man in a suit talked to his mother, pointing to a ship coming slowly, slowly in, a point of shining steel on the morning surface of the sea.

His mother clenched his hand very tightly. When the boat had slid to the dockside, two men came trudging down the gangway with a heavy stretcher between them. They all got into an ambulance and rumbled off. Peter hid his face from the being on the bed, who was grey and coughed weakly into its gas mask.

At the hospital, the stretcher was unloaded and they followed it through corridor after corridor. It was pulled into a room and the door closed. He and his mother had to sit outside. There was a lot of clattering and talking and hissing of snakes and the thing in bed kept coughing. Peter was very scared and made his mother take him to the toilet several times. There he felt safe.

Finally a man in a long white coat came out and said they could see the grey thing. So Peter, terrified, was dragged into the room. And there, waiting, lying on his back, his head lolled over to one side on the white pillow, tubes up his nose and down his throat, was his father. The eyes looked at Peter, who screamed.

Over the next month and a half, Peter got used to seeing his father like that. Gradually, the tubes were removed, his father began to sit up more, and then would shuffle around the ward when they visited. Eventually, he came home and suddenly the house was full of his father: his toothbrush in the bathroom, his clothes on the washing line, his plate and mug on the drying rack, his deep voice vibrating through the walls. The armchair in the living room became his father's chair, not to be used by Peter. Home life was irrevocably changed, everything turned upside down, twisted and bent around him. And yet it carried on.

He looked at the broken blood vessels in his left eye. Should he talk to Jane about the project? He didn't need her permission. He'd told her in an email what the schedule was.

His father was forty when he died.

The thought made his fingers drop away from his eye.

He tried to remember his father's fortieth birthday party, but couldn't.

—Mind yourself. Parked down here.

Peter trailed behind Mr Beaumont, their next-door neighbour, noting the weeds growing up along the path leading out of college. The sun was bright and hot for September.

—Let's get you home. Said Mr Beaumont. —Then your mum can tell you what's going on. Best coming from her.

As they passed a classroom window, Peter saw faces looking out at him, open-mouthed. They looked abstract; floating in the window. He glowed hot under their gaze and became conscious of his walk. Mr Beaumont stooped slightly to put his face on a level with Peter's.

—Y'know, it's alright to be sad, sometimes. He said, quietly. —You don't have to strut like that, not for me. My son is sixteen as well, same age as you; you and him are mates, aren't you? Well, I know what he's like at this age, what all you lads are like: not boys any more, but not quite men. Well, take it from me, the worst thing you could do is to act tough because you think you ought to, that will get you nowhere, believe me.

He pointed down the road. —'Fraid I brought the panda car. Hope that won't embarrass you in front of your friends back there?

As they turned and walked along the main road, they entered the shade of trees. Peter felt their chill. He had been shoplifting, just a few packets of sweets, but it was enough. Theft is theft, he thought, and I've been caught, and now I'm going to be punished. Beneath the worry of what his mum and dad were going to say, there was a sense of relief, the weight of hiding lifted from him.

When Mr Beaumont got him home, he was ushered inside to the living room. Sitting in his father's armchair was a female police officer, her hat in her hands, fingers plucking at the brim. His mother sat on the sofa, her face red-streaked with crying. They both looked up at him. He stood there, being looked at. Mr Beaumont gently laid a hand on Peter's shoulder.

—I think you maybe want to sit next to your mum.

Peter sat down on the edge of the sofa, looking at the TV set in the corner. He could see the four of them, grey and bent in the glass's curve.

—Sylvia? Said Mr Beaumont. —I think he'd be better off hearing it from you.

This was not how he thought it would go.

—Sylvia?

He felt his mother's fingers clutch at his t-shirt, trembling, pulling. She shuffled forward, wrapping her arms around him. He could smell brandy and... something bitter and sweet, like vomit.

—It's your dad. She whispered.

And he knew, suddenly, with a roaring in his ears, what was going on. His mother broke into sobs, leaning on his shoulder.

After a long while of no-one saying anything, Mr Beaumont cleared his throat.

—Come on Sylvia. Let's get this over with.

She nodded and got up, dabbing at her face.

Mr Beaumont took her elbow and led her out the door.

After they left, the policewoman smiled at Peter.

—What are you doing at school? She said.

—College.

—Sorry?

—I'm at college. Not school.

She pressed her lips together and looked down at her hat.

—That's my dad's chair.

She looked behind her, then shuffled awkwardly forward, to the edge of the seat.

—And your cup there? He pointed at the cold tea by her foot. —That's his best china. He brought it back from Hong Kong.

She picked up the cup and saucer.

—It's beautiful.

—He was in the Merchant Navy.

—Really? So was my father! She turned the cup round. —Our house was full of all the nick-naks he brought back. Always a present for us when he came home. I suppose you got that with your dad?

—No, not really. I only really remember him getting pneumonia. He didn't go back to sea after that.

—My dad retired as well, a good few years back. He does bingo-calling now.

She rested the china delicately on top of her hat.

—It'll sink in soon, y'know. She said, softly.

He looked at her stockinged knees.

—My mum died a few years back, dropped dead in a supermarket. Brain embolism. I was like you when I was told: didn't know what to think, didn't know how to feel. Just couldn't believe it. Didn't want to believe it. But it sank in eventually. She looked down into the cup. —When it does, it won't be pleasant: you may find yourself doing some pretty odd things. But don't worry, it's only grief, it's perfectly natural. Just let it happen, and move on. That's important, the moving on. But always remember your dad, remember the good times, you know? Forget all the arguments and what-not, remember him when he was at his best, yeah?

He twisted his fingers round each other, the knuckles strained white.

When his mother came home she was pale and quiet, but not crying anymore.

Mr Beaumont took Peter into the kitchen and gently told him what had happened.

As the two police left, Mr Beaumont assured Sylvia that he was only next-door and, with her permission, he would tell Margaret, his wife, what had happened, so that she could pop by, just to help out, if they wanted, would that be OK? Sylvia nodded, swinging the door shut on him.

She walked over to the drinks cabinet and poured herself a brandy from the bottle stood on the side.

—It was him alright. She said. —Laid out like that.

She gulped the drink down. —It's bollocks, you know, when they say that they look asleep. He didn't. He looked dead! He looked like a lifeless wax dummy!

Peter stood behind his father's armchair, his shaking hands holding the headrest. Leaning slightly, he breathed in the old cigarettes and cologne, mingled with ammonia from the tiling grout and the sweet vinegar of silicone caulk.

She sipped her drink and stared out of the window.

—They made me sign a form, to say it was him. I thought: what if I don't sign it? Does that mean it isn't him?

She laughed, and took another drink.

—Selfish bastard. Typical of him, isn't it?

She looked at Peter, then down at the armchair. She shook her head and up-ended the glass. She went back over to the cabinet.

—Come on, you look white as a sheet! I expect you could use a small one of these, couldn't you?

Pulling out another glass, she poured a small measure and handed it to Peter.

—You know, you look just like him. Spitting image of when he was young. He was a handsome man.

She glazed over, staring at the window. Peter sipped his brandy.

—I met him when he was, what? Twenty-one? Nineteen sixty-eight. There was a bonfire on a patch of old waste ground. He was there, his skin all brown, still in summer clothes from… where had he been? Singapore? Somewhere down that way. He had no winter clothes. A couple of us took pity on him and gave him some warm things: a scarf, a hat, a duffel coat. He said he'd bring them back, but I heard nothing for a week. Turned out he'd been trying to get them cleaned.

Peter drained the glass and held it, watching the light sparkle off the thin, oily dregs clinging to the sides. The familiar sensation of burning heat sank through him, threatening nausea.

—He was only ever half here, half in any place. There was always the rest of him, somewhere else, somewhere I could never reach him…

She sipped her brandy, looking at the window, eyes unfocused. Peter cradled his glass, watching her drink. He burped, unexpectedly.

—I suppose he was just 'dad' to you. You never knew any different.

She sighed. Peter looked at the bottle on the side. He knew it was all his fault.

She turned and looked at him. She flashed a trembling smile and wiped her cheeks.

—I… I'm going to phone mum. Tell her. She can come down…. Maybe… She stopped, frowning. —Do you think I need to phone his work? Someone has to tell them…

She wandered into the kitchen. The glass clonked onto the table and a chair scraped back. The phone clicked as it was dialled.

He stayed in the living room, looking at the brandy. Her voice wavered as she tried to explain that Jim had died. Peter stared at the bottle, feeling the acid itch of the box upstairs, under his bed. The box which had caused the death of his father.

He adjusted his tie in the toilet mirror, tightening the knot up over the top shirt button.

I ought to give mum a call, maybe meet up.

He paused, one hand tucking in his shirt.

She's got Michael these days. With his little beard, and his bicycle.

He shook his head. Maybe in the New Year.

He ran a hand through his hair, trying to heap some of it over onto the left-hand side, where the skull had been pinned into place. His right cheekbone was lower and shallower than the left and there was a kink to his nose. Pulling his hair round, he leaned into the mirror to look for the thin, white scar that ran along what had been his hair-line when he was twenty-four. As he moved his head, his right eye's gaze remained fixed, staring straight ahead. All the surgery putting his head back together had happened over nearly a year. The leg and the ribs and the fingers and the wrist and the collar bone had been simple, they said, but the skull was complex, needing several different procedures. They informed him there was likely to be brain damage, but the extent would only become clear over time. He sometimes had headaches and dizzy spells, and there were times when thoughts slipped away from him, like bubbles down a plughole.

He had woken up in a hospital bed, unable to move or see. A hand put something wet to his lips. There was a short intake of breath, words left unspoken.

Days later, he woke to find two policemen by his bed.

—Are you sure he's well enough to talk? One of them was asking a nurse.

—Oh yes, she said. —He gets very chatty sometimes. Keeps trying to tell me about boats and all sorts.

—Boats? Hello Peter! You're awake! What's all this about boats?

—Who…?

—Sorry, I'm Constable Steve Maplin, this is Constable Fuller. The other man nodded. —And you… are hopefully going to tell us how you ended up in here.

—Here? Err… I… I remember standing in a room, but… no, it wasn't a room, it was a cabin, on board a ship.

—A ship?

—Yes… I think. We'd been travelling.

—You and…?

—We… What?

—Where had you travelled to?

—All around the world… We saw a Buddha that was a

mountain. We saw people walk on water...
—Nurse?
—He is still heavily medicated...
—Right. Peter? Listen to me. You were found on the corner of Brompton Street, unconscious. There is a bruise on your chest in the shape of a size nine boot, so we know you were beaten up: less of the bullshit, eh lad?
The nurse tutted.
—Come on Peter, you know who did this to you, don't you? If you don't tell us, they'll do it again. I've had the dubious pleasure of seeing where you live. And despite the clean-up someone's done, it still stinks: vomit and filth all over the place, crusty socks and mould on the beds. I know you take a lot of illegal substances. I know you deal in those substances. I know you move in some pretty squalid circles, Peter, full of some right cunts, out of their skulls, unpredictable, dangerous people. I think you pissed a few of them off and I think they'll come back, so who was it? Eh?
—I... don't know.
—Next time, it'll be more serious, you know that, don't you?. We're already investigating the death of Benjamin Evesham. Can't be a coincidence, can it? You two live in the same house, he turns up dead, you beaten half to death? So what's the connection?
Peter stared at the policeman.
—Come on Peter.
—They never... they never said how he died. Just that...
—Peter, please... I'm a busy man. If you're not going to tell me... just say so, and we can arrest you for obstructing the course of justice.
—What?
—You heard.
Peter lay there. He looked up at the ceiling and sighed. He shifted about in the bed, his thoughts slippery, elusive.
—Alright... But... first I want to know Claire is

alright.

—Claire…?

—Claire Mulligan. She was… Ben's girlfriend.

—Where does she live?

—Same house.

The policemen scribbled in their notebooks

—Alright. She see anything?

—She was there. With me. Make sure she's alright.

Constable Maplin looked at him.

—You making demands?

—No… I…

—We'll be coming back. And when we do, you'd better tell us who did this. Understand?

—Yes.

—Don't run off now, alright? The policemen looked Peter up and down, snorted with laughter, and flipped closed his notebook. The two uniformed officers turned and left, boots squeaking on the polished floors.

Peter tried to picture Claire in front of him, her face as he had last seen it. But it was unfocused, blurry.

Smoothing down his hair, he walked out of the toilets, into the corridor. From the canteen came a babble of voices, and the chime and clatter of metal cutlery on steel trays. A greasy, meaty aroma drifted through the doors. He frowned and pushed them open.

To his right, at an angle, leading to the exit out to the offices, were stainless-steel serving counters, fronted by curved glass displays. In the middle of the room was the coiled staircase leading up to the encircling balcony, lined with tall windows. All around the room were smooth, grey tables: lily pads on a clear pond. People sat, reading, talking, hunched over plates and steaming cups.

Peter walked along the line of the serving counters, the queue between him and the glass fronts. At the far end, where the breeze from outside whistled in and the coffee machine hummed, he bent to get a battered brown tray.

Plucking a tea bag from a box, he dropped it into a

cardboard cup and poured hot, gurgling water from the machine. As it filled, the string tail of the tea bag flipped over the rim, into the water.

Shit!

He lifted up the cup and looked at the floating cardboard tab. He began prodding it with a wooden stirrer, trying to push it up the side

—Having fun? Said a voice behind him.

Peter turned sharply, the tab slipping back down into the tea.

—Oh! Martin!...

—Surprised you there! Didn't I? Said Martin, scratching his head, grinning.

Peter frowned. —Like you surprised Becky Ashworth?

Three Christmas parties ago, Martin had drunkenly arranged to meet Vanessa Thorpe in a disabled toilet. But he had gone to the wrong cubicle and walked in on Becky Ashworth, who was trying to retrieve an earring from beneath the cistern. The rumours varied about what happened next.

Martin grimaced. —Sorry, man, I... didn't mean...

—Yeah, I know. Sorry about... How are you?

—Oh, man, I'm good. Tired, but good, cheers. Yourself?

—Fine. Thank you. Said Peter, still trying to slide the sodden cardboard tab up the side of his cup with the stirrer.

—Oh man, I fuckin' hate it when that happens! Martin reached over and got another of the stirrers. —Here. Use this as well, like chopsticks. You can actually get a grip, y'know?

——Thanks. Said Peter.

Martin got a cup and put it into the machine. —Gotta get me coffee, man, can't function without it, y'know?

Peter pulled out the tea bag by the string, grasped between the stirrers, and swung it into the bin.

—There you go, man! Said Martin, slapping Peter's

shoulder. —Told you it would work! He picked up his coffee and shook a sugar sachet. —I was out at a gig last night, man. Fuckin' amazing band at The Trees: 'Static Ems'? Great band! Really great!

—Yeah? Said Peter, pouring in sugar as well.

—Yeah, you heard of them?

—'Static Ems'? No.

—Oh, fuckin' 'ell, man! They're brilliant! Really good. Still underground. Nobodies heard of them! I think there was just me, my girlfriend, and about three others! That was it, man! How cool is that?

Peter nodded, looking down the line to the hot food counter.

—How's Change? Asked Martin.

—Oh, you know... Fairly dull.

—I heard something happened to your office, like?

—Yeah... Peter sighed. —We've gone mobile. 'Deskless', they call it. Not much of a change to how we were before, to be honest.

—You what? Martin frowned. —You're working without...?

—It's like hot-desking. Kind of. We always worked in-department anyway, so it doesn't really make a difference.

Peter realised he was repeating what Geoff had said to the rest of the Change team, just over a month ago.

—It really won't make any difference.

—Well, with respect, it will. Said Alistair. —We do our research in-department, but all the analysis and project work happens here! Alistair waved a hand round their office, a second-floor corner with fifteen desks for only six people. —Where are we going to do that?

—Yeah, what about the conference calls with admin processing out in India? Said Simon. —Are we supposed to do that from the edge of someone else's desk?

Geoff held up his hands, smiling.

—All thought of. There are meeting rooms we will book for project work. Down in the canteen building there are excellent facilities: there's even a dedicated video-conferencing room, for when you need to talk to India. All there. So don't worry.

—Yeah, but... what about stuff we don't want anybody to know about? We find out all sorts of shit sometimes and it can just, y'know, pop up.

—Like I said: book a meeting room.

—We won't have time to book a...! Look; if you find something bad, I mean really bad, like... industrial-scale fraud type-bad, we can't wait for a meeting room! It needs immediate, forensic attention! Somewhere secure! We won't have time to piss about, booking a bloody meeting room!

—How many times has something like that come up? Hmm? And if it is that bad, then surely the first thing you should do is take it to one of senior management, shouldn't you?

Peter had been sat at his desk, looking down at the bottom drawer which contained his sandwiches and a book.

—The whole site is wireless now, so you have, and have had for quite some time, complete freedom. You can work wherever you like. Go and sit in the sunshine, in the canteen. Go and work in a cupboard for all I care. Work wherever makes you comfortable. The bottom line is, however, that this office is a luxury that the company can no longer afford. Look out the window! There's an international financial disaster happening out there which is bigger than any previous crisis in the modern era of banking! The company needs to utilise every resource it has, so it's going to use this office for something that will generate money.

—So... who's moving in?

—Broker database admin.

—How do they make any fucking money?

Geoff smiled. —You didn't think it would be straightforward, did you? They're moving from the ground floor of William Building, which they shared with Risk and part of Travel Insurance Admin, who're both moving as well, so that the diminished Sales team for Travel can take over that entire floor. And where Travel Sales were, on the second and third floors, will be taken over by the new, expanded, Income Protection team, and that is where they hope to capitalise. There's a lot of people out there worried about losing their jobs, about keeping up with mortgage payments, school fees and medical bills. IP has already seen sales increase by seventy-five percent.

He paused and looked around. —It makes good business sense.

—Do we have a choice?

Martin raised his eyebrows. —I suppose it kinda makes sense, but… Well, aren't you a bit pissed off? Losing your space, and all that?

—Nah, Peter lied. —Like I said: barely notice it. How's Telephony?

—Mmehh! Grunted Martin, shrugging. —It's alright, y'know? It's just that… well, no-one wants to be there, man, they all hate it. I mean, everyone gets the odd bad call, you know? But recently, we're getting flooded with them! It's like every other call, they're phoning just to moan at my guys, y'know? And the really bad ones? Know who they get passed to? Me. So I've got my team moaning at me, customers moaning at me, who do I get to moan at? Hmm?

He looked at Peter, eyebrows high.

—I… I don't know.

—Yeah, exactly: no-one.

Peter nodded, then frowned, and looked up at Martin.

The line moved forward again, the smell of food getting stronger now they were away from the draft of the door. The bacon was rich and strong, salty and meaty. There was the watery, earthy smell of the mushrooms, and the pungent sweetness from the boiled tomatoes.

—You going to get food? Asked Martin.

Peter nodded, feeling his skin go cold.

—Yeah? I'm going to skip straight to the till then, man. Need to get on.

Peter relaxed.

—Late getting in, man, bloody rozzers in town, blues and twos all over the road by the canal quay. Right pain in the arse, y'know? Traffic backed up all the way to the ring road. White tent out and yellow tape all over. Got to be a murder investigation.

—Really?

—Local radio said they found a body. They don't do all that when some old codger keels over, do they?

—Police say anything?

—Nah! You know what they're like: 'Move along please, nothing to see here.' All that bollocks. Anyway, yeah, look man, great to catch up. Where you working today?

—I'm doing follow-up for On-Boarding, so… I may end up working over there.

—Yeah? Well, if you fancy coming to work in Telephony…

—Well… it's pretty intensive work. It needs… concentration.

Martin winked, a thumb raised. —Know what you're saying, man. Know exactly what you're saying!

Peter smiled. —Yeah.

—Absolutely fine, hombre! Happy hunting!

Martin saluted as he turned and went to the till.

Peter turned back to the food, watching the people in front point and smile, accepting plates, or paper bags stained with grease. The server clacked and scraped her steel ladle round the serving trays, piling plates with hash browns, egg and sausages. The line shuffled forward.

Martin returned, winking as he passed.

Peter shuffled forward, sliding his tray alongside. Louise's whispers came in and out of his thoughts: her reasons, her accusations, her wearying, pitying, goading voice.

He was staring into the distance when a plate was clattered onto the glass countertop.

—Mind: plate's hot.

And then the dinner lady was looking straight at him.

He blinked. —Full English please.

She nodded and picked up a plate and dug the serving spoon into the beans. The red of her poppy stood out on the white of her overall.

The tomato looked, to him, rather watery and insipid, weeping a pale pink juice from its light-red pulp. He remembered the bright red bullets of the cherry tomatoes he and Louise had eaten on a warm evening in Rome. They were tiny, no more than half an inch across, but exploded with a sweet tang, almost as sharp as grapefruit. He remembered their smiles as their mouths puckered and tingled.

Peter stopped the serving woman. —Not the tomato, please. Thank you.

She paused with the tongs above the tray, nodded, and moved on.

His breakfast was served up. —Mind: plate's hot.

—Thank you.

Putting it down on his tray, he dragged it to the till, where Mary peered down at it.

—So... Full English? She asked.

—Minus the tomato. And a cup of tea.

She looked up at him. —No tomato?

—No. And a cup of tea.

—Four pound eighty, please.

He dug around in his pocket and pulled out coins, counting them out under his breath before handing them over. Mary clattered them in separately, then presented his change between two forefingers.

He walked over to the sideboard where the cutlery trays were stacked, alongside sauce sachets and paper napkins. He paused for a moment, staring at the knives and forks, momentarily seeing each individually, their every scratch a story. It was bewildering: there were too many to comprehend.

A voice behind him made him turn.

—Can I have the full cooked breakfast please?

Standing at the serving counter, two customers behind him, was Jane, wearing one of her tight jumpers. Turning back to the cutlery, he took his time selecting the right knife and fork, checking them for cleanliness, for quality of shine.

—Jane? He said, when she perched her tray alongside his.

She looked at him and flashed a smile. —Hi!.

—How are you? He asked.

—Not bad, not bad at all, thank you. She said, selecting a knife, fork and three sachets of ketchup. —And you? You're looking well this morning!

—Really? Peter laughed. —I… I must be covering it well! Look at me! I'm a mess! Barely slept last night…

—Yeah? Me too! What happened?

—Oh… Peter waved a hand, wafting the matter away. —No! Nothing! Just… y'know, a restless mind. Couldn't sleep. Must be guilty of something! Or not! No. He snorted a laugh. —You?

—We had a really strange evening last night. Very… She stopped and adjusted the cutlery on her tray. —It was just a bit, y'know, disturbing. No. Sad. Distressing.

He looked at her closely, watching her eyes for some clue.

—What happened?

—Well… do you want to…? Jane held up her tray and nodded to the seating. He smiled his agreement, picking up his breakfast.

—Up there? She said, and they walked towards the central stairs, winding their way through the forest of tables.

Peter felt as though the noises in the canteen had

gotten louder, the colours brighter. Words tumbled, rolled, meaningless, in his mind.

Their shoes clanged together up the staircase. Above them, two men were descending, holding empty trays. Peter dropped back to let Jane go first as they passed the men. He looked up from making sure his tea didn't spill, right into the gently undulating cleavage of Jane's backside, swaying its way up the stairs just beyond the lip of his breakfast plate. For a second, he stared. But when laughter erupted nearby, he quickly looked back down at his food, his face hot. When the men had passed, Jane stepped to one side and slowed to allow Peter to catch up.

—That's Ian and Mitchell. She whispered. —They meet every morning to do bible study and pray over their muesli.

Peter turned to watch the two men slot their trays into the rack for the dishwasher and walk to the door for reception.

—Sanctimonious little shits. She said. —Sandra told me that they refused to donate money for the floods in Pakistan because they see it as 'God's judgement on Muslims'. How sick is that?

They set their trays down on a window table looking out over the staff entrance. A glimmer of sun peeked through the drizzle and clouds, reflected in the windows of the buildings opposite.

—Weather's not great. Said Peter.

She laughed. —It's not the best, is it? Stupidly warm for November as well. And all this drizzle! God! It's that horrible stuff that soaks right through you, isn't it?

He smiled up at her as they started eating.

—How's your breakfast?

—Good, thanks. Needed.

—I wouldn't of had you down as a Full English kind of girl.

—No?

—Well... I don't know; I suppose I thought you'd be

more… y'know: healthy. Yoghurt, muesli, that sort of thing.

She pulled a face at him.

—God! No! Can't think of anything worse! Whatever made you think that?

He blushed. —Because… Well… you always seem so….

—I grew up on a farm with three brothers, all rugby players, two now in the army, so I always thought that this was what everybody had for breakfast.

She laughed, forking another slice of egg up into her mouth. He smiled at the image of Jane as a little girl, sitting with three big brothers at a table, digging into a mound of food.

—But you're right, I suppose. She said. —I don't eat like this too often. But I'm hungry: dinner got interrupted last night.

—Oh yes, you were saying…

She shook her head.

—No, not now. After we've eaten. Probably best…

He frowned at her.

They ate, cutlery moving back and forward, clattering and scraping from plate to mouth. Teeth chewed, scrunching and mulching loud in their ears.

As he ate, Peter tasted the salty unami of the bacon, and the herbed, juicy meat of the sausages. A Lincolnshire? He thought. Been a while since I had…

—Is this alright? Asked Louise as they pulled into a roadside café.

They had been driving through dawn light from the overnight ferry from Oslo. The dual-carriageways were quiet and blue mist gathered in the dips and hollows of the fields. They had declined food on the rough crossing, the North Sea lurching and rolling. So their stomachs, back on dry land, were growling and aching with emptiness. Seeing the white Portakabin in a lay-by, Louise pulled in.

Peter nodded.

Inside, there were white, plastic tables and chairs. The kitchen was a wooden table with blackened gas hobs and a row of chipped enamel pans.

A woman looked over from the window as their footsteps echoed in the bare, small space. She came and stood behind the table, picking up a pencil and paper.

—I'll have… the full English, please. And tea. Thank you. Said Peter.

—Fried eggs?

—Yes, please. The woman looked at Louise, who was frowning at the handwritten menu.

—Oh, just… err, scrambled eggs on toast for me. And coffee.

Louise and Peter sat by a window and looked out over the dawn fields, down a rutted track to a distant farm. Mist gathered in the leeward side of hedgerows and the long huts scattered over the field. Pigs nosed among mounds of hay, their feet lost in well-trodden mud. Rabbits and pheasants bobbed tentatively in the early morning, nothing more than silhouettes. A man walked up the track, carrying a picnic cool-box.

—Here's your tea and coffee! Said the woman, setting down the cups. She looked out at the figure, who stopped to rest the heavy box and stretch. —Oh, here comes my Richard. Lazy bugger, look at him!

—Is that your farm? Peter asked.

—Aye. Two hundred years of pig farming, and there's no money in it anymore. Bloody supermarkets. They want bacon and sausages as cheap as them factory farms over on the continent. And we can't do that, I says. We can't torture them little pigs! Can we? Happy pigs make decent meat, as any farmer will tell you! An' them CEOs all turning over billions of profit? Driving around in fancy cars? They're not getting it from the shoppers, no. They's getting it from the likes of us. She waved a tea towel round the cabin. —That's why we set up this place. Sell our own. Cut out the leaches and the vampires!

She watched the man pick the box back up and trudge onwards.

—Look at him... Poor bugger. He's got cancer. Gall bladder. I keep telling him to give it a rest, but... I reckon doing nowt'd be worse for him... She shook her head, turning back to the crackling, spitting frying pans. —I'll fetch over your breakfasts when they're ready.

Peter and Louise looked out over the countryside as the sun crept over the fields, sipping from their steaming mugs.

When Richard eventually clomped up into the Portakabin, red-faced, breath pluming in the cold morning air, he dropped the cool-box on the wooden table, making the pans rattle and the blue flames flicker and flare.

—Thank you, love. Said the woman. —Do you want a bit of bacon? Cuppa? Richard smiled and shook his head, leaning an arm across her shoulder and kissing her cheek. He whispered something that made her giggle. Still laughing, she gave him a playful slap as he walked away. He winked at Peter and Louise.

While Peter ate his breakfast, he could see stately galleons of pigs outside, walking imperiously around the field, faces hidden by long, folded ears. Cutting up the sausage and the bacon, it became impossible not to wonder which part they were taken from, and the slicing it had taken to get them out.

—They say, he said, in-between mouthfuls, —that the pig is very intelligent. And that our organs are so closely related that one day we might be able to use them for organ transplants.

Louise looked up at him from her eggs.

—Really? Well I'm never eating a fucking sausage again.

He grinned at her.

—So... How are things up in Change? Asked Jane.

Peter sighed. —I take it you heard?

—No? She frowned. —What's happened?

—They've shut down our office.

—No! Really? What? No more Change?

—Yes. I mean: no. Change is still going, we just don't have an office. We have to work 'mobile'.

—Oh, I'm sorry! She frowned. —That sounds rubbish! She scrapped some egg yolk onto her toast. —Where are you going to be based now?

—Don't know. Nowhere, I suppose. They assume that, because we always work within other departments, we don't really need an office.

—Well, surely you need space for analysis and… and what if you find they've done something illegal? How can you deal with it while you are in their office?

—Yeah… It's tricky. He admitted.

She looked at him, waiting for more.

—I miss my chair. He said. —My chair was really comfortable. It was orthopaedic. The previous owner had a heart attack in it. Peter chuckled. —I thought I'd scooped the best chair in the office, but no-one else would touch it.

Jane pulled a tight smile.

—It's a shame. She said.

She scooped up the final forkful of beans.

—You were hungry, weren't you? He said.

—Sorry! Disgusting of me, I know!

—No, no! I like a woman with an appetite!

She wiped her chin with the back of her hand. —Dave and I went to this restaurant last night and there was this… well, this old drunk guy there. It was really disgusting, actually. He made a right mess. So… in the end, we didn't eat much, y'know?

Dave? Thought Peter. Who's Dave?

—What happened?

—It's this new restaurant by the canal basin called 'Henka Tsumi'. Y'know the multi-story car-park? It's just up the road from there. It does all sorts of Pacific stuff, not just Chinese, but Hawaiian and Polynesian, that sort of thing. Really interesting, beautiful food.

She looked out of the window.

—Thinking about it, it was weird that we went there. We were celebrating Dave's promotion, and he likes his red meat, his pizza, stuff like that. But... he knows I like my fish, my squid, that sort of thing.

Jane sipped her tea, her eyes unfocused, glazed over.

Peter mopped up the last of his beans with a slice of toast.

—Anyway! We were waiting for our starters, just sitting there, y'know, chatting and stuff, when this old guy came in, stinking to high heaven! He must have been seventy or more, but it's always hard to tell with these alcoholics. He was as skinny as he could be, his clothes just hanging off him, skin all peeling and horrid. And the smell! It was the smell of mouldy, unwashed football kits.

She shuddered.

—And he'd been drinking. The smell of it streamed off him like an oil slick. Made your eyes water. I couldn't work out how he'd got a table, turning up like that. But Dave said that he was some children's TV star from the eighties, apparently. So they'll give a table to someone completely legless, if they used to be famous...

He got put near us, and sat there, burping and coughing, like he's on the cusp of throwing up. And he was muttering and growling to himself! Really weird shit like that. This teenage waiter went over, and the drunk ordered something or other, and then he sat there, chatting away to himself, all fearful one second, angry the next.

We were having our starters when the waiter brought out this huge, steaming bowl for the drunk. He put it down in front of him, and the drunk... God... he had a hand over his mouth, looking white! About to vomit! But the waiter just walked away! Left him to it! And he carefully picked up his spoon and... well, he managed one mouthful and then... well...

Jane spread her hands, wrinkling her face. —He tried

to keep it in, bless him, clamping both hands over his mouth, but... He jumped up, running out, knocking over his table, sending his bowl of soup everywhere, little bits of fish all over the place! The smell was revolting! Hot fish and wet carpet!

Jane looked up into the overcast sky.

—They offered us free glasses of wine, but... Dave doesn't drink and I... I couldn't stay there. I felt really queasy. So we left. Paid up and went home. Couldn't really face food after that. Watched some TV, nothing too taxing.

Peter watched her as she gazed out at the clouds reflected in the windows across the car park.

—There's something about seeing someone really lose control that can pull the rug out from underneath you. She said, wiping tomato sauce from the back of her hand. —I wandered round the flat all night, trying to make sense of it, but I simply can't. I can't describe it. I can't find the words. An old man came in and was sick. That's all that happened, y'know? But... I don't know, it's like the whole world is a bit more delicate this morning. Like if I poked it too hard, I'd rip it.

She shrugged.

Peter nodded. I know that feeling, he thought, when sanity is as slippery as a wet bar of soap.

Sitting there quietly, he became conscious of all the people in the canteen, that each was an individual with their worries and joys, all of them eating and drinking, chatting about their family, what they saw on television, the gig from the weekend, their holidays.

—...and I said 'no way is that legit!' and she laughed, right? Because...

—...I just don't know what it is that he wants from a relationship.

—...what the scan showed was a build-up in the left ventricle...

—...they crossed, passed in before me, and later I saw

them in the...

—...I honestly didn't! It was all Marcus! Nothing to do with me!

Some read newspapers or books, their phones or e-readers.

—Remembrance Day Protestors Banned

—Economic Meltdown in Italy Threatens Contagion

—Frankie: I'll Be Star Without X-Factor

A table of four men erupted into loud laughter, the noise echoing around the huge room. One of the men stood up and mimed riding a horse, bucking and snorting. The other men rolled around in their seats, helpless.

All that stands between being human and being an animal is language, Peter thought. Language narrates our consciousness. That tiny voice in our heads. And with lips and noise, vibrations in the air, it allows us to transmit our thoughts. Telepathy.

He turned his cup back and forth, rolling the cardboard ridges.

But it only works so long as we can find the right words. Cup. Tea. Terror. Disgust. What happens when we can't? When what we feel can go no further than a jumble of emotions, boiling around inside us?

He looked up at Jane, trying to read her face.

Because that's where the slippery moment comes in, that complete failure to communicate, to understand, and everything stays locked up within us. That's the moment we descend: when we stop being human and drop into the realm of the animal. Un-languaged. Mute. Dumb.

Peter looked back out over the canteen.

Anyone here could be bubbling away, seething with something they can't express. Who knows when they may... flip their table over, and sink down into the bestial. Everyone is only ever on a small raft of sanity, kept afloat by language. When the ocean grows rough we grasp at words, fling out our emergency phrases, our inflatable clichés. But sometimes they don't work, and we tumble into the deep, dark ocean of our subconscious animal-selves, tearing off clothes and convention, mutating into something with long teeth and lidless eyes.

And all it takes is for language to stop working.

—Sounds like you had a rough night. He said.

—Oh, I'll be fine. I saw worse when I was on nursing placement. But I expected it at three AM on a Saturday night, y'know? This just surprised me, that's all.

—You were a nurse? Said Peter, getting a sudden mental image.

She looked at him, and tipped her head back, laughing. He frowned, unsure what was funny.

—Yes, yes, I was! For my sins. Anyway. Less about me. What are you up to today? In your new working paradigm?

—Ha! Well, actually, I'm starting the follow-up to that project I did with you guys six months ago.

—Oh, was that the one where the brokers had to fill in the forms or we cancelled the policy?

—Well… there were other elements… But yes, that was the main outcome. You?

—Well, the new version of SysOn is going online next month, so I have to get on with sorting out the training for my team. It's all been revamped, so the interface is totally different, and it's going to be a bloody nightmare! Do you know how hard it is to get people to accept something totally new? She slapped her head. —Of course you do! That's what you do! But yeah, that's my day today: looking at the training models, setting up rotas, stuff like that.

—Do you know how to use it?

She laughed. —Err…? No! Not really! Ridiculous, isn't it?

—Then they'll learn as you learn. I'm sure you'll do OK: you taught me to use the old version, a couple of years ago, and I thought you were a very good teacher. Just have a play with it on demo mode, you'll figure it out.

She nodded, pursing her lips and narrowing her eyes.

—You speak wisely, sensei!

He smiled at her.

She grinned back, then started to put her plate and cup back on the tray

—So... Are you working with us today? Said Jane, standing.

Peter looked along the top of the table to the Y-shaped cleft in her trousers. He felt a roar of blood in his ears. Christ! He thought, looking up at her eyes, her big, brown eyes, so soft inside her frame of hair. Her breasts were pert mounds inside her tight jumper, and her fingers were wrapped loosely around her cardboard tea cup. He imagined looking down into those eyes, her hair bobbing back and forth, breasts wobbling, her mouth clenched around his... He shut his eyes.

Louise was in his ear again —Really? Feel free, but remember: you always disappointed me, so you'll only disappoint her.

Peter smiled up at Jane. —No, it's OK. I don't need to be in department. Thank you all the same.

—OK, well, there's a desk if you change your mind...!

—Wait! Jane? Before you go? The famous guy in the restaurant, the drunk? What was his name?

—Dave said he was called 'Arthur Finchley'. I didn't recognise him. Name ring a bell?

Peter remembered sitting on the carpet as a child, clutching his father's old wool cap, watching Arthur swim with sharks, sit with gorillas and clutch venomous snakes. Peter could still hear his voice, his face looking up out of the sea, sunlight glinting from the waves.

—Yeah, I used to watch him all the time. Was it really him? He... He did some amazing programmes... ; He was a proper scientist as well: Dr Finchley. He won awards. And now he's... wow...

—Blast from the past, eh?

Peter nodded.

—Things change, don't they? Time keeps ticking over and nothing stays the same.

Peter nodded, again, still staring down at nothing.

—Well. OK. Cheers, Thanks for listening, Paul. Said Jane.

She smiled at him and walked away, her footsteps clanging down the iron stairway, getting lost in the hubbub of the ground floor. He watched her deposit her tray then walk out, the double doors closing gently behind her.

Peter pushed away his dirty plate.

And he felt something within him…

                                                        fall.

two

In a pale green, sparkling ocean, light arcing down through the water, hung a man, made long by his flippers and his floating, smoke-like hair. Behind him, an enormous, dark shape emerged out of the emerald haze.

—The Whale Shark is the largest of all the fish, being around thirty-two feet long. Said the voiceover. —And yet, like the majority of its namesake, the whale, it eats only the smallest of the oceans' inhabitants: plankton. Which is why John, our cameraman, and myself, were perfectly safe.

The shark slowly undulated through the water, leisurely cruising past Arthur Finchley and the camera. Its wide, speckled upper filled the screen, the flickering light from the surface danced across it. A tiny, black eye winked white.

—Although the sheer strength and size of it can still be a hazard!

As the tail swept up to them, it flicked suddenly and camera and presenter were blown back by a cloud of bubbles. When the water cleared, Arthur was reaching out to the lens, grinning behind his snorkel mouthpiece. The view swung round to watch the shark glide away.

—Whale Sharks originated some sixty million years

ago, long before humans existed, around the time of the extinction of the dinosaurs, making them a wonderful link to this planet's ancient past. Each individual can live for seventy years or more! This one could have been around longer than me, so I was happy to leave him to his wanderings.

The shark gradually disappeared back into the murky haze of the ocean.

Peter stared out of the window, watching some faint patches of blue appear in the grey of the sky.

—Before you join me next time on Wild Life, go outside and see what wild you can find!

Birds flew over the top of the office block opposite. He saw them as fluttering black flecks. In the distance, the dual carriageway was a roaring, tidal river; a shuddering rumble of lorries and cars.

He turned back to the On-Boarding quarterly figures and their long lines of numbers and coded shorthand. He realised that when the early accounts in this group had been on-boarded, Louise had been healthy, life had been normal. The mundanity of their innocence made him stop and stare, accusingly.

Below him, small islands of people sat at their tables, clutching cardboard coffee cups. Low murmurs drifted round as informal meetings were held, pens clicked and sheets of paper shuffled.

Peter clicked through the details on one account and created a new column in his spreadsheet: 'Delay due to insufficient information'. Inquires had been made, messages sent: On-Boarding needed the name of the next of kin.

Sunlight glinted in the windows opposite, making him tighten up his eyes and turn slightly, putting up a hand for shade.

Looking at his watch, he counted down the hours until three that afternoon, thinking of the sun gradually arcing over him, unstoppably leading to that moment. He imagined the drive home, the careful, cautious walk up the path to the front door, the shuffle of his feet on the carpet inside.

He remembered the carpet at his parents' house, the feel of the sofa, holding his father's seaman's cap, watching Wild Life on TV, the sound of Arthur's voice crackling from the speakers in the wood-pattern casement.

—In the deserted remains of this European settler's house, is the home of one of the most fearsome creatures on the Indonesian Islands. The dominant predator, whose mere name strikes fear, largely due to its association with myth and legend: the Komodo Dragon.

Viewed through a broken window, a long-nosed lizard, elbows out, as big as a man on all fours, stood in the doorway of a room, littered with the wreckage of broken furniture and fallen ceiling-plaster. Its tongue flicked in and out as it examined the room. On the opposite side, beside the front door, was Arthur, whispering toward the camera, eyes locked onto the dragon.

—Because of their size, they are not fast, but they are very dangerous. Their true weapon is not their teeth, or even their bulk, but the septic pathogens that are in their saliva. They create their own carrion by infecting their victims and then following them around, sometimes for weeks, until disease takes them. Then the Dragon, really just the largest of the monitor lizards, will swallow the carrion whole, much like a snake, with its semi-articulated skull and jaw.

The dragon weaved its head around.

—It has good eyesight, but has difficulty discerning stationary objects: which is why I'm standing very still. I have the door to the left here, so, if he attacks, I can escape. Many of the locals in this corner of the island of Flores have built their huts and houses on stilts, since the Komodo Dragon cannot climb. It doesn't hunt humans, but has been known to kill and eat them when...

With a flurry of claws, the lizard surged forward,

kicking up a cloud of dust. The view jerked and wobbled as the cameraman ran to the corner, where Arthur was stood, staring back at the doorway.

—Did you get that? Incredible burst of speed there! Purely territorial, of course. Not a female with eggs. They're usually laid in a specially dug hole in an embankment, much like the crocodile. She would never lay here, in a house. Careful John!

The camera spun to see the dragon stood in the doorway, tongue flicking in and out. Arthur and John backed away carefully.

—Maybe we've outstayed our welcome! We'll leave this magnificent animal to its house. An odd dichotomy between the modern, human, western world and an ancient, almost… mythological past. A simply wonderful beast! Wonderful!

Peter clicked to the next account and opened the notes, reading through the codes and references. A one day delay, he thought. Just one day.

He watched a small group of three men and one woman on a table downstairs.

—I think we can probably guess that the result is going to be… disappointing, but… it's whether we do anything drastic at this stage?

—We can't rule out just a slight anomaly; that this was caused by a flaw in the figures. Do we have any proof that they have behaved like this in the past?

—We have to push on. We have to. If we give up now… well, we're sunk, aren't we?

—No. The only way ahead is to freeze out PostCo. They're dead in the water. Michael expects them to be wound up anytime soon.

Peter pursed his lips and ran the flat of his hand along the cool, grey top of the table, imagining it to be an icy ocean, stretching out to the horizon.

—Here, within the Arctic Circle, is an environment which exists for much of the year at an average temperature of minus forty degrees centigrade. But among this vast expanse of ice and snow, there is, however, life.

The Danish icebreaker pushed slowly through a fractured, grey-white expanse, blocks of jagged ice rocking in its wake.

—There! John? Look!

A Polar Bear stood alone on an ice floe, looking over at the humans with tiny, black eyes. It walked forward a few paces, still staring at the boat.

On the foredeck stood Arthur, dressed in an orange, padded parka, thick mittens and a black wool cap. He had turned to the camera, the bear a dot in the background behind him.

—The Polar Bear will spend much of its life alone, wandering around a vast territory, looking for food. It is… err, unlikely that he can see us, but he can certainly smell us. They have one of the most sensitive noses in the animal kingdom.

The bear, still staring towards the boat, slipped easily into the sea.

—Look at that! They are, of course, excellent swimmers and have been spotted far out at sea… most probably in search of fresh hunting grounds. And their fur is a wonderful insulator: each strand is not white, but a transparent tube, trapping air… Look, look, John! There's a seal, just there!

Peter could remember clutching his father's black, woollen watch-cap, smelling the salty, metallic brine of the North Atlantic as he watched the TV.

—I… I don't think the bear knows it's there! Can you see? There's the seal, on that chunk of ice to the right… but the bear appears to be… concentrating on us! Do you think it's our corned beef sandwiches, John? He's still swimming towards us!

Peter could hear the low whine of an engine getting louder. He looked up to see a lorry, the sides decorated with images of lettuce and tomato, come leaning round the corner and pull up by the side entrance. The driver jumped out, pulled a fluorescent jacket over a faded black t-shirt, and walked slowly up to the building, flipping through the pages on a clipboard.

Peter turned back to the spreadsheet, cupping his hands round his eyes, blocking out the rest of the world, frowning at the list of figures.

When he was a child, he read in bed by the light of a small lamp: a pool of brightness amidst the blackness of his bedroom. On the open page before him was a pencil and watercolour drawing of a Red Lionfish, its long, venomous fronds brushed gently by the current, an imperious, haughty look upon its striped face.

There was a knock at the door.

—It's nine o'clock, love. You ready for sleep?

—Is dad home?

—No, he's still out. Don't wait up for him.

—Mum?

—Yes love?

—You know the Stargazer Fish, mum? It can give you an electric shock, as well as poison you!

—Really love? Why does it do that?

—So if you step on it, right? You'll go 'OUCH' and hop away!

—I bet you will! Best not go stepping on any Starfish then!

—Stargazer, mum! And a Starfish isn't even a fish!

—Why's it called a fish then?

Peter shrugged.

—Well, time to turn your light out love. Come on now, sleepy-time.

—And the Reef Stonefish can shoot venom out of its spines!

—Yeah?

—Did you know that it's the most poisonous fish in the world?

—I suppose nothing will step on it then.

—Well, actually, they're eaten in Hong Kong and Japan. Do you think dad's eaten any Reef Stonefish? I want to ask him.

—You'll have to wait till morning. Sleep now.

—Mum?

—Yes?

—Where is dad?

—He's out. I'm sure he's fine. Don't worry yourself. Now, light out please.

He clicked the light off and rolled himself up in his covers, listening to her go back down the stairs to where the TV blared the canned laughter and theme-tunes of American sitcoms. Eyes shut, he turned his attention to the pavement outside, waiting for footsteps, the snick of a key in the lock. But he kept seeing his father lying in hospital, tubes going into him, the quick legs of doctors and nurses running past, his mother gripping his hand tight.

He clicked the light back on, and opened his book at the chapter on Coral Fish. Many of the fish among the corals are ray-finned fish, he read, which are known for having sharp spines in their fins. These are used for defensive purposes, such as wedging themselves deep within a crevice. Small fish will quickly hide should danger threaten.

Turning the page, to Deep Water Oceanic Life, he wanted to shut the book, because he knew what was eventually coming. First there were the Jellyfish, their domed bodies and trailing fronds drawn as yellow-tinged gossamers; ghosts of the sea. And then there was Fish Behaviour, with the silver herrings that swam across the page, none exactly the same. Beyond that was the Cartilaginous Fish and the thin Blue Shark with its long pectoral fins and onyx-black eyes. There was the Spotted Eagle Ray, spread wide, like a beautiful, fleshy butterfly. Then there were sections on Bony Fish, then the Baleen Whales, throat pleats bulging. But then, after all that, there came the black pages he hated, the images he feared and dreaded: the Deep Water Fish. Transparent-skinned nightmares, their lower jaws yawning wide, hinged like sprung traps, long needles of teeth jutting out unevenly below lidless eyes. The Deep Sea Viperfish, the Scaleless Dragonfish, and the Anglerfish with its bright lure poised before its gaping maw. It terrified Peter that such things could exist. They appeared rotten, undead. They waited in the deep for him, teeth sharp and skin raw. From the corner of his eye he could see the carpet ripple and furrow as they swam towards him.

He sighed and slowly closed the book, putting it up on the shelf above his bed and getting Wild Jungles instead, with its long-armed Gibbons, balletic birds of paradise and the little frogs that hid away in secluded ponds, deep within the folds of giant leaves. Opening it up, he settled down within his own isolated pool, shutting out the creeping, scratching things of the night.

The lorry driver banged through the side doors into the canteen, frowning down at his clipboard. He wandered over to the glass counter, folded back several pages and clicked a pen.

—SHOP!

Mary came out of the kitchen, wiping her hands with a cloth.

—Hello Keith! You want me to sign that?

—Ta.

She took the clipboard and read through the sheet, slowly starting to frown. —White potatoes? Again? She shook her head. —I keep asking for King Edward, or Red. Much better: there's actual flavour to them.

—Aye, but twice the price, aren't they?

—Yeah, well… 'Price of everything, cost of nowt.' You know? These buggers might appreciate decent food if we got the chance to serve it.

She beckoned to Keith and leant across the counter.

—There's a lot of talk about them shutting this place

down, that we're not 'cost effective'. But is it any wonder people don't eat in here if we're serving up food without any flavour?

The driver nodded over at the coffee machine.

—I bet they make sure that's kept well-stocked, don't they?

—That thing? Scares me, it does. Grinds its own beans, makes a dreadful noise.

—No sense of perspective, some people. Said the driver, shaking his head.

—I'll get the fire escape open for you. Said Mary, walking back into the kitchen. —Save you traipsing all your mud and muck through here…

—PETER! His mother shouted from down the stairs. —What have I told you about treading mud through the house!

He looked down at his sodden trainers, hands still clamped around a squirming frog, and saw they were black with dirt.

—Peter! I know you're up there! Do not play silent with me!

His hands shook as he attempted to get the frog feet-first into the jam jar.

—Come on! He hissed.

—PETER!

She was coming up the stairs.

He turned the frog round to put it in head-first, and it blinked its white eyelids, which he knew were called the nictitating membranes. He felt it squirming through his fingers; the fine skin soft and oily, the bony hips and the inner organs sliding across his palm to the spindly legs.

—PETER? For crying out loud!

She was stamping up the stairs and he couldn't just drop the frog since it would land on its nose, and Peter could feel in his own face how much it would hurt. But there were her footsteps, just outside his room, and he let the poor frog drop, its nasal squeak echoing up, its eyes tight shut.

—Have you seen the mess you've made down...

And as the door swung open, he watched the frog lying on its face in the bottom of the jar, feet kicking above it.

—What the hell are you doing? She said, as he tipped the jar on its side. He looked up at her. The frog found its feet and sat there, blinking.

—For God's sake, Peter!

She dragged him downstairs before he could cap the jar, and yanked his shoes off in the kitchen, dropping them in the backyard. She went to the living room door and stood there, hand on forehead.

—Can you see what a mess you've made? She cried, pointing at the carpet. She turned and ran up the stairs, shouting: —You get the hoover out! We've got twenty minutes 'til your father comes home!

Peter opened the cupboard under the stairs and untangled the vacuum cleaner from the ironing board. Above him, her feet boomed back down the treads.

—This'll do it. She cried, waggling a hair-dryer. She plugged it in and dropped to her hands and knees, playing it over the splodge nearest the kitchen.

—Get hoovering! She cried. —Starting here!

When his father got home, his mum calmly said that dinner would be ready in ten minutes, and did he want a drink? Peter spent those ten minutes trying to get the frog out from under his bed.

From the window, he saw the delivery driver pull a loaded trolley, five foot tall, off the lorry, the hydraulic lift wheezing them down. The trolley rattled up the ramp and out of sight, into the kitchen.

He clicked an account number through to his spreadsheet, logging it on one of the columns after he had read through the notes.

Outside, the driver pushed an empty trolley back to the lorry, the frame rattling and crashing, the sun glinting off the metal frame, dancing among the bars, tarnished and scratched.

Peter opened the next account. Delayed by four weeks. He read through the notes.

Another trolley rattled down from the lorry, laden with boxes and hessian sacks.

It was a small business account. There appeared to have been an attempted buy out by a much larger company. Peter's eyes widened, reading on with interest. It had failed, a legal loophole had been found, the noose dodged. Peter felt himself smiling.

The delivery man rattled and clanged the empty cart back up into the lorry, sunlight glinting from its metal.

—Anyone who dives in the open oceans always has the same fear, that they will one day be faced with one of the ultimate predators that nature has created: the shark.

Arthur was sat in bright sunshine on the front deck of a small fishing boat.

—While filming on the sandy shelves of the Western Pacific, just off New Zealand, it was our turn to face one of the most terrifying animals on the planet.

The scene cut to footage of Arthur swimming close to the sandy, shallow floor, around him swam a few silver fish, glinting in the refracted sunlight. The film had a bleached, corroded quality to it: little specks and streaks flickered across it. He pointed urgently at an octopus that scuttled along, kicking up little wafts of sand with its arms.

—We had been following a Veined Octopus, a fascinating creature which I have previously observed using shells as tools, and I admit I was desperate to capture this utterly remarkable behaviour.

The fish around them suddenly scattered. The octopus burrowed itself into the sand.

—Myself and the cameraman, John, had swum too far from the boat to hear the warnings. In such waters it is always essential to stay close to your support vessel, a lesson we learned all too well that day.

The camera picked up a dark shape moving slowly

behind Arthur, emerging out of the blue. John's hand pointed from beside the lens, his skin white, soft, and dappled in sunlight. Arthur turned, and saw the shark swimming towards them.

—This particular shark is the Shortfinned Mako, which was bad news for us, since it is probably the fastest fish in the sea, so out-swimming it was impossible. It also has a fearsome reputation for attacking humans, having little or no fear of us at all. So we couldn't flee from it, nor scare it away.

As the shark got closer it appeared a dark, oily, blue above, with a white underbelly. Its mouth was a wound of jagged teeth.

—There was, however, another way out...

Arthur slowly swam backwards to the camera. When the shark was six feet away, he pulled out the mouthpiece of his scuba gear and vented a thick stream of bubbles straight at it. He then grabbed the camera and flung it just to the right of the shark. The camera caught a few frames of Arthur's and John's flippers as they kicked away, before it was bitten by the shark, teeth darkening the lens. The shark shook the camera back and forth, thrashing it in the water.

—The Mako hunts swordfish, mackerel, and tuna: all fish with a silvery, metallic sheen to them. I knew that bubbles would confuse it, just enough that it would attack the silvery, metallic camera, rather than us.

The shaking of the camera stopped and it slowly sank to the bottom, the shadow of the shark moving away across the sand.

The scene cut back to Arthur on the boat deck, cradling the bitten and battered metal camera case.

—And this is the camera which saved our lives. When we went back for it, we were rewarded with this fascinating footage.

Back on the sea floor, the sand several feet in front of the camera started to shift and the Veined Octopus emerged, clutching a clam shell over its head like a helmet.

—Isn't that remarkable!

—There you go, Mary, all in. Said the delivery driver, tapping the clipboard on the countertop. —Mind if I get meself a quick coffee?

She waved her hand while looking over the list.

—Best coffee I ever had was in Italy.

—You've been to Italy?

—Oh yeah! Go every year. Been round Rome, Florence and Venice. Me and the missus, we like the culture, the art, y'know? We go and see the museums and the galleries. It's all over the place there. Can't bloody miss it.

—Well, well, Keith. I never had you down as such a man of culture.

—Hidden depths, me. If you want me to pick you up a genuine Italian handbag, just ask.

She grinned. —Genuine?

—Genuinely from Italy.

She laughed.

—I bet you'd look good with a bit of crocodile skin hanging off your arm. He said

—Genuine Italian crocodiles?

—Of course.

She laughed again, leaning back.

Peter clicked onto the next account and opened up the notes.

—I don't think there are crocodiles in there. Said Dan, looking over the shallow pond, which had dried in the summer heat to a muddy swamp.

—Yeah? Well, after you then.

The two boys stood side by side, looking down at the blackened weeds and sludge, strange shapes poking out of it, made stranger by the dim light of evening.

—Well, there aren't crocodiles… but there's bound to be something nasty in there. Said Dan, frowning.

—I'm telling you, somewhere in there are some small

crocodiles, maybe Caimans, or baby Crocodiles. They probably escaped from a handbag factory.

—Handbag factory? Where?

—It happens all the time: 'alien species' they're called.

—Have you seen them?

—No. Jimmy Worthes saw one: he swore on his sister's life.

—He hates his sister.

——So? He might still have seen one.

—Where? Here?

—I think so. He said it was around here.

—Yeah but… these woods are massive, it could be… y'know, anywhere.

—No, 'cause this is a pond: there's no river running in or out.

—So?

—So if an animal that lives in water gets in, there's nowhere else for it to go.

Dan screwed up his face.

—If it gets 'in'?

—Yeah, in the rainforest, when a river floods, fish, like piranhas, swim into the new areas and are cut off when the waters go down. And then, trapped, they run out of food. Starving, they'll leap out of the water if they see you stood by the bank. They go straight for the throat.

Both boys stepped back from the quagmire, eyeing it with suspicion.

—Yeah, but, this ain't the Amazon, is it?

—'Alien species'.

They walked round the edge of the pond, picking up a couple of fallen branches and poking at clumps of reeds, grassy tussocks, muddy mounds and the black holes amid twisting tree roots.

—Can you smell that?

—Yeah, you farted again?

—No: that. Something rotten?

—Yeah, kinda. Suppose.

—That'll be their recent kill.

—Oh shut up about your bloody…

—LOOK!

Peter pointed, urgently, eyes wide. Dan looked.

——What…?

—There! Just there! Peter went over and pointed with his stick to a thin clump of mud sticking up.

Dan shrugged.

—Look at it! See how it forks? Four toes coming off from it? Said Peter.

—What? No way…

Peter prodded the mud a few times, then levered the stick in and under the body. With a sucking squelch the lump emerged with four limbs bent out from it, a bony tail and, leering up at them, a skull still matted with fur but with gaping sockets where the eyes once were. Peter whined without meaning to and suddenly felt sick.

They stared at the corpse, wrinkling their faces up.

—What is it? Asked Dan.

—It's too big for a rat. Doesn't have the teeth for it: look, those are canines.

—Canines? Is it a dog?

—Could be. Got to be recent anyway, still got fur on it. Can't have drowned, not in this.

He tentatively poked the side of it, feeling the bone beneath the spongy flesh. He shivered and dropped the stick.

—Something got to it.

—Didn't eat it though.

Peter nodded. —Good point. Maybe we're dealing with some sort of poisonous animal, a snake maybe. Peter looked up at Dan. —Some of the most venomous snakes in the world are aquatic.

They stood up and looked out, across the remains of the pond, watching for anything small and slithering, among the intricate and slimy surface.

—THERE!

They leapt back, one of them kicking a log that pivoted round to hit the other's leg.

—AAAAHHH!

And they were both running back through the woods, crashing through the darkened trees, following an irrepressible instinct to get home.

Keith and Mary were leaning on the counter, talking, when a middle-aged man and a young woman walked in. He was clutching a padded leather folder, while she was looking down at her phone.

—Coffee? He asked, picking up a cup.

She shook her head.

—No… No, me neither. He said, putting the cup back.
—Shall we… find somewhere to sit?

—Rebecca Parker's brother keeps a gun up here. Said Dan as they walked through the woods to the old quarry. Sunlight flickered through the pine trees, the sweet scent of sap all around.

—Really?

—They come up here and shoot cans with it.

—George Fox does that. But he's only got an air rifle. It could still kill you though. He says it's the most powerful air rifle you can buy. He's killed a cat with it.

—Yeah, well, Rebecca's brother has a proper gun. A magnum. He can shoot through trees.

—Why would you want to shoot through a tree?

—What if someone was stood behind it?

Peter thought about this, then nodded.

The two boys got to the lip of the quarry and climbed down to the edge of the deep green water.

—What do you think we'll find? Asked Dan.

—All sorts: Terrapins, Goby Fish, Eels, you name it. Place like this, they'll love it. Although… Maybe not the terrapins. Reptiles. Cold down here.

—Fish?

—Oh yeah. Catfish, trout, carp, pike or… He thought.
—Sticklebacks.

Peter stripped off his trainers and socks and stepped into the shelf of shallow water.

—Oh! Oh! Cold!

He giggled slightly as he paddled, swishing his net back and forth, liking the sound it made.

Dan sat on a boulder at the side and unwrapped the fishing hook from its paper wrapper and began tying it to the line. He looked around and sniffed.

—Should of brought some worms. If you catch a worm, give us it.

—Good idea. It'll be what the fish in here eat anyway.

—Yeah? Yeah… that's what I meant.

Peter dipped the net in and out of the deeper water, beyond the edge of the stone shelf, swishing it through, making long trails of bubbles. He pulled it out and inspected it closely, the brackish, stale water running down his arms.

—Not getting anything. Maybe they're deeper down.

—Yeah? I'll put a weight on the line then. My grandad has weights that look like fish. Always thought that was weird. Why'd they eat themselves?

—Big fish will always eat smaller fish.

—What? Just smaller versions of themselves? Like… their kids?

—Yeah, I suppose. Survival, though, isn't it?

—That's disgusting.

—That's life. It's why they have hundreds of babies.

Dan finished tying the lead weight on and stood up.

—Here goes.

He spun the weighted end and flung it high up against the blue sky; an arcing thread of silvery plastic, briefly a rainbow, a prism in the sunlight. Peter watched it go, having only ever seen someone fish on TV. There was a 'plop' as the weight entered the deep water and the line rattled off the reel. Peter watched his net under the water, slowly turning this way and that, the mesh caught in slow motion. Dan slowly started to wind in the line, the way his grandfather had shown him. The only sound was the gurgling of water from Peter's net.

—Bugger! Said Dan.
—What?
—Hook's caught.
—You've caught something?
—No. It's… solid; it's not… pulling. You know? No you don't, do you?
—I do! Just… didn't hear you, is all…

Dan let out some line and flicked it, then wound it in again.

—Oh bloody hell!

He splashed down into the water and waded out to the edge of the shelf, peering over into the deep.

Peter watched Dan waggle and tug the line, then looked back down at his net.

There was an intake of breath, and Peter turned to find just a ripple where Dan had been, the quarry suddenly silent.

He stared at the water, imagining the cresting shapes of the deep sea fish, the glowing lure of the Anglerfish, the lidless eyes and pin sharp teeth of the Dragonfish. He backed away, hurrying out of the cold, cloying water, up onto the rocks, still staring at the ripple.

There was a burst of white-foamed bubbles and Dan flopped up onto the shelf, spluttering, puffing and blowing. He pushed himself to his feet, slimy and soaking, t-shirt sagging.

—Got. It. He panted, grinning, holding up the reel of fishing line with the hook and weight still attached.

A loud phone ring echoed round the canteen, silenced with a beep.

—Sorry! Sorry… I…
—That's OK, Felicity, don't worry about it. Said the man with the padded folder. —These things happen. So…? Your timekeeping. You've always been brilliant, one of my little early birds, always there before everyone else!

But recently you've been coming in late, haven't you? Several times in the past month or so I've seen you coming in past log-in time.

Peter looked over through the railings, but they were underneath the balcony.

—Yeah... It's just been... traffic, y'know?

—Really?

—Yes! Honestly! I swear! Just... bad luck. Keep getting caught by red lights. Road works. They've been doing a load of road works near our house.

—Right. Well... that's fine. But... errm... you do need to improve on...

—Yeah, yeah. I know.

—OK, well... you've also been off sick several times in the past couple of months.

—Yeah. Only a couple of days though.

—Yes, well... It was seven days actually. I know it seems like just a day here, a day there, but it adds up. Have you been to the doctors?

—What? God...

—Are you going to the doctors for medical help when you're off sick?

—It was just, like, a stomach bug. I was throwing up, then... then I felt better. I...

—It's OK! It's... fine! Don't worry, no-one's accusing you of anything! It's just that...

—What?

—Well... If I was being that ill, that many times, I'd go to the doctors. If only to set my mind at rest. Stop me worrying it was something really serious.

—OK... Yeah. I see your point.

—So, if it happens again...?

—Do you know how hard it is to get an appointment?

—Well...

—I mean, I phone up, and they say they have nothing for a week! No need, is there? Be better by then!

—Yes. OK. Maybe if it's a recurring problem though...

—They just never listen.

The phone rang again, loudly shrill, making Peter frown. The driver and Mary looked over.

—Sorry! Look… I'll… Hi Tony… No… No I… I don't want to talk to you. I don't want to discuss it… Not here, not like this… No. Look… I'll call you later, alright? Sorry about that, Michael.

—That's… Everything alright?

—Yeah, yeah, yeah. Just… No. It's nothing. Sorry.

—It's fine. Don't worry.

There was a shuffling of papers. —Moving on. Team work. You've been brilliant at this in the past, always offering help to new members, organising team nights out, stuff like that. But lately… you've been a bit more… withdrawn.

—Really?

—Is there… anything upsetting you? Something you feel is… holding you back?

—No… Everything's fine.

—No problems with anyone on the team?

—No.

—You had a bit of an argument with Chantelle the other day.

—Did I? Oh that! That was nothing… No… Nothing to do with work.

—Do we need to sit you and Chantelle down together and sort this out?

—No! It's all sorted. Sorry… Sorry about that.

Again the phone rang, sudden and alarming.

—I'm… Hello? Didn't I say I didn't want to talk to you? Did you not hear me?… No… No I'm not going to take down the post… No… I put it on Facebook and it's staying there… Look, I have to go, I'm at work, Tony. I can't talk now. I'll call you at lunch time. OK? Please don't call me again. Bye. Sorry. So, so sorry, Mike.

—Don't worry! Boyfriend problems?

—Oh… God no! It's nothing. Sorry.

—That's... alright. Do you want to talk about it?

—No. No thanks.

—OK... Right. Customer Care. You've always scored really well at this, always had people falling over themselves to praise you! But recently... there's been a few complaints. Nothing major. A couple of people saying you sent them the wrong information, and someone else complaining about your telephone manner... although I personally think that may have been... mixed signals... but...

—Yeah, I know about the wrong quotes... I just got them mixed up. I'm sorry. It won't happen again.

—I think you may just need to stay on top of...

The phone chimed loudly again.

—Sorry! Hello? Tony? No... No! I said I can't talk! The post is staying up! It's staying. I'm not... No. No I'm not taking it down because... Because it's true! No. Look... No! I'll talk to you later. I'll talk... No I will not take down the post: I meant it... Why should I apologise? What have I done wrong?... Well, if you find it embarrassing, then maybe you should pay back the money?... Yes, yes you do owe me: you owe me two hundred quid, Tony... So? Look... Pay me back the money and I'll take it down. That's fair... It is. It is fair, Tony... It's fair. I... I don't care! You can't go around telling everyone that you've got me wrapped around your little finger and then expect me to just ignore...! No... No! Look, I have to go. I'm not going to answer the phone to you again. Alright? I'll just hang up. So don't bother ringing back.

—Are you OK?

—Yeah. Why shouldn't I be?

—No... of course. Maybe... could you switch your phone off?

—I... My mum might be calling. I need to... Sorry.

—OK... err... That's... fine.

Peter felt his heart thump a little quicker, a little louder.

He turned back to the spreadsheet, holding his hands steady for a second over the keyboard. He tried not to think of that house, where once there had been shouting, blame and footsteps thumping up the stairs. He got the chalky taste of pills in his mouth, making his saliva run, his head start to pound.

The driver raised his eyebrows at Mary.

—Well… best be on me way.

—Alright then Keith, see you next week.

The driver strode out, barging the door open with a fist.

—The trouble with your father is that he wants everything done a particular way.

His family always holidayed at a campsite on the Norfolk coast, where the sand from the beach blew through the Marram Grass, right into the tents. When his parents argued, Peter would be taken down the road by his mum, to the village where quiet, cold children shuffled in and out of sweet shops in sandy flip-flops, eating candy-floss.

—All he does is fuss and moan and complain. As though nothing is ever right. And he thinks he knows everything about camping just because he's slept on the docks in Argentina.

Brightly-coloured plastic buckets and spades spilled out onto the pavements. Above the shop fronts hung inflatable boats, dancing in the breeze.

—He keeps saying he wants to go back to sea. Times like this I wish he bloody would.

She stared at a bucket in the shape of a castle.

—Sometimes he's just so… stubborn. No: particular. Like… Like…

—Mum? Can I get that boat?

When it rained, the three would sit silently in the damp tent, watching it fall, the steady drumming on the cotton and the drip, drip into a puddle outside. All around them they could hear the other families talking and squabbling, calling and shouting, laughing and crying. In their tent there would be silent voices inside heads, sighs, and pages turned impatiently of novels not really being read. Peter would clean the sand out from between his toes and try not to look at his parents.

The phone rang again, sudden and urgent.

—Sorry! Hello? Hello? Rich? Who is this? Tony? Tony, is that you? Why are you on Richard's phone? Yes, I said… I said I wouldn't talk to you… No, I don't care if people are saying stuff about you because of Facebook… I don't care: you pay me the money back, then I'll take it down!… Well, you should think more before you go around, flapping your mouth!… Yes! You should! I talked to Chantelle, I found out that you and her had been texting, and Mitch told me what you said the other night, and that you've been chatting to some woman on Twitter! It's not right, Tony! It's not right at all! Pay me back the cash and then I'll take it down… What do you mean you've got no money? You keep saying you've got no money, but you bought a new exhaust for your bike! What was that? Three hundred? Four? And you said you'd go to Prague with Damien. So don't tell me you ain't got no money! You've got plenty of money! Pay me what you owe me and I'll take down the post… No… No!… No, I won't… I don't care… Look… Tony, you're just winding me up now… I've been really clear with you… That's it, I'm hanging up now, alright? Sorry Michael.

—That's… that's OK, Felicity. Do you… do you think, maybe, you could turn your phone off, just for a few minutes?

—Yeah, maybe.

—OK. Great. Now. Final section: Moving Forward. What actions do you think we can take to fix some of the issues raised? Hmm?

—Err? Yeah. What were they again?

—How about you try and leave home a bit earlier? Just in case of road works?

—What? Oh! Yeah... Alright.
—I also think you need to be engaged with your...
Again, the phone rang, screaming for attention.
—Mum? Tony!? I told you not to phone back! I was clear with you! You owe me money... Yes, and until you do, that post is staying up... Fine... Fine! Alright, if that's how you're going to be, I'll expect you packed and out of my house by tonight!... Yes, I can do that! I pay the mortgage and all the bills!... I don't care what she thinks! I want you out of my house! That's it! It's over! That... No. What?... You what? You can't threaten me!... Well that's just bullshit. You know it, and I know it. You're a lying, conniving, back-stabbing, little shit, you really are... No! I'm not! I'm doing no such thing!... I'm not jealous of you and mum!... How am I splitting you up? I'm kicking you out because I can't trust you! Neither should she, but I'm not telling her that... So I'm not splitting the two of you up! Am I? I'm kicking you out!... Well... be someone I can trust, and you can stay. No... No. You do this every time, you protest and whine, then you drag my mum into it and make it all about her! Sort your life out! You're supposed to be a grown-up! Goodbye!

There was a bang of something being slammed on the table.
—Sorry Michael.
—It's... OK... Are you alright?
—I... He and I...
—Is he your...?
—Yeah...
—Things aren't great at home?
—No...
—By the sounds of it, you and your mum will be better off without him.
—Yeah.
—Look. Maybe...
—I wanted to ask a question...
—Of course! Whatever! Fire away!

—I wondered... and this is... private...
—Of course!
—What maternity leave can I get?

There was a creak and voices. The main doors of the canteen banged open as the red-haired receptionist walked in with an old man, carrying a leather briefcase.

—I really am dreadfully sorry sir, but...

He frowned at her. —Do please spare me your ghastly pleasantries! If this fellow has done some sort of bunk, then get me his manager! Quickly!

—I... I'm sure he's around somewhere Mr York... Please, just... She hurried over to the counter and called for Mary.

—I'm a very busy man. I'm only here as a favour to your CEO, Tim Dennings. I have better things I could be doing!

—Mary here will get you any drink, or snack, you want while you wait...

The man with the padded folder walked slowly towards the old man.

—Excuse me? Ahh? Mr York? My, err, name is Michael Jones? I'm here to...

—Ah! Michael! Yes! We spoke on the phone! Very pleased to meet you! They shook hands. —Yes, I was just explaining to the young lady here that I'm good friends with old Tim Dennings. Play golf together. Do you play?

—I try to get out... but... more of a football man, really...

—Oh dear! Not that ghastly bunch of preening foreigners shagging their way round Newcastle and Manchester? Eh? Ha!

—Er... yes. Well... I mean, no. I play golf, yes. Sorry for keeping you waiting. I was down here...

He held his hands open to the receptionist, shrugging apologetically. She sighed and pressed her lips together.

—Shh, now. Tuck your shirt in, here he comes. Said Peter's mum.

A dark shape loomed in the glass of the front door. It opened with a clatter and a gust of cleaning products. Grandfather was a stooped old man looking yellow in the pallid April sunlight.

—Come in. He mumbled, slurring the words together.

They stepped up into the house. Peter noticed the carpet was gritty beneath his trainers, and the smell of bleach was stronger.

—Do you, err… want anything…? To drink?

—No. No, thank you George. We're fine.

Peter wanted to ask for a Pepsi, because that was what he drank. He was a Pepsi man. And when he drank it, he always went 'ahh', just as they did in the ads. But he stayed quiet.

They stood in the front room. Years later, when Peter read about this house and the old man, who peered at him through yellowed, bloodshot eyes, he found it difficult to equate that history with the place he had stood in. The room was nearly empty, with an armchair in front of the television, and a stained sofa underneath the window. There were no pictures on the walls and a shelf above the fire had only a small plastic clock and a lighter.

—How was the… journey?

—Good, thanks. Yeah, the train was fine, wasn't it Petey?

Peter nodded.

—Trains these days, all the… never as… Good. Did you… with the bus? Up here?

—Yes. We asked at the station and they pointed us in the right direction. Yes, it all went fine. Thank you. How are you?

—Please, please… sit. He waved to the sofa.

They sat, gingerly, on the edge of the seat.

—Yes…

They looked at each other. His grandfather had slightly runny eyes, all expression washed out.

—Jim… Can't make it.

—Hmm? Oh! I... Yes... I didn't...

—He has to work.

—You said... on the phone. He pointed at a blue plastic phone on the floor beside his chair.

—Yes.

—I don't... expect...?

—No... It... It was too... He isn't... hasn't...

—No.

—But this is Peter! Peter, say hello to your grandfather.

—Hello.

—We've been looking forward to this, haven't we?

Peter nodded.

—Come all this way to see grandfather!

—It's... err... good that you... yes.

—I just thought, really, you deserved to meet him.

—Before I...?

She looked at him for a bit, then nodded.

—How are you feeling now? She asked.

—Ohh... fine. Better now I'm out of... there. Nurses were all foreigners. Couldn't understand a word. Doctor was a... girl. Teenager. Didn't know what she was... talking about. Gave me... some pills. Waste of time.

His mother sat for a minute or so.

—The doctor's were worried enough to ring Jim. They told him to come and say his... They thought it was serious...

He waved a hand.

—Didn't though... did he?

She sat, hands in her lap.

—No. But... we're here. Now.

—Yes. Yes... and it's good to see you. It was... a shame... he... I thought maybe...

She nodded. Through the open door of the kitchen Peter could see black plastic sacks, bulging with rubbish, piled up by the back door. He wondered why someone would let their rubbish build up like that. It must have taken weeks.

—If he did, and it's a big 'if', would you see him? Calmly?

—I would… I would forgive him… yes.

—Oh… OK. Well… I think he sees you as…

—As what? As…? I heard what he… said about me… His accusations…

George curled a lip and stared at the fire. Peter watched his fingers pick at the arm of the chair.

—Was any of it…? She asked.

—True? Him? Truth? No. He's a… fantasist. Always living in a dream world!

—But you would forgive him.

—Of course! Of course I would… I never knew why he… ran. It broke his poor mother's… He could always have come back…

They sat silently again. George looked down at his fingers, plucking loose thread from the arm of the chair.

—Why does he…? Never understood…

—I know. She said quietly.

—Just wish he'd…

—George?

—Hmm?

—What did happen?

The old man sat, staring into the fireplace.

—He ran. Things went to pieces round here. I did what I could… But Rose… she doted on that boy. Spoilt him. When he left, it hurt her. Killed her, in the end.

—How? How did she die?

—Why are you…?

—It's important.

He looked over to the poker, lying on its side beside the fire.

—Stairs. She fell down the stairs. I was… out. Came home. Found her. Terrible.

She sat still. Her feet together, hands clenched around each other. Peter did not know where to put himself. He did not understand what was happening.

—George?

—Hmm? He looked up, wet eyes looking at first the boy, then the mother.

—How did Jim not being here kill her?

—What?

—Sorry... I... I was thinking out loud. Ignore me.

There was another silence. George stared angrily at Peter's mother.

—She took to drink. Should of stopped her. But...

Sylvia unfolded herself, breathing out.

—Sorry. I... I shouldn't intrude. She took another deep breath and slapped her thighs. —How are you keeping? Since... the hospital?

—Fine. Said George, and looked away.

—Are you... do you get any help with the... around the house?

—Maggie. Comes in every now and then.

—Oh... that's good. Must be nice to...

—I'd like you to leave now... He said. —I... I don't feel so well. Please... leave.

——Is there anything...?

—No, no. Please... Go. Thank you.

He heaved himself to his feet and stood behind his armchair, his fingers scratching and plucking at another tattered thread on the headrest. Peter and Sylvia stood and edged along to the front door.

—Well, thank you for having us. Say thank you, Petey!

—Thank you.

—Say 'thank you grandfather'.

—Thank you grandfather.

The old man ushered them to the door, but his mother kept talking.

—It was nice to... finally meet. I was hoping we could... stay in touch?

George looked at her, opening his mouth to say something, then looked down at Peter. He shook his head, closing the door.

—Wait! I... I'm sorry! I didn't mean...!

But the shadow moved away from the glass. Sylvia stood there, staring in. Finally she looked down at Peter and raised her eyebrows.

—Well, it's good to see where your father gets it from. She whispered.

—Look, Mr York...

—Call me Francis.

——Francis. I just have to... I have a management issue that I just need two seconds to wrap up... He pointed behind him.

—Two seconds? Hardly important then, is it? I've been waiting for ten minutes out there! Do you mean to keep me hanging around all day? Eh? I've got a meeting to attend!

—I... I do understand, but it is rather important.

—Really? More important than the future of this company? Than either laying off some of the staff, or all of them? He glared at Michael. —Tell the little slut to keep her knickers on and be done with it!

Michael stood still for a second, staring at the old man. —It's really not... She's...

—Oh for God's sake, man! How precious can she be? This is the sharp end of the business world, Michael! Sink or swim! It's teeming with sharks out there and if you want to stay in one piece then you have to be harsh! No namby-pamby, tip-toeing around! Tell her to grit her teeth and get on with it! He pointed a finger at Michael. —Do you think this company has time to treat people with kid gloves? Eh? No! Everyone needs to earn their place here! It's not a sodding charity! We can only have the brightest and the best. Survival of the fittest! If she can't handle it... well... that's her problem, not yours. Same with all these young girls. He looked at the receptionist. —Come into these jobs, expecting it to be lovely, then start crying as soon as it gets tough. And bloody Europe demands we be nice to them! Make allowances! Doesn't help them at all! Have to toughen them up! Only way to survive!

—Look, Mum! Look! The terrapins!

Around them was the slosh and splash of water filtration, the echo of children calling amid the great cement structure, the acrid smell of chlorine and brine.

—Really? Oh yes! Look Jim, terrapins!

—Yes, yes. Come on, we'll be late for the Sea Lions.

—These ones are Diamondbacks, they're American.

—Petey? Do you want to see the Sea Lions?

—The word 'terrapin' is from America: the Red Indians called them that. But Americans call them turtles.

—Peter? Your mother asked you a question.

—I mean, they are turtles, they're all turtles, even tortoises, but terrapins are freshwater turtles. Except when they're not.

—Peter! Sea Lions? Yes or no? Quickly! It starts in five minutes!

—Daaa-ad! We saw them last time!

—Yes! You like them!

—But it's hardly natural behaviour, is it?

—Petey! Don't talk back to your father like that!

—But it's not. They're trained!

—Exactly! Otherwise they'd just be sitting around, not doing anything, wouldn't they? Who wants to see that? Come on Petey, let's go see the Seals.

—Seals are totally different. They don't have ears.

—What?

Peter stopped and stood, transfixed by what was happening in the tank of Terrapins.

—Oh... Mum? What are they doing? Look! They're...

—Come on Petey, best... No. Don't look Petey, dear...

—But mum, they're... biting him...

—Let him watch, Sylvia.

—But... it's a terrapin as well... a little one...

—Sometimes it happens, Peter.

—Jim, I really don't think he should be seeing this...

—But this is the natural world, Sylvia. If he wants to see it: this is it.

—I... I really don't...

—Look! They're... eating him?

—That's what they do, Peter.

The smaller terrapin struggled for a while as the rest began to slowly swim up to it, the water growing murky with blood. Mouths latched onto the saggy, grey flesh, ripping chunks off with their serrated lips. The small shell slowly sank down, trailing tissue like soggy cotton wool. His mum put a hand on his neck. His dad remained impassive behind him. Peter twitched when the body hit the bottom.

—For God's sake Michael, come on! I need to go through some of the turnover figures and the forward projections. Is the room set up yet?

—Ah, good question. I need to contact Steve...

—Well let's go to your office, you can phone or email or whatever it is that you have to do, while I try and save everyone's jobs!

—Yes. I will just say two words to... He pointed over his shoulder.

—Good God, man! I'm being paid by the hour, and each minute is more than she makes in a week!

—Yes, I'm aware of that but... with the greatest respect... He stepped closer to Francis, leaning in. —If I don't, then... she could sue! We have an obligation...! He held up a hand. —I'll just be... two minutes. Two minutes that could save us... hundreds of thousands...! He walked quickly back to the table.

—Hallo dear! How are you?

They had walked through long, green corridors, taking lifts to other long corridors, eventually finding his dad propped up in bed. Peter sat in the chair by his feet.

Jim nodded at her. Peter looked at the tube coming from his dad's side: a frothy, yellow liquid oozed through it.

—We brought you some oranges.

His father pointed to the bowl on the side.

—We got the bus down OK. Same as last time, isn't it Peter?

Peter frowned. This was the first time they had visited.

—Do you not remember the last time he was in? You were only little…

—Oh! Do you mean when they rushed you home from Chile?

—Rushed? His father croaked, gasping. —What nonsense … did you tell him? Did you say we went … round the cape? They did … nothing of the sort, they went the slow route: they picked their way through … the Straits of Magellan from Punta Arenas. They crawled up the coast, passing all the … ports where they could have flown me home from, but didn't. He coughed, spluttering.

—Calm down, dear, you're…

—Peter, I got ill because they wanted bird guano. Bird shit. From a penal colony. That's Punta Arenas … Captain knew I was ill, still made me work. I collapsed during docking. He had the first mate assign me … to cleaning out the head for the voyage back. Medic put me to bed. He knew what was wrong with me! Pneumonia. With … this shit … He knew! Gave me penicillin, but … I needed fluids draining. Nothing he could … do … Confined me to bed. Fed me brandy and soup. While I drowned in this shit … He waved a hand at the tube.

—Jim! They got home three days ahead of…

—They planned on bad weather! You always do, coming … east across the Atlantic! And they had good! Captain thought I was faking it. I needed a hospital! You remember what I was like when I got in? … I was like that all the way across, and they never tried to get me home any quicker … That would have meant docking, and the bird shit was more precious!

—Jim! I know you're… but not in front of…

—I could have died! And they know they're lucky that

I didn't! He looked straight at Peter. —They made me sign a compensation form.

—Jim… We've talked about this…

—While I was fevered, delirious, they made me sign a legal document to say they were right.

—They also gave us more than enough to pay off the mortgage, so please, Jim, stop this!

—Blood money. They knew they were wrong. There was a line in that form saying I couldn't sue them for perpetuity. Why put that in if they'd done nothing wrong? Hmm? He collapsed into red-faced coughing, a shaking hand reaching for a kidney-shaped bowl by his bed. —If only… I hadn't… Could have… sued. Got… millions… for…

A nurse came in, shushing him and leaning him forward.

Peter and his mother left, not even waiting in the corridor.

—He's just… frustrated, Peter. His mother said.

Michael came back, clutching his padded folder, walking slowly up to Francis.

—Shall we go then? The old man asked.

Michael nodded.

He held a hand out towards the side doors, letting Francis go first. At the door, he turned back, glancing over at Felicity, before turning and leaving.

Peter clicked through another account, reading the notes, assigning it to a column.

The sky outside clouded over and a smattering of rain rattled on the glass.

There was a scrape of a chair and Felicity walked slowly over to the counter, staring down at her phone, avoiding the eyes of the few people she passed. Peter watched. There is more, he thought, to being alone than merely being without other people.

—Your father's gone beachcombing. Said his mother, sitting in the tent.

—What?

—Just leave him be. Peter looked up over the sand dunes to the out-going tide. There was a figure stood there.

—He's just staring out to sea.

—Yes.

—Why?

—He… does that. Have you never noticed? Maybe you never realised it was anything to take notice of. She went back to reading. Peter looked out at his father; a single black stroke against the grey North Sea.

He could see that Felicity was on Facebook, scrolling up and down, reading comments. She sighed and tucked the phone away, staring down at the stand of brightly-coloured packets of crisps. She ran her finger among them, flicking the wrappers, watching the light dance across them; like jewelled coral, twinkling under fluorescent tubes. She stood there, an impenetrable black form. Peter stared, seeing the clouds and waves behind her.

She took a deep breath and walked to the doors, leaning against them, pushing them open.

three

—So I went round the back, and Tim's noshing down that fucking pizza...
—The one...?
——The one we threw out!
—He's a fucking nob is that Tim.
—We said that! We said: 'You're a fucking nob, Tim'!
—He didn't care, did he?
—Course he fucking didn't: he was eating cold, uncooked pizza from a fucking wheelie bin!

Peter stood in the queue, the lunchtime rush in full flow, the canteen full of voices: competing and shrieking. People filled the area around the counters, pushing and hurrying, the floor rumbling with their hooves.

—He said he was really fucking hungry and that it was a fucking crime to chuck something 'perfectly edible' away.
—Did he know that...?
—That Kelly spat in it? Dunno. Doubt it. I mean, not even Tim would...

The man in front of Peter was tall and broad, his suit jacket bulging with waves of flesh at his sides. On Peter's eye line was a roll of skin just above the man's collar, short hairs bristling out. Each time the head moved, the skin rolled, fanning out the hairs.

—Wouldn't he? I've seen Tim walk fucking miles to get food.

—When's he done that?

—Last year, don't you remember? We was camping out in Wales. Got back to the tents after the pub and Tim's, like, begging everyone for some food, but we haven't got any...

—Oh yeah!

—So Sam's like: 'just go kill a sheep, Tim' and he's like: 'how do you kill a sheep?' and trying to find a penknife and shit...

—But he couldn't find anything, so he said he was going to walk to Cardiff or something to find a fucking kebab shop.

—And he just wandered out. Midnight. Middle of fucking nowhere. Walked for miles till he found a fucking all-night café or something.

—There's something tapped in that boy's head, there really is.

Peter held his tray at his side, tea in his hand, fingers running up and down, too hot on the cardboard cup. He looked along the queue at how many were before him for the hot food counter. Too many, he sighed.

—I mean, fuck me, that lad does some weird shit, like when he asked that stripper if she'd shit in his mouth?

—No fucking way!

—Yeah, straight up. She was giving him a lap dance at Spearmint's and he was, like, whispering in her ear. Then she looked at him, like, 'what the fuck?' and walked away. Next second he's being hauled out by the fucking bouncers! It was fucking hilarious! Tommo got a dance off the same lass, she told him what Tim had said. Fucking weirdo.

—Oh yeah. Didn't he try to tell us that he'd actually said she should come 'sit in his booth' or some other bollocks?

—He probably said that, yeah, but this is Tim, he's guilty of doing something weird, isn't he?

Peter could smell bitter, unwashed bodies. The pungent odour of sweaty flesh under winter coats, seeping out to fill his nostrils. Tilting his head down, the aroma got stronger. He sighed and looked around, trying not to catch the eye of people pushing closely past.

—Do anything last night?

—Jonno and I played squash.

—Good game?

—Nah, the twat cheated. Kept tripping me up whenever we crossed court.

—It's the only way he was going to win. Isn't he like forty or so?

—I still beat him! Yeah, he's old enough to be my fucking dad, but he thinks he can act like that!

—Cheeky cunt.

Someone pushed past, pressing Peter up against the glass of the sandwich counter. Looking down, he saw the bright greens and pinks in their little trays, sliced and ready. Behind a chopping board stood a bored woman, waiting.

He drummed his fingers on the cup, thinking of a fifth-floor private office in which Geoff would probably be sat, eating a lunch which had been delivered.

A woman staggered sideways into him, pushed from the queue.

—I… I'm terribly sorry about this! She stuttered, eyes wide.

He stared at her, lips pressed together.

—But there… there really isn't much I can… do! So… many people!

He looked around, at the faces surging past, frowning.

Still pressed up against him, she grinned. —Maybe… do you think? If we… y'know… blew some balloons, we could have a party in here? She snorted with laughter and looked around.

He stared at her. There had been balloons at his father's wake. They were pink. They had been left in the function room at the crematorium from an earlier event. He had stared at them while people talked and drank, a low murmur humming in the air, the chink of glasses and an occasional laugh. There were vol-au-vants.

—You know, Peter, your father was a wonderful guy.

Peter glanced up at the man who had sidled up beside him.

—He was… The man looked upwards, clutching at air. —Y'know, really great. Really great.

Peter stared, until the man's smile faltered, and he looked away, to the food spread out on the table. Peter sighed. People kept talking at him. His suit was hot and uncomfortable.

—I err… I knew him quite well. The man continued. —I worked with him, back when he was at Wilson and Son's. He was a good man. A really good man. Always had time for him.

Peter poked a sausage roll, crushing the pastry.

—You, err… you shouldn't think bad of him for what he… for what he did.

Peter looked up at him, sharply.

—I mean… you should always, y'know… think of the good times you and him had together.

Peter frowned.

—How he… I mean, what he… it was shocking, truly… shocking, what he did, but that's… that's not… not all of who he was, was it? You loved him, didn't you? He was your dad. Everyone loves their dad.

Peter turned and walked away. He wandered into the milieu of chattering people without any plan or intention. Faces turned to look at him, eyes filled with worry, or pity. Hands reached out to grasp at him.

—Peter, Peter… How you doing, son?

—Oh, there you are! Have you had enough to eat? There's a cake still to be…

—Peter? Come meet Gwendoline, she was the secretary to the purser on... err, *The Adamantium*, wasn't it?

—Oh ... The woman was crying, trembling hands reaching out to him. —You look so much like your father! So much like him!

He backed away from her thin fingers.

—I'm so sorry. You just... It was all just such a shock...

Peter stared at her and turned. He walked away, edging through the crowd until he found himself back at the buffet table. He looked at the food once more.

—Hello there Peter! How are you?

Peter looked at the man, all bronze skin and yellow teeth.

—Christ! His face fell. —Sorry pal! Stupid thing to say! Of course... you feel terrible, don't you?

Peter looked down at the bottle of whisky in the man's hand.

—Yeeees... The man nodded. —Shocking; isn't it? We're all... in shock. I'm sure you are too?

The man cracked open the seal on the bottle and poured out a splash into a glass.

—Tell me, he said, raising the drink to his lips. —How is your mother? One eyebrow went up.

Peter's lip curled.

—She's fine. She's over there, if you want to talk to her. He pointed behind the man, who turned, peering.

When the man turned back, Peter and the bottle had disappeared.

—So Damien said that this lass turns to Tommo, right? and asks if he wants a blowjob!

—Yeah?

—And he, like, says: 'no', 'cos, y'know, he's there with Michelle.

—Yeah, course...

—But the thing is, right? Michelle was sucking off some guy out in the car park!

—No way!

—Damien saw them! Half the fucking pub saw them! And Tommo's being all, like: 'No, my misses is here and I love her!' And she's outside, meat down her throat, spunk on her chin! Y'know?

—Christ!

Peter sighed, looking away from the black polyester of the fat man's back. His fingers drummed quicker on the cup.

A woman passed, her perfume sweet, sharp and floral, a chemical sketch of flowers. Her woollen coat was a swirl of bright red, gold and blue. She was quickly swallowed by the crowd.

Feeling energised by the whisky, he had wandered through the crematorium to the hallway, where cellophane-wrapped flowers covered a table; bright petals shone through crinkled plastic. He bent back a card and read the inside:

'Dear Jim, I will always love you. Sandra'

Turning, he saw his mother coming from the function room. He ripped off the card and stuffed it in his jacket pocket.

—Who are they from, love? She asked, standing next to him.

—Err… I don't know. No note.

—Shame, they're beautiful.

—They kinda look like white poppies.

—Hmm. I thought that, first time I saw them. Your father used to bring them back from Hawaii. They're called 'Lei'; see how the petals overlap? Like a propeller, he always said. Are you sure there's no note?

—No… Nothing…

—Oh well… She sniffed. —Must have been someone special: these aren't easy to get hold of…

She frowned and poked around amongst the cellophane, searching. —Hmm. No. She conceded, straightening.

—Oh look! She pointed. —Hibiscus! The one that looks like it's sticking its tongue out. She reached over and turned over the card. —'To Jim, you will be very much missed, love Pam and George.' Ahh… They're good friends.

She stared at the flowers. —They're from the Pacific as well. Probably expensive in this country. Your father would always have a story about where he'd picked them: on a hill overlooking Honolulu, the lights of the town twinkling in the twilight; or from a dense forest beside a volcano; or a white beach, water lapping over bleached coral and the washed-up wreck of a boat…

She went back to the Lei, stroking the petals. —I know they were probably from some tart's garland, but…

She lifted the bouquet slightly, looking at the table underneath. Peter watched her. She shook her head.

—Look at that. Terrible.

Underneath, the dark wood was stained white from water dripping from the flower stalks. —They're going to murder us when they see that… She muttered, dropping the flowers and walking away.

Peter turned and went back to the toilets, to the cubicle where the whisky was hidden. There he flushed the card from the flowers.

—That is so fucked up. Said one of the men behind him in the queue.

—You know Michelle is bisexual, right?

—Oh?

—Yeah, but she won't let Tommo watch!

—Christ! Why does he stay with her?

The fat man in front of Peter eased himself from one leg to another, flexing his knees. His heels came up, brushing Peter's shins. Looking down, Peter could see the thin soles of the man's shoes, worn down to nothing more than a line. Peter hoped the fat man would not step backwards.

—Look at them! Said Louise, pointing at a man

carrying his girlfriend in the orange evening sunlight.

They had been for a meal, their first anniversary, and were walking home through the autumnal park, mouths still tingling with the sharpness of dessert.

—Forget it, I'm not...

—Oh come on!

—My back...

—Oh your back is fine!

He sighed, and looked at her. She grinned and nodded, going behind him. As he bent over, he shook his head. He heard her heels click and scrape as she took a short running jump, her weight knocking him forward. He grasped her thighs, pressed tightly around his waist, her arm round his neck, breath panting loudly in his ear. He could feel the bone of her crotch rubbing against his lower back.

—Fuck! He gasped, clumping forward.

—Yeee Haaw! She cried, waving an arm in the air.

He walked, her legs slipping, his fingers clawing at her skin as she slid lower and lower. He stopped when her heels clacked along the ground.

—No, no! Come on little horsey! She cried, trying to climb back up.

He shook his head, leaning forward, hands on knees, breathing heavily, his head throbbing. She laughed, staggering back, and slipped an arm round his waist.

—Do I need to carry you home?

—Yeah, well, Tommo didn't tell the police that the burglars left a stack of porn in his sitting room! His kids found it!

—No way! ... Why would they bring porn to a break-and-enter?

—I reckon it was his. The burglars found it and, y'know, made it public...

Peter was jostled from the side. He tutted, glancing down at his tea, then up at the person trying to push past. They kept their gaze firmly ahead, ignoring him.

The fat man shuffled forward, swaying from foot to foot. Peter followed him, peering round to see the hot counter, the food laid out in steel trays, glistening with oil, sparkling in the strip lights. The menu clipped up on the side listed: 'Home-Made Meat And Potato Pie', 'Fish Fingers In Crunchy Batter', 'Vegetable Curry (Vegetarian)', 'Chips', and 'Gravy'.

I've had all that before, he thought, remembering when he had bitten into the pie and found more potato than meat: soft, favourless lumps of potato. And the meat was cheap, scrag-end stuff, full of gristle and stringy lumps. The vegetable curry was lumpy sauce and rice, reminding him of baby-changing rooms. He wondered who could be vegetarian if that was the option? And the chips, a bland crunch and soft insipidness.

He looked at the food. Fish fingers, he thought. Two left. Two deep-fried orange lines of battered white fish, swimming in oil. Only thing here to eat.

He shook his head. When this place is sold off to a contractor, he thought, this'll all change. It'll have to.

The woman who had served Peter his breakfast, ladled chips onto a plate with a slice of pie and placed it on top of the glass cabinet.

—Mind: plates hot.

The fat man shuffled forward, put a hand up onto the counter and opened his mouth. The serving woman held up a finger and bent down to open a hot cabinet beneath the counter. The fat man closed his mouth and watched as she brought up a fresh new tray of chips, slotting it onto the empty one beneath the glass counter.

Please don't go for the fish fingers, thought Peter.

—Two fish fingers and chips, please. The fat man asked, a strong Birmingham accent elongating his vowels.

Peter sighed, watching sullenly.

The woman nodded and picked up a pair of tongs, but paused.

—Do you mean two plates of fish fingers and chips?

Or two fish fingers and a portion of chips?

The fat man stared at her.

—Just... just one plate. Please.

The server nodded briskly and plucked two fish fingers out from the tray and scooped chips onto the plate.

—Mind: plates hot. She said, sliding it onto the top, already turned to Peter.

—Do you have any more fish fingers? Down... underneath?

She slowly shook her head.

He stared at her.

—So you've none left at all? He pointed. —In the cabinet?

She pointed at the meat and potato pie.

—We've got pie. It's good pie. Made it meself.

She looked beyond him, at something more interesting in the crowd.

Peter looked down at the pie, drying in its deep steel tray, seeing only the white flesh of the potato, encased in thick, pale, short-crust pastry. His heart was thumping, arteries in his neck ached with pressure.

Peter stared, eyes going from dish to dish, always returning to the empty one on the right. The woman server tapped the counter with the tongs, looking down, then back up again. She turned to the two men behind Peter, just as he looked up at her.

She raised her eyebrows at him.

—Err... He stuttered, going back to the curry, or the pie, or the chips.

She sighed and stepped to her right, raising her chin at the men behind.

—Hmm? Oh, it's alright. One of them said. —We'll let this guy go first.

Peter's eyes flicked between the trays, his head starting to shake.

He looked up at the woman and saw her at the end of a long tunnel, light bending and twisting around her as she moved slowly away.

He clutched at the counter, reeling, the canteen tilted and rocked around him. A quick swell of nausea flushed him with sweat.

Raising his hand, he stepped back from the counter, into the crowd, letting the two men take his place.

—So my lad, he's like, three now? And talking! What? Oh, sorry love. Err. Pie and chips please. Yeah. Mate? Do you want owt? Yeah? Alright, twice please, love. With gravy. Ta.

Peter stood among the moving waves of people, wondering where to go next. He looked down at his tea, steadily cooling in the cardboard cup. Someone barged into that arm, knocking a slop of tea out of the small hole in the plastic lid.

He tried to breath slowly, steadily. Louise was laughing: a callow, merciless cackle that flew around the canteen, zooming tight into his ear. He turned around, spinning, staring at the others in the crowd, looking for who would join in the laughter. A skinny woman was beside him in a white fluffy jumper; a young man in a blue shirt and tie next to her; then an old man in a v-neck jumper carrying coffee; a man in a green army parka talking on the phone; a pair of women in dark blue uniforms; the woman in a fluffy jumper; young man in blue shirt; old in v-neck; the green parka; two women in blue; the fluffy; young blue; v-neck; parka; blue…

—…I have been trying to explain to my daughter the importance of proper breastfeeding…

—…there was absolutely nothing there! Seriously! I went all over! Where did you go?

—…these home-grown, socialist theories of macroeconomics are nearly always comic, absurd in their…

—…It was ridiculous, man. Guy was a complete muppet. Yeah? What you want? Fuck you, pal.

—I swear: laxatives are the best way to lose weight…

And then he saw a flash of red jacket, moving quickly past him. Ben! Peter reached after him, grabbing out, missing. Ben turned and flashed a grin, lips pulled back from teeth, eyes wide.

And then someone walked in front and the red jacket became a woman's top, Ben's brown hair someone's woolly hat.

Peter stared, his hand curling up into a fist.

There was a break in the crowd, revealing the sandwich counter, with its pink meats and bright greens. Trembling, he pushed his way through the queue to the glass front.

—Hello? He said to the bored woman stood by her chopping board. —Err... can I have... a... corned-beef salad sandwich, please?

Startled from a daydream, she nodded. —Brown or white? Her hands hovered over the pile of bread buns.

—White, please. But no tomato, thanks.

—Certainly. She said, blushing. Peter frowned at this, watching her work quickly, hands spreading, plucking and layering, her eyes down, concentrating. He leant against the glass, breathing deeply.

—For God's sake, Sylvia!

His father stared at the sandwich lying in the paper wrapper. The winds coming up the cliff tugged at it.

—What's wrong this time?

—It's... You know I hate corned beef!

—Since when?

—Since...? How many times have I been to Uruguay? Hmm?

—God... I don't know. She bit into her own sandwich, waterproof up tight around her neck.

—Too many times. He turned to Peter. —You see, Peter, what your mother is wilfully disregarding is that when a ship carries cargo for the Liebig Extract of Meat Company, the crew eat nothing but bloody corned beef all the way from the port of Fray Bentos to here! He stared at his sandwich. —Just the smell of it makes me want to vomit. He turned to Sylvia. —As I've often said.

—I'm sorry. She said, chewing. —Feel free to chuck it away and go hungry.

He looked at her, sighed, and turned to stare out at the horizon. He leaned forward and bit down heavily into his lunch. There was silence, except for the rustling of paper.

The sandwich maker pressed down the bun-top and slid it into a paper bag, scrunching up the corners and stretched to present it to him on the glass counter top.

Peter picked it up delicately, holding it by the bag, and pushed his way to the till. Mary arched an eyebrow at him and picked up the sandwich.

—What do we have here then? Eh? Sandwich? On a miserable day like today? Thought you'd want a nice hot meal, wouldn't you? She opened the bag and peered inside.

He saw her warm, moist breath going into the bag, sinking into the bread and the beef. His face wrinkled with disgust.

—Corned beef salad? Very nice, I'm sure. Not as nice as a bit of pie would be, eh? Three pound fifty all in, please.

Peter put the cup down and dug down into his pocket for change. A flash of orange from the plate beside him caught his attention. He turned and saw fish fingers on the man's plate, nestling beside chips and green peas. He stopped and looked into the hot counter, finding a fully loaded tray of fish fingers there.

—Three pound fifty. Please. Mary said.

He looked at the serving woman, taking another order for fish fingers. He turned back to Mary, still with her hand out, staring at him.

—I'm sorry, he said, keeping his voice level. —But I was told there were no more fish fingers, but there clearly are. He nodded at the counter.

She frowned. —What?

—I queued up, earlier, for hot food. I spent a long time waiting, only to be told there were absolutely no fish fingers. None at all. So I went and got a sandwich. He held up the paper bag. —But you do have fish fingers. Plenty of them.

Mary looked at the tray of deep-fried batter.

—Do you want a fish finger, love? Is that it? Because... well, there's a queue behind you.

—No. I can't, can I? I've got this sandwich now... But I wanted...

—Right... So... do you want to pay for the sandwich and move on then? Eh? Let some other folk through? There's a love.

—But... It's... How about you try and serve people properly! Try a bit harder! Who do you think pays your wages?

—Oh come on now! We all work for the same company, don't we, eh? All part of one big happy team? We're on the same side! None of this, eh?

—Yeah. For now. You wait.

Her smile dropped. She stared at him. He counted out money from his pocket and handed it to her. She dropped the coins into the till and slammed it shut.

He pushed his way out through the crush of people to the stairs at the side of the canteen, which ran up a narrow canyon to the balcony.

At the top he looked down at Mary, jabbing the keys on the till. He wanted her to look up, to see him. He wanted to grin down at her from on high. But she carried on working, serving and smiling at the customers. He walked along to his table and set the tea and the sandwich down, pulling out the chair and flopping into it.

He did not move, but stared blankly at the tabletop, his hands together on his belly, shoulders slumped. He looked at his computer, fingers tapping. He dragged it over and opened it up.

Clicking on his email, he tore the bag open and looked at the bun. Some shredded lettuce hung out the side, a white sheen of salad cream showing. He opened the composing screen and began to type.

Dear Karen,

He paused. Which way should he take this?

FUCK YOU AND YOU'RE FUCKING USELESS UNTS SERVNG SHITY FOOD WHY DO I HAVE TO PAY FOR THAT SHIT ITS SHIT AND EVERYONE ONE FUCKING NOWS IT YOU STUPID FUCKING BITCH I HATE HAVIGNN OT EAT HERE.

He sat back. Anything more? He thought. No? He selected the text and pressed 'delete'.

Peter picked up the sandwich and bit into the soft, floury bread, crunching through the lettuce and the cucumber, a slight salty tang on his tongue from the meat.

Dear Karen, he read.

It is with some regret, he typed, that I must inform you of an incident in the canteen today. I was misinformed by a member of your staff as to the availability of fish fingers. When I saw they had run out, I politely inquired if there were any more. I was lied to, and when I highlighted this, was rudely rebuked. This is very poor behaviour on the part of staff that you are responsible for. Please note this and consider implementing a training session based around customer care to rectify this.

Yours sincerely,

Peter Simpson, Change and Process Excellence.

—You can't lose your temper in a company like this. Said Andy, sitting down on the side of Peter's desk in Credit Control. —Not over some shitty bureaucracy like that. He sighed and scratched the back of his head. —But stuff is going to happen that makes you angry, so here's what I do: I write out two emails. The first is the angry one, the emotional, incoherent, over-the-top, ridiculously bile-filled one. Kind of like the one you sent to Lawrence in Sales Admin the other day. The one where you get everything out, all the hate, all the shouting. Hammer it into the keyboard. And then, and this is the important bit, the bit I cannot stress enough: you delete it. Select it all and calmly get rid of it. Then you write out the other one, the sensible, considered, thought-through one, the one you will actually send, the one you should have sent to Lawrence. Except, in that instance, you wouldn't, you'd send it to their bloody boss and get them to sort the awkward little shit out. And I can prove it works, because that's exactly what Lawrence did. Which is why I'm having to talk to you, and you can't delete me like you would an incoherent, rambling email, can you?

Peter read the email again. He preferred the first version. He always did.

He crunched on the sandwich, his chewing loud in his ears. Looking around, he watched the other diners as he ate. Several people wandered round the balcony carrying trays, looking for somewhere to sit.

He tried to picture Karen, the catering senior manager, striding into the canteen and angrily confronting Mary, surrounded by a circle of diners, fingers pointing, voices raised, feet stamping. The two women would prowl round each other, growling and hissing, hackles raised, claws drawn. And then they would charge, slashing and hacking, yowling with anger.

—Alright?... Is this err... Maureen's party?

The girl stared at him. He knew his eyes were half-shut from the dope he had been smoking.

—Charlene. It's Charlene's party. Yeah. She looked at him, frowning. —You Peter Simpson?

He nodded.

—Heard about your dad. I'm... Sorry. You... you want a beer? She held out a can of lager.

It was two months since his father had died and he was used to this sort of reaction. He took the can and nodded at her as he pushed past into the house, out of the damp, cold November night.

In the dark hallway, kids from college leaned against the walls, drinking cans of low-alcohol lager, clustered in twos and threes. They sat on the stairs, chatter and noise everywhere. Some girls pushed past him, going outside, wearing sheer cotton tops, bra straps showing, skin glowing pink from heat. He wobbled, swaying into the living room door frame, peering in at people perched on furniture, milling, leaning, swigging, screeching with laughter. Stock, Aitken and Waterman pop played on a large cabinet stereo.

Peter walked in, having to shove hard to get through. The far end of the room opened up into a conservatory, something Peter had never seen. He stared at the glass walls and ceiling: shiny slabs of onyx-black November night. He picked his way over legs and limbs, tripping and stumbling, falling into people. —Sorry! Sorry, man. —Get the fuck off me! —Sorry! He got to the sofa in the conservatory and leaned back, looking at the ceiling, lost in the sparkle of evening stars, till he toppled over backwards onto the cushions, laughing. It was then that the stereo played Rick Astley. He swore loudly. —FUCK! Astley? People around him turned and stared. He laughed and opened the can with a flash of spray. —Sorry! Sorry mate. He said to the boy in front of him. —Sorry about that. He took out a small wrapper containing three ready-rolled joints. —Here... do you want a smoke? It's good shit, man! The boy shook his head and looked away. Peter turned to the two girls next to him.—How about you?

—No thanks. Said the one with long hair, sitting closest.

—No? No? No?! Why the fuck not? Why would you not want this? This is supposed to be a party, isn't it?

—I'm fine thanks. She held up a can of lager.

—Pfff! That stuff is full of chemicals. And sugar. It'll rot you from the inside out, it will.

—Really? My dad drinks this stuff all the time.

—It'll kill him. It will. You mark my words.

The other girl pulled on her sleeve.

—Don't say that. Are you drunk? Why would you say that?

She tugged more insistently.

—Because it will happen. Now this? This is natural, herbal goodness, it will make you feel mellow and relaxed and open your mind to... everything in the... That, that shit that you and your fucking dad drink, and you! Yanking her elbow! That shit will make you loud and aggressive and stupid! STUPID! You want that?

—I think you're drunk. I think you're the one who's stupid. She turned to the other girl. —What? What is it?

There was whispering. The girl with long hair looked back at Peter, who was looking round the room, trying to see if anybody was staring at him. *Never Gonna Give You Up* came to an end, another track began.

—Oh for FUCK'S sake! Whitney Houston? Can you believe this shit?

—Are you Peter? Peter Simpson? She asked, her friend staring at him with wide eyes.

Peter pulled out a lighter and sat there, flicking the wheel, watching the sparks. He nodded.

—I... heard what happened...

He lit up the biggest of the joints. —Can't they put any decent fucking music on? I mean, this fucking shit isn't music, it's just warbling! Listen to it!

—My cousin, she... my cousin Adrianna, she... she died.

People were turning and looking at where the smoke was coming from. A short girl came through the crowd and stood beside him, staring angrily down at the joint.

—Are you...? You're... And then she was gone.

The girl with long hair watched her go. —It's OK. It's OK to be angry. You know? But...

Peter watched the smoke drift upwards in a thin stream, rippling and fluttering. People started to leave the conservatory.

—Do you know how he...? He started, but found he couldn't finish the sentence.

He took another long drag, sucking it all the way back,

filling his lungs, swelling his alveoli, the smoke fizzing into his blood like a sodastream.

He looked around, wondering how long he had been there. There was still a crowd, but they had all moved out of the conservatory and were crammed into the living room, trying not to look at him.

—Yooouuurrrrr'ee aalllllll ppiigggg igggnnnoorrrant. He said, and was surprised by his voice. He laughed, but found himself spluttering instead, flecks of spit spraying out from his mouth. He bent over to see where they'd landed, but couldn't find them on the beige carpet.

—Careful! The long-haired girl cried, trying to stop the lit end of the joint touching the sofa.

—Whoooah! He pulled his hand and the joint up, not realising how light they really were, how powerful he was. He worried about controlling his arms: where were they? What were they doing?

He stood up, too quickly, and found the wall of glass come suddenly up to his face with a bang.

—Oh my GOD!

—'M allrrright, 'm allllllright!

The girl was stood over him, he could see up her skirt. He pushed down, pushing the ground and the wall away. She bent down and picked up the lit joint from the carpet and rubbed the mark with her shoe. Peter looked down the room, at people trying not to look, stealing sideways glances.

—Come ON! This is supposed to be a PARTY! He said, waving his arms at them.

Paul Simon's *Graceland* came on the stereo.

—Oh... fuck this! He said and barged through the crowd, looking for the stereo. People staggered out of his way all too readily, mouths open, unsure what to do.

He found the stereo and a pile of tapes. He began rifling through them, throwing the shit ones aside. Some of these hit people. —Sorry! Sorry about that. Whoops! Sorry! But no-one said anything, did anything. And the less they reacted, the harder he threw.

—Ah HA! He cried, finding *Pump Up the Volume*. He noticed the too-young-girl was stood in front of him. He waggled the tape at her frowning face, and bent to fumble it into the stereo. He clicked 'play', and turned up the volume, just as it told him to do, till the sound was deafening and distorted. The girl barged past him and turned it down. He tried to push her away, but she grabbed onto the stereo cabinet and wrapped her arms around it. Everyone was looking. He stared at her, feeling his lip start to tremble, his fingers clenching and clawing. He grabbed under her arms and pulled, but she clung on, and the whole cabinet came toppling over sideways, cables yanking speakers over, hitting the ground with a crump. There was silence, music stopped.

The girl lay on the floor, one arm still under the stereo, eyes wide, skin pale. People lifted the stereo, helping her up. She was trembling, eyes welling up, lip wobbling. No-one touched Peter. The girl stood in front of him, unable to look at him.

—Get... out. She whispered, voice hoarse. —Get out of my house.

She pointed, finger sharp and thin. The crowd shifted around him, bristling, readying, eyes still everywhere but on him. He looked at them, then shrugged, and swung his hardest kick into the stereo. Hands grabbed him, grasping at his shirt, his arms; angry voices in his ear. He swung another kick, and another, toes hurting, someone screamed, and an arm went up around his neck, choking him. He wriggled and fought, lashing out with fists and feet, but a punch to his stomach stilled him and hands gripped him. He was dragged along. He saw balloons up by the ceiling, people looking down from the stairs. Yelling and shouting everywhere.

Suddenly it was cold and wet and he was released onto the pavement. He could hear shoes moving around him, his cheek pressed against the cement. Looking across the road, he could see the glimmer of orange lights reflected in the puddles, sideways to him, and the stars were on his other; faint pin-pricks above the sodium glow. The feet walked back inside the house, leaving him. The door slammed.

Peter slowly pushed himself upright, onto his knees, then further up, swaying, to his feet. He looked at the shut door, the noise of voices behind it. He slowly turned and began walking down the street, finding it tilting and turning.

A shriek of women's laughter echoed round the canteen. Peter turned, seeing six of them on a nearby table, huddled together on borrowed chairs.

He read through the email again. Was it worth getting management involved? His finger pushed the pointer over the 'discard' icon.

They're just fish-fingers.

He tapped and the email winked away.

Shutting down the laptop, he covered it with his coat and stood, his chair screaming across the floor. He walked quickly across the balcony to the stairs at the side, jogging down them.

When he was halfway, three younger men came round the corner, and began climbing up, their trays nearly filling the narrow gap.

He stopped. What the hell are they doing? Shaking his head, he pressed himself against the wall, sucking his gut in to allow them to pass.

—…honestly never eaten so much, it was fucking immense. Oh! Cheers mate! Thanks! Yeah… It had fucking cinnamon and currants, man.

—Yeah? Cheers, mate. Sorry 'bout this. 'Ere, John, what were it about Amsterdam that made you so fucking hungry? Eh?

The third man had red-hair, and thick-framed glasses. He winked at Peter as he passed.

—Can't be a fat cunt round here, can you? He said.

Peter blinked at him and looked down at the floor after he had passed. An image of the man tripping on the stairs ran through his mind: the tray crashing down and his red head clattering onto step after step, limbs bending the wrong way.

He sighed and carried on down the stairs, turning left through the door at the bottom, into the corridor, and walking down towards the toilets. There was a man in shirt sleeves washing his hands and a pair of ankles in the right-hand cubicle, shrouded in trousers. Peter pushed into the left-hand stall, gently closing the door and pushing across the loose bolt. Hanging his jacket on the back of the door, he unbuckled his trousers and sat.

He saw himself standing on the stairs, feet apart, hands up, looking down at the three men, who cringed and turned around, allowing him down. He gently squeezed and there was a hollow splash from below, a warm smell rising up from between his thighs. Then he saw them again, this time not turning round, so he leapt and kicked, punching them back down the stairs. He squeezed again and more weight dropped, and water from the bowl jumped up to surprise him. All fresh, he assured himself. Flushed fresh, completely fresh.

He waited, then pulled sheets from the dispenser, reaching behind himself to wipe without looking, the taste of corned beef and salad cream still in his mouth. He wiped again and again, before pulling up his underpants and trousers, buttoned and buckled, zipped and adjusted. He shrugged on his jacket, flushed, and opened the door with a flick of the bolt.

He briskly washed his hands in the sink, not wanting to look at himself in the mirror. He rubbed water on his face and neck, drying himself with a paper towel. He walked out quickly, going back down the corridor, through the door and up the narrow stairs to the balcony, where he stopped and looked. He could not see his table. He frowned. It should be empty, except for a black coat on top, he thought. He looked across, going from table to table. Were his eyes tricking him? None were empty. But then he saw that one table, with three men at it, had a bundle of black in the corner.

He stared. One of the men was the red-head with glasses. He walked over, fingers twitching. He stood at the end of the table, looking down at them. They paused in their eating and glanced up, still chewing. Peter saw that the ginger one had fish fingers. He pointed at his coat.

—You... You've got my stuff.

—Is that...? Red-head pointed. —Is it yours?

Peter sneered, rolling his eyes. —What? Yes! His hands clenched, a lump in his throat.

—Sorry mate! Do you... I dunno... wanna sit down?

The other two went back to their food.

—No, no... Peter looked around the balcony. —Could you not have...?

—What? Sat somewhere else? The red-head shook his head. —Sorry. There was nowhere... We looked, didn't we boys? Nowhere else to sit. You here, all on your own? We saved you a seat... if you...?

Peter looked at the spare seat, in the corner. —It's just a bit... rude. Isn't it? Taking someone's table.

Red-head looked at Peter, eyebrows furrowed. —Sorry mate, but... you can't have an entire table just for yourself... I mean, there's a seat... if you want it.

—No, no, no! You're welcome to it! Enjoy! Not like I'd been sitting here all morning, is it?

—You don't have to be a cunt about it.

—Can I just have my stuff. Please.

One of the other two men grabbed at Peter's coat, which snagged on the laptop. Frowning, he yanked, flicking the coat out, dropping the laptop with a bang. One sleeve landed in a plate of pie and gravy.

—For fucks sake! Be careful!

—Don't 'ave a fuckin' go at me, mate...

Peter took his coat, wiping the cuff. —My laptop.

Please…

The man picked up the computer in one hand and swung it at Peter. —There you go.

Peter turned to leave.

—Here, mate? Said the red-head. —You ought not leave your laptop lying around! He grinned at his table mates. —Someone might hack in, have a look. Know what I mean?

Peter stopped. —Have you… fiddled with this?

The men laughed.

—Nah, mate. Honestly! Just… passing on advice. Steve here knows what I mean!

—What have you done? This is a company laptop… if you've…?

—Seriously! We've done nothing! Just being friendly. You seem like the type of guy who might want to keep his browser history as private as possible…!

The other two men looked up, grinning.

Peter looked at them.

—Wh… What? He stuttered.

They snorted with laughter, looking right at him. He frowned and walked away, his arms full of coat and computer.

Why should looking up Arthur Finchley be wrong? Peter thought. Unless… maybe they think I'd do the same. Copy him. Lose control. Kick off.

He stopped and looked back at the three men. Maybe it wouldn't be such a bad thing.

He started down the stairs, trying to look past the bulk he was carrying.

Shit, he thought, stopping.

The laptop bag…

It's still under…

Shit!

He stood on the second step down. Should I go back? Shit! I have to… Don't I? Could I not just get another one? How much do they…?

Shit!

The power adapter!

This is not my fault! I was put in this position! Geoff and his sloppy fucking management! Poor risk assessment! He should have known this might happen!

And now I'm... He went down a step.

I... I...

Shit.

I need that adapter.

He turned slowly on the step, took a deep breath, and started back up. Looking over, he saw the red-haired man hurrying towards him, holding the laptop bag. Peter stopped, and glanced back down the stairs.

—Oi, mate? You forgot this.

He held out the bag, smiling.

Peter reached out and took the handle, dipping his head.

Red-head nodded, turned, and jogged back to his table. Peter watched him go, hand white-clenched around the handle of the laptop bag. He started back down the stairs.

Smug fucking cunt, he thought. Fuck him, fucking cock. He shook the bag, wanting to swing it from wall to wall, whirl it round and round, battering everything.

He sagged against the side. Why bother? You can't win. There's always someone with a quick comment, a snide look. A snigger behind you. Challenge them? They just laugh. Put you in your place. Too many of them. He shook his head.

—I'm going to have to get a better job, Peter.

His mother was sat in the middle of the living room with bills and bank statements in an arc around herself. The Christmas tree blinked in the corner. Too much tinsel covered the room. Peter watched her, sullen and miserable.

—Dad should've sued...

She looked up, frowning. —What for?

—Y'know, when he had pneumonia, on the boat, and they, like, denied him treatment.

—Oh… yes, well. She went back to the bills. —If he had… he would have lost… She moved a sheet to another pile.

—No he wouldn't: Millions.

She sighed. —It wasn't quite as… simple as he made out. He was ill when he got on board, in Argentina. He signed a contract saying he was fit to work. He wasn't. He thought it was just a way to get home and get paid. And so when they changed course for Chile, he argued against it. Well, he dressed it up as a protest against the military dictatorship, which, to be fair, did bother him, but…

She picked up another bill, turning it over, eyebrows raised. —When you're a sailor, at sea, you can't do that. They have a special word for it: mutiny.

Peter stared at the dark, grey TV screen. —But they knew he was ill… and they didn't try and help him.

—By rights, technically, they could have dumped him on shore and let him make his own way home. As it was, they confined him to quarters, gave him the antibiotics, fed and watered him. They could've pressed charges. They didn't. They paid him compensation, which was… more than generous.

—So… we ought to be grateful because they could have done much worse?

She looked up at him, blinking. —Yes.

—But… his health? He never went back to sea because of it.

—No… I'm afraid he was blacklisted. True, his lungs were never the same. Bronchial Obliterations. But how much of that was smoking? She shook her head. —Never heard him talk about suing the tobacco companies… And you met some of his shipmates… None of them were exactly athletes, were they? They still got work. She picked up pile of bills and flicked though them. —Besides, the industry was laying off people left and right back then. Containerisation made everything quicker and cheaper and easier. Less boats, less men to sail them.

Peter sat there, staring out of the window. After a while, he got up, went to his room, and shut the door.

He turned the corner at the bottom of the stairs and looked out at the canteen: a jostling, rippling tide of humanity; moving, eating, talking. Eight hundred eyes, he thought, looking around, searching for something to stare at. All of them looking back at him, the other side of the divide, the man who is sunk, stained darkly by the drowning waters, whilst they think themselves safe on-board a shallow raft.

Peter craned his neck, standing on tip-toe, searching amongst the crowd. Beneath the stairs he saw the small counter that, five or six years ago, was used for tray returns. Is anyone…? No? He edged into the crowd, dodging round people carrying trays, fetching cutlery, moving among the low forest of tables and chairs. Elbows and legs jutted out, coat sleeves and handbag straps trailed the ground. He stepped and shuffled through, heading ever closer. When he got there, he claimed it quickly with his coat and laptop.

People around him glanced, then went back to their phones, food or gossip.

There was no chair at the counter, and its surface was stained and chipped. He turned and saw a spare chair at another table.

—Excuse me? May I…?

A surprised look, then a dismissive wave.

He hoisted the chair up and over, into the shadow of the stairs, setting it down and wrapping his coat around the back. He pulled it out to sit, then noticed someone walking towards him.

Shit!

Mary's stained whites were pushing through the crowd.

What does she want? The sell-off? Shit!

She looked at him, brow furrowed, urgently picking her way through the tangle of diners.

Oh fuck… He put the bag next to the laptop,

unzipping, putting it in.

—Excuse me…?

He turned to her.

—I just wanted to say: them fish fingers?

——Yes?

—They were still cooking.

He stared at her, open-mouthed. —Oh. OK.

—So there weren't any when you first asked, but there were when you came to pay, because they'd come out the fryer by then. She smiled at him.

Peter leaned back, raising his eyebrows. —That… Yes. That's fine.

She watched him, jumping from eye to eye.

—Well… He continued. —I'm sorry. I… I… got it wrong. Sorry.

He breathed out, relaxing his shoulders, snorting with a laugh, smiling at her.

—That's OK. Just thought I'd… explain, is all. She said, as he got his laptop back out.

—No. Absolutely. Thank you.

She stood there.

He stopped and looked back at her.

—Sorry. But… She asked.

—Is it the table?

—What?

—Am I not allowed to sit here?

—Oh… no, no. No, you can sit here if you want.

Oh shit.

Here it comes.

He stared at her, laptop half-out.

—I know you can't really talk about it, but… please, what did you mean?

—What?

—You said… You seemed to hint… that there may be… changes coming…

He pushed the computer back in, pulling the Velcro strip out from underneath.

—Hmm? Did I? I don't remember that.

She sighed. —Yes, you did. I said: 'hey, we're all on the same side, aren't we?' And you said: 'For now. Just wait'.

Peter stood and zipped up the case.

—Oh that! I just meant that... well, from an interdepartmental point of view... We're not, are we?

—Well, no. But... that's now. You implied a future in which we aren't.

He struggled, the zip caught on a thread.

—I... just meant that... in the future, each department will need to make separate... defendable business cases for their... erm, budgets.

—So they are going to make cut-backs?

He stopped and turned. —I think this is something you need to talk to Karen about. Your manager?

—We're stripped back to the bone as it is. There isn't anything more we can trim!

Peter zipped down, then up, down, up.

—It's just one of the... unfortunate pitfalls of working...

—Of what? Working in the same place for thirty-odd years? Giving your... life to one place? She glared at him.

He picked up his coat and the laptop bag and began walking back through the crowd. He heard her following.

—Please! Before you... Wait! Please! Stop! You have to...!

He stumbled over a bag, his foot caught in the strap, and staggered against someone's chair. A hand pulled him upright. Laughter was loud in his ears.

—I think I know what they're going to do. Said Mary.

He looked at her serious face. Nobody at the table was laughing, and yet there it was, chortling and chuckling, sniggering and screaming, bellowing right beside him.

—And I know it's not going to work. She said, helping him up. —Can I...? Have you got time to talk?

Peter looked around, going from face to face. He shook his head as he turned for the door.

She followed.

—It's misguided, is what it is. Fanciful ideology, dressed up as efficiency. If they... do.

He barged through the door and crossed the corridor.

—It'll... it'll not be any better. It'll be worse! And more expensive! Think about it! They'll have to turn a profit, which means saving on overheads and ramping up the prices!

Peter went to the door of a meeting room and listened. Was there laughter coming from inside? Voices?

—As it is now, we can run at a bit of a loss, it's OK, the rest of the company absorbs it, but whoever you get in will not only have to get that profit, but they'll have to pay rent, won't they?

He walked down the corridor to the next meeting room.

—The company is looking to make money off of this, isn't it? That's why they do anything, right? So they're going to sell off the canteen, get someone else to run it, they don't care how.

He opened the door. Two men looked up from sheets of paper laid out on the table.

—Sorry. Peter muttered, closing the door.

—I'm right, aren't I? So there's your first flaw: for every pound spent now, you get a pounds worth of ingredients and staff. Right?

Peter looked up and down the corridor, trying to hear what the whispering was saying. Was it talking about him?

—But when you've sold this place to a contractor, every pound will have to be divided between food, wages, profit and rent. So... they'll have to cut costs. They'll cut us lot and hire staff who'll work for less because they're worth less. They'll get in cheaper produce, but they'll sell it for more.

Peter turned and walked back down the corridor, hurrying away from the laughter, the bright, shining laughter.

—People will stop eating here so the contractor will pull out and then you won't have a canteen. And you know what the really ironic thing is? You know who'll really profit from this? The lawyers. Commercial law. Them buggers are paid more than anyone else. And they'll go over the contract for weeks. Months. It'll cost everyone a fortune before the first coffee has even been poured.

He stopped outside the toilets —It's nothing to do with me! He said, loudly.

—Oh, but it is! It is! You can do something about it! Argue against it! Make a business case for keeping the canteen!

He shook his head and pushed into the men's toilets.

—You have to tell them they're making a mistake! You're part of them lot, aren't you? Aren't you?!

Peter leaned against the white tiles.

—Please! Just... talk to them! You have to!

He staggered over into the left-hand cubicle, the lock was down a long tunnel, his hands floating, disconnected from his body. The floor pitched and swayed.

He stood there, hearing only his own breathing. In, out, the soft hush of air in his throat.

Don't look at the bowl. He thought. Don't look down there. If you do... Don't think what might happen.

Cold sweat stood out on his skin, his mouth grew slick with saliva.

Breath calmly.

His hands shook as he hung up his coat on the back of the door and then delicately bent to put the laptop on the floor. He swallowed. Putting the seat down, he sat, putting his head in his hands and trying to think of something else.

Nausea. Sign of heart trouble. Adrenaline. Stress, he thought.

—Hey! Jumpy! Said a voice right behind him.

Peter flinched, nearly dropping the tin he was holding. Sam stood to his side, his face split with a grin.

—Oh, I'm sorry, Jumpy... Surprise you? Just wanted...

these! And he reached into Peter's trolley for the shelf labels. —No need to over-react so much! Man, you're so... jumpy!

He stood there as Peter slotted the can onto the shelf and reached for another.

—Peaches? Hmm...? Sam picked up one of the tins from the shelf. —Don't you think they look like arses? The peach: it looks like an arse, doesn't it? Do you think about arses, Jumpy? I bet you do, you look like a man who enjoys arses. Emma says you like men's arses. Do you? Do you think about men's arses, Jumpy?

—No, no I don't.

—You calling Emma a liar?

—What? No. But...

—Because that would be an insult to Emma, and then, Jumpy, I'd have to teach you a lesson, wouldn't I? Can't have you going round insulting people like that, can I?

—I don't...

—I think you're walking on very thin ice there, Jumpy. Insulting people like that. I'd watch it, if I were you, I'd be very careful indeed, because...

And then, from the main aisle, came the squeaking shoes of Wilkins, the night manager.

He paused, looking at Peter.

—Everything alright here... ahh? He consulted a clipboard. —Peter?

Nodding, Peter turned, but Sam had already skulked off round the corner.

—Make sure you, ahh, finish by two. Move on to dry produce after break. There's a good fella.

In the staff sitting area, Peter sat on the second table, looking over at the first, where Sam and Emma and David and all the ones who boasted of nightclubs and gigs, of sex and drugs, lounged about, giggling and laughing, sharing in-jokes and flirtation. Sam was whispering into the ear of new girl Tracey, who was snoozing, her head on her arms.

—Your dad ever go to Afghanistan?

Peter looked at Scott, sat opposite. Theo and Denise were also on the table.

—Err... Dunno. Does it have a port?

—Yeah, think so.

—Well... probably then.

Denise leant over.

—Why do you keep looking at them?

—Why do they think they're so fucking brilliant? He said. —They swan about the place, doing fuck-all! They look down on us as though we're shit! Fuck them!

Sam looked up at Peter and whispered something to Tracey, who shook with laughter, lifting her head to look over as well. Peter turned away with a sigh.

—Forget about them... Said Denise.

—How can I? They're always right there! In front of me! They pick apart anyone that's different... that's not one of them...! If you're outside their... then you're a target! Hardly fucking fair, is it?

—Yeah, well... I don't want to be one of them...

—Well they wouldn't have you, would they?

Peter frowned over at the other table, his face growing hot and red. Denise sighed, got up, and walked back out to the warehouse. Theo followed, shaking his head.

—Well done. Said Scott.

Sam stood, licked a finger and stuck it in Tracey's ear, making her squeal, her hand slapping his. He laughed, walking away, passing Peter and Scott.

—Come on, come on, ladies! Rise and shine! Time to stop kissing and do some work!

At six AM, when the sky was lightening, Scott and Peter walked out of the staff doors and round the corner to the railway arch. There they stopped and Peter pulled out two joints, handing one to Scott. Without talking, they lit them and stood for a while, breathing in the smoke in the darkness of the tunnel. Then they carried on walking, the streets nearly empty, an occasional car coming past.

—You going down the park this weekend? Said Peter.

—Dunno… Need to save some money. Rent and that.
—You pay rent? I thought you lived with your mum!
—Yeah. Still have to pay me way though. Don't you?
—No… My money.
—Lucky twat!
—Ha! Yeah! Look, I want some more weed for this weekend, maybe some whizz as well. Know of anything going?
—Shouldn't you, like, offer her something? Contribute to the bills, you know?
—What? Nah, it's fine! More money to get out me skull! So… know of anything?
—Nah, sorry.

They walked on a bit further.

—It's a shitty job, Pete. No-one does it for long.
—Yeah?
—I've been doing it six months. I'm going to have to move on.
—Shame. Seriously.
—Just the way it is. And no-one, 'cept maybe Wilkins, wants to be there.
—Yeah…
—So you have to either get out before you go nuts, y'know? Or keep your head down until the arseholes leave.

Peter nodded.

—But just don't become one of the arseholes.

They stopped at the corner. Scott took a final drag on the joint and crushed it underfoot. —Laters. He turned and walked quickly away down the hill. Peter wandered along, smoking his joint down to the quick.

Clutching his head in his hands, sat in the toilet cubicle, Peter tried to breath slowly and steadily, thinking calm, peaceful thoughts.

Should I call someone? Is this what a heart attack feels like? No… What about… arrhythmia? Aneurysm? There's all sorts of ways…

He imagined the knock on the door at home.

—Louise Smith? Can I come in? I'm afraid I have some bad news. Do you want to sit down? Your partner, the co-habitee of this address, Peter Simpson? I'm so sorry, but he was found dead earlier on today. Yes, I know, it's a shock, don't worry, unusual reactions, such as laughter, are common… He was found in the toilets… Actually, yes, he was sitting on the… Well, we think it was caused by being chased there by a member of the catering team. Yes, I suppose it would be quite funny, if a man hadn't died. Are you going to take this seriously? We think he was literally frightened to death. Yes, by a dinner-lady. Why is that so funny? Please, pick yourself up! Peter is dead!

He leant back, loosening his tie, blinking at the light bulb above him, clenching and twitching his fingers.

four

It was two hours and nineteen minutes past three PM when the screen went black and the fan stopped whirring. There was a moment of silence in the toilet cubicle. Peter's hands still hung above the keyboard, tips poised to continue his last sentence.

He frowned.

It's supposed to tell me. Isn't it? A little thing pops up to say it's running out of battery…

He pressed the power button, holding it down. Nothing happened. The screen remained blank and dark.

Is it the battery? Or is it something else?

Lifting the computer, he sniffed the vents just under the screen.

Doesn't smell of burning.

He jabbed at the power button again, shaking his head.

This is the trouble with these fucking things: they need power to work. Can't we have a clockwork version? Wind-up laptops? Work anywhere then.

Ahh, but we did, didn't we? Back in the dim and distant past. And lo, the Lord looked down and gave unto Moses the holy typewriter. And He said unto him: go into the desert, and there ye shall write, but only if you can find ribbon and paper...

—Be careful, Peter!

His smudged-black fingers shook trying to delicately tuck the ribbon into the clip. Behind him, in bed, was his father, watching, his breathing rasped and laboured.

—Come on Peter, get on with it, times ticking.

—Sorry! It won't... won't go in!

—For God's sake... let me. You get the box out.

The heavy machine was grabbed from him and big hands tensed the ribbon, the edge slipping easily into the clip. Peter got resentfully off the bed and pulled out a battered cardboard box from underneath. The picture on its lid was of an old jigsaw puzzle. His father took the box and opened it, rifling through the papers inside.

—Don't you want to go and play outside? He muttered.

—It's raining. And I'm fourteen.

—Rubbish: it's only spitting. Go on. I want to work.

—But... Mum said I had to sit with you...

—Oh for God's..! Get out of here! Go outside and pretend you're in a rain forest or something.

Peter slouched out of the bedroom, hearing the cylinder clicking paper round.

He paused at the door.

—Peter? The voice cracked and rattling. —Outside. Now.

Peter turned and ran, suddenly frightened, out into the street. He ran through the steady patter of cold water, up to the top of the road. Turning, he listened. There, in the breeze, came the tock-tock, tickity-tock of his father typing, pouring out his mind into a machine with violent, spindly arms, punching paper. Peter turned and walked quickly away.

He slumped on the toilet lid, staring down at the screen. The shutdown had happened very quickly, almost instantly. There was an autosave function. The file would have saved, wouldn't it? He glared at the screen. Wouldn't it?

He shook his head. I've lost it all. Gone.

He imagined driving home, car headlights on the road, sliding into their drive ahead of him, shrinking down to bright shapes on the garage. The clunk of the car door echoing down the street. Footsteps crunching to the front door, the snick of his key in the lock, and the empty, silent darkness of the house.

He saw himself tip-toeing up the stairs, to sit by her bed and watch her sleep, as he had done several times. But it was different now. There was no going back. Maybe he would run up the stairs and bang open the door, loudly emptying the drawers of his clothes. Maybe he would scream at her, tell her what he thought, then walk away.

When she slept, her breathing was so slight and delicate; a fragile movement of air. He would watch, then gently wake her. Maybe she would smile at him, be glad, and cry. He would tell her he really loved her. Then he would pick up his pillow, from his side of the bed, the bed he hadn't slept in for three weeks, and hold it tight across her face until she stopped struggling.

He slammed the screen down on the laptop. If I had a plug... he thought, looking along the skirting board of the cubicle.

He stretched, reaching up to the ceiling, pointing his toes. How long have I had this? Two years? How long are they supposed to last? Planned obsolescence. Make sure they're out of the way for the next generation. The next new thing.

Beyond three PM now. Will she know? Would they call? Would they say it over the phone? Thought they preferred to say it to your face. Tinny human voice down a wire, sounding oh-so distant: —I'm sorry to have to tell you this, but...

He imagined a little flat, with a view of a river. A small apartment several floors up, walls lined with books and paintings, a sofa in front of a coffee table. Big bay windows overlooking the city and the trees along the water. On a winter's night, rain lashing down from coal-grey clouds, he would lie on the sofa, wrapped in a blanket, drinking tea, reading a book under a single lamp. And on summer mornings, he would cook himself a breakfast in his small kitchen, where everything was laid out how he wanted, then walk along the river, nodding to the fishermen, smelling the green of it, inhaling the natural.

Everything had been sick and diseased for such a long time.

Or he could get transferred. Run away, yet again. Avoid all the painful memories lurking round corners, waiting to punch him down. He would go to London. Leather shoes tapping down stone steps into the underground, voices all around, adverts on the wall, on his way to the West End, rush of air on the platform, doors hissing open. Taxis, buses, rushing round the streets. Lights and darkness, shiny metal speeding by. Oh-so-much speeding metal roaring past.

—Good morning, children. It is with the deepest regret... that I have to tell you... that Andrew Edgars, of year four, has... passed on.

Behind the headmaster stood a policeman, his peaked cap in his hands, buttons bright on black uniform.

—I know Andrew had many close friends among you, and I'm sorry I can't make this any easier... hearing it like this. And he was a part of so many peoples' lives that... He was our classmate, our pupil, our friend. A bright and clever boy, one with a glittering future, so carelessly, stupidly cut short. He will be sorely missed by all here, as well as by his parents and sister. A true, true tragedy. The headmaster paused and looked at a sheet of paper, his hand shaking slightly. —Now... erm... in the light of what has happened, we have Sergeant Richardson here this morning to talk about road safety, and how it is immensely important to be careful when crossing roads. How the consequences can be so... yes. Sergeant?

The policeman smiled at the headmaster and stepped forward to the front of the stage.

—Good morning, children. Yes, what happened to Andrew was terrible. I was at the scene myself, I saw... I saw how dangerous roads can be. But all it takes is a few simple checks before you cross, and you'll be safe. It's easy. Stop. Look. And listen. I drum it into my own son. He's about the same age as Andrew. Crosses the same road for football practise. Wears the same sort of... same... The policeman fiddled with his tunic buttons, fingers trembling. —Yes. Stop. Look. Listen. Do that, and we can avoid another tragedy, can't we?

The policeman looked at the children, eyebrows raised, mouth in a slight smile. He turned and smiled at the headmaster, who nodded and came back to the front.

—Well, there we go, children. An important lesson for us all, I feel. Sergeant Richardson will be doing some road safety classes in the playground today, just to practise your road-crossing. Your teachers will now escort you out.

When they were out of the hall, Peter overheard Norman Nicholas: —Bill Dorsten saw it happen! Andy got hit on Western Road where Bill lives. Said he got hit by a lorry! They were picking bits of him out the radiator grill!

—What?

—The lorry hit him so hard, there was only a hand and a foot sticking out of the front! And a bit of his head!

—Really?

Another voice chipped in: —Amanda Graham said it were a bus and he went right underneath and got wrapped round the wheels like spaghetti!

As Peter walked through the corridor, he saw Andy Edgars coming the other way, face down, small, dark eyes behind glasses, blazer slightly too big for him. He saw him slowly step out into a road, in front of a car, his nostrils filled with exhaust fumes, bonnet shining, traffic roaring, school shoes crunching on grit and tarmac. Then glancing, so slow, muscles not working, driver's eyes widening, knuckles tighten, foot stamping. And Andy felt the hot air ahead of the engine, the trombone slide of it right beside him, sunlight glinting from the paintwork. And then it was upon him, kicking him under, rattling him between the drive shaft and the road, his body fluttering in the wheels and the gears and the dirt, grease and blood everywhere. Peter felt pain wash over him, skin burning, tearing, ripping apart nerve and tendon, bones crunching, splintering, jaw bone biting up through his skull, teeth popping out through his nose…

Peter snapped back into the day, Andy gone, the bustle of the corridor continuing.

At dinner that evening, his mother asked him why he was so quiet. As he told them, his father listened, his fork held rigidly in a white-knuckled fist.

—Do you really want to know what the final few seconds of life are like? He asked.

—Jim… Said Peter's mother.

—He won't have had time to have any profound insight into life, nor any fear of what was happening. He would have just had time to react. Gut instinct. No thought at all. There was a container that fell, in Singapore, three guys underneath and one just stood there, wondering why the others were running away. He may have registered that it was getting dark… but…

—Maybe this isn't the time, Jim.

—It's a better way to go though. Quick. No time to be scared, to suffer. There was one time in Sao Paulo when I saw a man get his arm caught in an winch. Slowly started reeling him in, wrapping coils of steel cable over his hand, wrist, forearm… And he was screaming and shouting, praying, pleading, but the other men were too far away. He was being pulled right in, and when it reached his shoulder, he set his feet square and pulled. He knew exactly what he was doing and what would happen if he didn't. He let out this almighty scream and fell backwards onto the deck, blood pumping out of him. He'd seen what his death would be like, and he was prepared to do anything to avoid it. Like I said, you want it to be quick, rather than slow. Torture if it's slow.

—Jim... the boy died. Just...

—Yeah. And I'm sorry for that... but what I'm saying is, he won't have suffered too much, if that helps.

Peter stared at the laptop. What was the last thing that went through its mind? What nugget of spiritual truth could we derive from 0011011010? He hefted up the machine, weighing it. So much scrap, at the end of the day. Bits to be recycled.

He turned it around, looking for screws.

Maybe they could get the spreadsheet from the harddrive. If I could get it out, they might be able to just plug it into something else. They're clever. There are ways and means.

—And so we reach here, a death in the Kalahari. And this magnificent bull elephant, who, after wandering these lands alone for much of his life, has now come to the end of his journey.

It was sunset on a savannah plain. An elephant lay on the orange ground, its ear flapping feebly. Its trunk flicked, once. One leg scraped the dust.

—Death here, for the largest of the land mammals, is of old age: a natural end, a life fully lived.

The elephant stopped moving.

—And when any animal dies on these plains, there are those around whose job it is to take care of the corpse. But when the animal is as large as this, then... well, it simply requires a team effort.

The camera cut to birds, circling high in the darkening sky.

—Vultures are the first to spot the carcass, as they usually are: their eyesight is remarkably accurate over very great distances.

Long-necked, black vultures hopped along the ground by the dead elephant. One plucked at the limp trunk, shaking it, then hopping away.

—But they know they will not be the first to deal with this particular body, for the elephant's skin is too thick for their beaks to rip open. They are waiting for help.

As night fell, camera lamps lit the carcass. Dark shapes ran across the background, four-legged and shaggy. One walked up to the rear of the elephant. Eyes glowed green in the darkness.

—These are Spotted Hyena, with jaws strong enough to crush bones and tear through thick hide.

Several of the dark animals bit into the thighs and stomach of the elephant, their teeth bared, legs pushing, ears flat back.

—Hyenas will primarily feed on the elephant's muscle. But sharing does not come easily to them.

Two of the Hyena, heads soaked near black in blood, squabbled, lips pulled back, making hacking, high-pitched yaps.

—And, if fighting amongst themselves was not enough, the vultures are now keen to join in the meal …

Picked out by the lamp-light, a huge ruffled bird stood on top of the elephant, looking down at the hyenas, still tugging and ripping at the rear. The bird hopped forward, flapping its wings. Another was on the ground beside the corpse.

Suddenly, the camera cut to a flurry of black shapes flapping and fighting around the belly. There was a close-up of a vulture tugging at a long, stringy piece of intestine.

—These birds are the ultimate waste-disposal systems. Evolution has fine-tuned them to fill a vital role in this environment's eco-system. Bald heads keep flight feathers clean, and their stomachs contain incredibly strong acid, capable of digesting almost anything, as well as destroying otherwise deadly pathogens which build up in corpses.

A vulture tilted its head back, swallowing a wedge of meat.

—These birds will gorge themselves, bolting several

kilos in a single sitting.

A hyena and a vulture snarled and snapped at each other, wings flapping, jumping, both covered in gore.

—This raucous dinner party will continue for the rest of the night.

The scene cut to the very early morning. The elephant was ripped and blooded, palid white intestines open to the flies and the dust. The hyenas had left and only a few vultures were pecking at the stomach innards.

—Come the first rays of sun, and more diners come to call.

Long legged, blotchy dogs jogged in, noses pointed at the corpse, huge, bat-like ears attentive.

—African Wild Dogs. Killed by humans in cattle country, they're now a rare sight in the Kalahari.

The dogs tugged meat from the elephant.

—But being dogs, they will scavenge, and they would never pass such a feast as this.

Several puppies trotted in, and senior dogs made way for them. The camera zoomed in on one pup, its mouth smeared with blood.

—African Wild Dogs are unique in allowing their young to feed first.

The pack ripped and bit and fed. There was barking and playing, running around, mouths open. Then they trotted away, a ragged line of dark shapes.

The sun rose higher.

A tall stork picked its way slowly towards the elephant, its long, thick bill emerging out of a bald, mottled head, looking burnt and disfigured.

—The Marabou Stork. It has the largest wingspan in the world, equal only to the Andean Condor. It is known as the undertaker bird, both from appearance and behaviour.

The bird towered over the vultures, looking into the carcass. It bent, and snapped its huge bill.

—Other, smaller animals join in. Like these Pied Crows

and Bat-Eared Foxes, as well as a few lizards.

A large bird, black with a white bib, stood high on the flank, looking down at a small, sandy fox with enormous ears. Both were cautious.

—But much of the disposal will be being done by insects, flies laying eggs, beetles burrowing, lines of ants creeping, crawling under the skin, slowly breaking down this huge animal.

The sun slowly dipped, casting the landscape in a vivid orange.

—At sundown, a different set of hyenas come to feed, the much rarer Brown Hyena.

Several shaggy animals came jogging in, mouths held open, scattering the crows and the vultures.

—These are more wolf-like than their spotted cousins, and are pure scavengers. Spotted Hyena are unlikely to feed on the Elephant now, after it has been dead for so long.

The sun set, putting furry shapes in silhouette, the elephant an angled, tatty outline.

The camera cut to bright sunlight and a patch of darkened ground littered with brown bones. Empty eye-sockets looked down the lens.

—It is two days since this animal lay down here, and died. And now, from this magnificent bull Elephant, all that is left are these bones, and skin. And this, on its own, is remarkable for its speed, but is not what is so special about this death. It's what happens next.

Arthur walked across the camera's field of vision, which panned to follow him.

—Over there, under that Acacia Tree, is where the Brown Hyena pack are sleeping off their meal. And in the branches of that tree over there, is where the vultures roosted overnight.

The camera cut to the hyenas, looking sleepily out from the shade, tails flicking away flies.

Arthur bent down, squatting in the hot sun, pointing at

a small curl of faeces amongst clumps of yellow grass.

—This is hyena dung. Under that tree will be more.

He pointed at another patch of faeces, more liquid, near-black.

—And this is from the vultures. So under that tree, and that tree, and scattered all over this area, will be a lot more of this. And it will feed those trees, working its way down into the soil, being absorbed through the root system, up into the leaves which will… He turned and pointed to the horizon, where a family of elephants pulled down the Acacia branches. ——feed the next generation of elephants.

Arthur paused, looking down at the skull.

—This animal, all animals, end up back in the food chain. It may be unpleasant to think about it, but that's how it is. In the wild, nothing is wasted. As humans, we could learn a lot from the natural world.

Peter held the laptop. We don't really repair things anymore, do we? Everything's got to be new, bright, shiny. —Cheaper to get a new one… they say. Mass-produced. Churn them out at three a minute. How long to fit a new motherboard? No idea. An hour? And scratched and chipped after. Better to get a new one.

He sighed, and bent sideways to slide the computer into the case leant against the wall. Maybe something recoverable. Get the IT guys to look at it tomorrow.

Standing, his knees and backside complaining, grating and numb, he staggered slightly, then arched his back, stretching his arms up to the ceiling. Alleluia! Praise the Lord! And shrunk back down to himself, scratching his groin. For he is risen, sayeth the Almighty Father.

Getting his coat down from the door, he opened the lock with a ping and walked out, into the sight of the mirror, and stood there, staring at the crumpled, dishevelled man before him. He reached up and gently moved his eye until it was facing forwards.

Shaking his head, he walked over to the door, and out,

into the corridor. He could hear the gentle chimes and clatter of dinner being served in the canteen, high-heels tapping over the wooden floor, chairs being scrapped back, voices chattering, a man laughing, raucously.

The doors swung open and two women come striding out into the corridor, smiling at each other. One of them looked at Peter, her smile dropping, a slight frown forming. And then they were passed and began talking again. —Yes, I've been to a place in Nottingham where they do something similar. Terrifying, isn't it? And the other woman laughed.

It's five-thirty, thought Peter. I could just go home. See what the news is. See what...

He looked down at the laptop case.

I ought... really, to see if it still works. Just... just quickly.

The smell of sausages and rich, warm gravy came drifting out from the canteen.

Can't eat that at home. He thought. Smell of cooking makes her sick.

He stepped back. I ought to go.

He looked down again and shook his head. No. A little more time won't make any difference

Pushing open the door, he peered in at the serving area. It was not Mary behind the till, but a younger woman with dark hair. He walked slowly in.

A new shift. Eight hours from seven AM would see them leaving at... three, he thought, frowning at the coincidence.

Everyone leaves me at three. Creating pain and annoyance in their wake.

He got a cup and fumbled a tea bag into it. Might not be three, exactly. And they'll be back tomorrow.

And at some point I have to go home...

He carried his tray and tea along to the hot food counter. There were slices of grey roast beef, threaded with translucent gristle; solid mounds of buttery mashed potato, sprinkled with herbs; honey-coloured roast potatoes, edges darkened; a black, cast-iron pot with a sign in front saying: 'carrot and coriander soup, with olive bread'; and a steel tray full of lamb curry. Peter looked over them all, frowning. And then, at the back, he saw a tray filled with brown batter, waves washing over half-submerged sausages.

He looked up at the serving woman.

—Toad-in-the-hole please, with mash and gravy.

She nodded and picked up a plate, slicing and scooping and ladling. Before she gave it to him, she wiped away a smudge of sauce from the rim.

—Thank you. He said, accepting the plate. —Thank you so much.

She smiled, tilting her head to him and keeping eye contact. He smiled back as he dragged the tray over to the till.

—Four pounds fifty, please. Said the woman with dark hair. He looked up at her big brown eyes as he handed over coins warmed by his pocket.

—Thank you, thank you for this. He said.

—That's alright love! Have a good evening. She said, as she dropped the money into the drawer.

—Thank you! You too!

He walked away, still smiling, to the cutlery stand.

—Pete! Hey!

He stopped, hand reaching into the basket of forks.

—Pete? Hey! Mate?

He turned. At the counter, being served a plate, was Martin. He grinned at Peter. —Here we meet again!

Peter turned back to the baskets, slowly picking up a knife and fork.

—Yeah... He said, putting the cutlery onto his tray with a clatter, and turning to look at the seating.

—Wait! Peter...? Wait, I'll just... Wait there! Martin said, giving coins to the woman at the till.

Peter stood by the cutlery, watching Martin come

hurrying over.

—Hi! Yeah! So… how are you?

—Fine. Thank you. Said Peter. —You?

—Oh… Martin picked up his cutlery. —Y'know… He said, with a shrug, throwing the silverware noisily onto his tray. The fork rattled over the edge and clattered onto the floor. Martin stamped it into silence, blushing. —It's… errm… Y'know, y'know… been better. He kicked the dropped fork under the stand and got another from the basket. —Right! Where d'ya wanna sit?

Peter stared at him.

—Hey, how about…? Said Martin, pointing at one of the low-slung sofas under the balcony.

—Well… I'm not sure… Said Peter, looking at a vacant table just to one side.

But Martin was already walking over, pushing through the tables, squeezing past people already sat. Peter looked down at his tray, and followed.

Martin shuffled round the low coffee table and slowly lowered himself onto the sofa, landing with a grunt, a jingle of cutlery, and his plate sliding towards him.

Peter put his tray down and pulled over a dining chair from a nearby table. Settling himself, he balanced his tray on his knees, the smell of his food rising up to him. He looked across at Martin, hunched over his dinner on the table, legs spread wide to push his belly closer.

—Man! Fuck me! I am starving! Said Martin, slicing up his food, knife scraping on the china. —Feel like I've not eaten for, like, a month! Y'know?

—Really? Did you not have any lunch?

Peter watched as Martin forked batter and sausage into his mouth.

—Well, yeah!… Like, I had a sub… But… Said Martin, voice muffled. —It's just a sandwich: not proper food, is it?

—Mmmnn. Peter replied, nodding. The sausage was, he thought, definitely a Lincolnshire this time: herby, without being peppery. The batter was firm but fluffy.

—Yeah, went out to that place near Argos. Does Tex Mex Subs: chilli meatballs with melted cheese in a footlong. Fucking oozing sauce all over the place! Bloody gorgeous!

Peter nodded again as he scooped up mash on the back of his fork, letting it slide off onto his tongue, tasting the butter , the sweet tang of salt, and the meat of the gravy.

—I went with Daniels. He said... Martin covered his mouth as he started laughing. —He said it was 'like licking a Mexican's exploded nuts'! Martin grinned at Peter with his eyes closed.

—Do you often have dinner here? Peter asked.

Martin swallowed and coughed.

—Sometimes. I got a training session tonight. Got to take the evening shift through new FSA guidelines. He waved a knife at the rest of the canteen. —Coalition are bringing in a new organisation. Have to make sure people know the law.

—Is that why so many people are in?

—Yeah. Box ticking formality. Fifteen minutes. A B C, y'know? Anyway... dull, dull, boring, yawn. How's your day been?

—Just putting together follow-up data for On-Boarding. Number-crunching. Pretty... mechanical.

—Hmm. Groovy. Said Martin.

Peter frowned at him.

—But you like all that number-y, statistics stuff don't you? I mean... that's your job? Right?

Peter looked at him, surprised. He shrugged.

—Mexican testicles aside, how's your day gone?

—Oh... The usual: fighting fires, mostly. I get my staff moaning at me. I get the callers yelling at me. It's always something simple, like: 'Why are you taking money from my account?' It's for your insurance. 'Oh yeah...' We once had this caller who said it was illegal to take the premium because they hadn't received the notification. Becky told them the letter had gone out. I said the same, and then they dropped the bombshell that they can't have received it as they'd moved house! They hadn't told us! Were we supposed to guess? To read his mind? Like we're bloody magic or something! Always our fault, never theirs. He shook his head.

—Be funny if it was for home insurance...

—It was! Spluttered Martin, mouth full. —It was for home insurance! A home he no longer owned! How fucking stupid is that?

—Cancel and refund?

—What? Oh, yeah. Cee-x'd and refunded. Sent him over to Retention, but... nah. Goodbye and good riddance!

He poked at his food, spearing strands of green-leaf salad.

—Bizarre, isn't it? He said. —He was happy to call us to have a go, to accuse and yell and get angry... but not to tell us he'd moved! It's like he enjoyed being angry.

Peter smiled. —Yeah. He lifted another forkful and chewed. There was a silence between them.

—Got this one call today... I probably shouldn't say anything, but... Martin looked around, shuffling forward. —Ever heard of Derek Shrimpton? He's a broker, real small time stuff: few business policies, couple of personal liabilities, that's it. Martin lowered his voice. —Barely fifteen grand a year. That's it!

Peter shook his head.

—Well, he wanted to talk to Roddy, make a few tweaks to a policy, because renewal is, like, tomorrow, and Broker Accounts can adjust the premium. But... Roddy's off sick with gastro enteritis. And I took the call, so I've heard him puking: I know he's fucking sick! And when we tell Shrimpton this, he starts yelling and screaming and saying he's going to get us reported to the ombudsman and everything! He gave Catherine a right old ear-full!

Peter frowned. Catherine? He remembered a pretty,

dark-haired woman sitting at a window desk, patiently explaining to someone that of course Dickens had a political side: how can a writer of such clear moral boundaries be described as anything but political?

—So, anyway, I step in because Catherine's hands are up: she can't get a word in edgeways. I get to play the 'I'm the manager…' card for about three seconds before he's biting my head off as well! We can't put him through to Dave Carter, Roddy's boss, because he's engaged, and nobody else is picking up and Derek refuses point blank to leave a message, or send an email! At one point he's even insisting, right, that I give him Roddy's home phone number! Like he's going to be able to do anything from the side of the toilet? And I'm sat there thinking: if you'd put these changes through last week, mate… But he's just going on and on and on, telling me all the different ways in which we're cunts and he's going to take us to court and yadda, yadda, blah, blah. And Catherine's crying and everyone's crowding round…

—Sorry? Catherine was in tears?

—What? Yeah… well… no. Just, y'know… quiet. But I know what you mean: who's the most unlikely to get wound up by some arrogant, self-righteous twat? Right? Who's the last person who would let someone get under her skin? But yeah, we were all pretty shaken up by him. I mean, she's made of fucking granite that girl is, but the way he went on… she got the worst of it, all the threats and the…

—He threatened her?

—Well, that sounds… dramatic, but… yeah. He said he was going to get her sacked. Said he was going to sue her for 'deliberately preventing him from his rightful ability to manage his client's money', or some other such bollocks… y'know? He did much the same with me when I took over. Martin put his head on one side. —Put me in the interesting position of having to file complaints about Catherine and meself!

—Really? Surely you can't…?

—I checked, actually. Didn't say anywhere that I can't log a complaint about myself…

—No… I mean log a complaint against Catherine.

—What? Well… I… I had to…

—But she'd done nothing wrong!

—Yeah… yeah, I know! But the customer 'expressed dissatisfaction.' It's FSA rules…

—That's ridiculous…

—I know! Tell me about it! But anyway, so I was just repeating: 'I can take a message, Mr Shrimpton' and he kept saying 'Are you going to put me through?' So I… I just gave up. I stopped talking. And there's this silence on the phone line, this golden silence, after all the agro and the arguing. And… I dunno man, something in me had just about given up. I just didn't feel it was worth fighting with him anymore, y'know?. And then I started telling him about when me gran died and I had to sort out her flat with the council and how I could never get through to the right person and it was all a fucking nightmare, like they were trying to piss me off when I was grieving, y'know? And I'm, like, telling him all this stuff, so he knows we're not robots or something, and there's just silence. I think it's working. Then I hear: 'I don't give a shit about your fucking gran!' And I get to slam the phone down. What an absolute waste of skin. He just wanted to be angry. He wanted to scream and shout. We could've taken a message but… no: that would have solved the problem.

—How's Catherine?

—Oh… better. Been sat with her for ages, man. Trying to talk her into staying, but… Nah, she's going to quit, I reckon.

—Really? Because of the complaint?

Martin shook his head. —There's only so much abuse someone can take before it just stops being worth the money. She's a bright lass. I'll give her a glowing reference. She'll get another job, easy.

—But the complaint...

—The complaint's got nothing to do with it! We've all got complaints against us! It's just... procedure!

Peter finished his mash and looked at Martin.

—You didn't have to take it. He muttered.

—Yes I did. FSA guidelines say we have to log a complaint if a customer makes one. What happens if they ask for a copy of their complaint and we can't produce it? We're had up for breach and it's a fucking thousand pound fine!

Peter shook his head. —Surely there's something about abusive behaviour...

—There is! And he didn't threaten physical violence, or swear: he knew the rules.

—You're still basically letting her get bullied out of a job.

Martin stared at Peter. —Yeah? Well... Maybe. But we have to take the complaints. Imagine if you protested at what you saw as bad service and the company turned round and said 'well, we ignored you because we don't like you very much'. You can't punish people for making a complaint. Like being the fucking Stazi or something, crushing all dissent under a fucking jack-boot, y'know?

—I take it you're going to bring this up with Account Management? Get them to take some action.

—Could do. I mean, I did pass them a message. Didn't exactly say the guy was a cock. Should I have? Wouldn't make any difference. Everyone's backs are up against the wall, particularly in insurance. All these websites cutting out the brokers? That whole side of the business is going to be dead in a few years. And when Shrimpton and his kind are gone, Roddy will be gone as well. Martin looked sharply at Peter. —More efficient, isn't it? That's your department, always trying to make things more efficient. Cut the waste. Well... Shrimpton has read the writing on the wall. And he is fucking panicking, isn't he?

Peter slowly placed his tray onto the table. Sitting back,

he folded his arms and looked at Martin.

—Change and Process Excellence. We make sure that what processes are in place, work well. And in my professional opinion, if you're losing staff because of abusive phone calls, then you need to do something.

Martin sighed and stretched his arms. —We lose staff because they're all nineteen and don't want to be saying 'Good afternoon, Safe Atoll Finance, how-can-I-help-you?' They all leave to go do something more interesting with their lives, y'know? Julie and Simon left to join a circus. A fucking circus. Seriously, how bad is it when being a genuine clown is preferable?

Peter shook his head.

There was a clatter behind them. Turning, Peter saw a woman in a short skirt bend over to pick up her spilled handbag. As she leaned, her skirt rode up her thigh, exposing curved muscle under thick, dark tights. Peter turned quickly back round, blushing, to be met by Martin's grin and salacious wink. Peter frowned, his fists clenching.

—Look... He reached down for his laptop. —I really need to get on.

—Yeah? Sure, man. Knock yourself out.

Peter stood and began looking along the skirting board for a socket, peering under tables and across the room.

—You looking for a plug? Said Martin.

Peter nodded. —I'm hoping... He held the case higher. ——It's just the battery.

—There's one right there. Martin pointed into the gap between the sofas.

Peter leaned, and saw it, hidden in the darkness.

He nodded at Martin and got up, dropping the case and his coat onto the next sofa along. He pulled out the power adapter and leaned deep into the crevice, straining to push the plug in. Martin was still smiling at him when he came back up.

—Well... I'm going to... He pointed at the other sofa. —I don't think the cable will reach... And he pointed to the chair he had been sitting in.

Martin waved a hand. —Go right ahead! I'm just gonna let me dinner go down. He patted his belly, grinning, and pulled out his phone.

Peter smiled politely and got out the laptop, setting it down on his table and settling into the middle of the sofa. Plugging in the power, he waited, watching a little light at the side of the machine. Seeing it glow orange, he smiled and pressed the 'on' button.

Looking up, over the screen, he watched the diners chatting, eating, cups and plates and plastic bottles around them. People laughed and chatted, smiling at one another. His eye kept sliding towards the counter, where it was brightest, the glass and the steel shining under halogen lamps.

There was a sudden crash as a tray was dropped, plate and cutlery crashing to the floor. Everyone turned and craned their necks to see a man looking at the floor beneath him. There was a ripple of mock applause. Peter glanced sideways to see Martin clapping. He grinned at Peter, nodding at the unlucky diner, then went back to tapping on his phone.

The laptop screen flickered, lines of white text appeared: 'Please wait while drives are checked…'

—Now, we move on to the Robert. J. Flaherty Award, for: Best. Television. Documentary. Film. And a warm welcome to present this to the award-winning film-maker, Christopher Swann!

The band struck up a jaunty tune as a tall man with a small smile came striding out onto the beige-gold set, haunted by twin images of a one-eyed theatre mask. He carried a statuette and a gold envelope which he held up to the audience. There was applause and he shook hands with Michael Aspel, setting the award on the podium.

—Nice to see you, Chris. Said Michael. —Here are the nominees for Best. Documentary.

The screen cut to a blue, streaked background, the

same mask floating beside an inset shot.

—'David Lean: A Life In Film' by Nigel Wattis.

The inset showed a wiry man, sat at one of the large round tables in the audience, clutching a wine glass.

—'The Frozen Ocean: Part 1 - Kingdom Of The Ice Bear' by Mike Salisbury and Hugh Miles.

The inset cut to two men sat at another table, sharing a joke.

—'Marilyn Monroe: Say Goodbye To The President' by Christopher Olgiati

It cut to a black and white photo of a square-jawed man wearing glasses, looking intently into the camera while touching his temple.

—And 'Wild: Human' by Dr Arthur Finchley.

Arthur was dressed in a dinner jacket and tie, toying with a napkin and gesturing to someone across from him.

The whole screen peeled up from the left, to reveal Arthur, dressed in his usual safari shirt and trousers, sat in a restaurant, surrounded by posh diners.

—But the most interesting comparison is in the field of un-spoken communication. Observe those around me. Watch them.

The camera panned around the assembled diners as they laughed and chatted, looked serious while listening, or calling over a waiter.

—Because you are human, you can tell what they're feeling without even having to ask them, to interrogate them: you can pick it up through their facial expressions and body posture.

A large man at another table was telling a story with lots of arm waving and face-pulling. A woman listening rested her head on her palm.

—But imagine if you were, say, an alien: could you make sense of this communication? To help me decode more on the subject, I'm here having dinner with, certainly not an alien, but our closest relative and one of the best non-verbal communicators in the animal kingdom.

The camera panned right to reveal a chimp sat across the table from Arthur, his place laid out with all the cutlery, plate, and wine glasses for a formal, three-course dinner.

—This is Mr Cávet, a Bonobo Chimp from Zaire.

The ape looked at Arthur, then at the camera and pursed his lips together while picking at the dried insects on the plate in front of him.

—See what he's doing? Chimps have incredibly expressive faces, communicating nearly all their emotions through their lips, and eyebrows. Hello? Hello? How are you?

Arthur tapped the table to get Mr Cávet's attention

The chimp hunched over his meal, baring his teeth.

—That may, to us, look like a grin, but it can, in fact, be read as a warning: he wants to be left to eat. Teeth are a weapon to the chimp. It can, also, be read as a sign of submission. The difference depends entirely upon context. And the difference is extremely important: he could easily kill me with his bare hands! Being able to understand communication in context can mean the difference between life and death. For both humans, and chimps, eating here at this restaurant, or eating together in groups, is both a friendly, civil activity, where society can gather and enjoy some good food and conviviality, but it is also an arena in which to assert status, to cement our place within society. Mr Cávet is warning me away, politely, since in the wild, obviously, food is a precious commodity and he wants to keep all of it. And he does it, just as everyone here around me does, with silent, coded, facial expressions.

Arthur sat, watching the chimp eat.

The image tumbled away against the blue background, changing to the next clip.

—And the… best documentary? Who is it, Chris?

Christopher Swann opened the gold envelope as the camera cut to four inset shots of the nominees.

—The winner is... Arthur Finchley! For 'Wild: Human'!

There was an eruption of applause. Arthur nodded and dropped his napkin. Getting up, he kissed the woman next to him, who clutched at his shoulders. He picked his way among the tables to the four short steps up to the stage. He greeted Christopher with a handshake and accepted the statuette, looking down at it with a smile, before shaking hands with Michael.

—My, err... my agent, Jules, made me promise that I'd write something, just in case I won. I assured her I would... I assure my agent many things! There was laughter around the crowd —Only some of which are true, and I'm afraid... this wasn't one of them.

The camera showed one of the other nominees, pulling a tight smile into the camera.

—I'd like to thank Jules for helping push this project with Thames, as well as the production crew: Michael, Freddie, and Susan; and all in the Department of Social Anthropology at Cambridge University, especially Ray Abrahams, without whom I... well, I wouldn't be stood here. I'd also like to thank my wife and son, who put up with a husband who is nearly always on the other side of the planet.

The camera cut to the woman Arthur kissed, who was looking up to the stage with hands clasped togther.

—I made 'Wild: Human' because I believe much can be understood about ourselves when we see where and what we evolved from. It explains our instincts and fears, as well as the ridiculous tribalism that still leads us to war and genocide.

A ripple of muttering went round the room.

—There is a very great need for us to see ourselves within the natural world; that we were created by it, are sustained by it, and yet stand to be the most destructive force upon it. We have come so far, created such astonishing machines, and harnessed the very limits of science; but unless we look back, and remember that we are all just animals who have learnt to speak, then we are in danger of believing ourselves as Gods; which we are not. 'We are nothing but apes with tin openers', as my old cameraman, John, was fond of saying. God rest his soul, he is much missed. I only wish he could've been well enough to be a part of this. I'd like to think he is up here now, beside me in spirit, camera on his shoulder... Thank you very much. Thank you!

He held up the award and, beaming at the crowd, walked off through one of the arches at the rear of the stage.

The numbers on the laptop screen kept whirling round. Checking... Checking... Pathways and files flickered past.

Peter drummed his fingers on the arm of the chair. It might not have saved. It could all be lost, gone. Whole day's work all down the tube, flushed.

He heard a snort and muffled sniggering from Martin, and glanced sideways to see him clutching a hand over his mouth, turning purple, watching something on his phone. Martin turned and held it up, tears trickling down his cheeks.

—Hilarious! He wiped his eyes. —You on twitter? I'll send it to you...

Peter shook his head. —No. Sorry. He pointed at the laptop. —Got to get on.

Keep your head down, ignore him, he thought.

—What you've got to admire, I mean really admire is the sheer fucking brilliance of the tech they've got these days. Said the guy with the neck tattoo. Orange streetlights made him look jaundiced.

—Yeah?

Peter drummed his fingers on his hip, bored and cold. Blank suburban homes arced away from them along wide streets cluttered with cars.

—Oh yeah! They have rockets that can be aimed so accurately they can be flown in through your front door and explode right on your favourite spot in front of the telly! Imagine that!

Peter could just make out that there was lettering around the tattoo: 'He who dares, wins'.

——Why use a rocket then?

—What?

—Why fire a rocket? Why not just shoot them? If you know they're sat in front of the telly, why not just shoot them through the window?

——No, no, NO. Don't fucking pick holes, alright? Don't do that...! I was just saying... that, to try and describe how fucking good they are! Alright?

—Yeah... Sorry, man.

—I mean, them Iraqis never stood a chance, they really fucking didn't, did they?

—Guess not.

—You 'guess'?

—I mean: no, no they didn't.

—The collected might of the American and British Armies, Navies and Air Forces against them and you 'guess' they didn't stand a chance?

—No, I said they didn't.

—Abso-fucking-lutely they didn't. Most sophisticated army to ever walk the planet, you're damn right they didn't stand a chance. Makes you wonder how stupid Saddam Hussein is, eh?

—Yeah.

—Can't just wander into Kuwait without someone noticing, can you?

From around the corner came a young man dressed in a purple shell suit, carrying a heavy plastic bag.

—Here he... Jesus! Said Tattoo.

—Alright guys.

—What the fuck do you think you're doing?

—What?

—Just... carrying it around like that? Right past... He waved his hand at the houses.

Shell Suit looked at the dark houses, with their glowing, curtained eyes, then down at the bag in his hand. —I think they're cool with it…

Tattoo grabbed his arm and pulled him over to the car. —Just… just fucking get in and drive, alright?

Peter got in the back, yawning from having not slept the night before, when he was working, and not sleeping that day, when he had been looking for somewhere to live.

Shell Suit put the plastic bag in the back with Peter.

—No offence, but I think it's better to have that up front with me. Isn't it? Said Tattoo, grabbing the bag and setting it delicately, carefully, between his legs. Shell Suit shrugged and started the car.

As they drove, they passed a police car.

—Fucking slow down! Slow down!

—What? Them? Don't worry about it…

—Worry…? We can't let them pull us over! Can we? That would be fucking stupid!

—Chill out man, it's not like they're going to do a Rodney King on us, is it?

—Shut the fuck up. Just shut up. You don't know the shit I'm in, alright? So don't tell me to 'chill out', just fucking drive and don't get us pulled over!

They carried on in silence.

They got to a junction where the lights were red. Shell Suit indicated right. They waited, the tock-tock of the indicator the only sound in the car. The light turned green and the car didn't move.

—What the fuck are you doing! The fucking lights are fucking green! Drive!

—It's not…

—It fucking is, look at it! It's fucking green, what are you waiting for, cunt face?

—It isn't. It's a… I live just round the corner, I use this junction all the…

—I don't fucking care where you fucking live! Just fucking drive, you stupid fucking cunt! CHRIST! I'm going to be fucking arrested, because you don't know how to fucking drive! JUST GO!

—It's only green to go straight on, there's…

Another green light came on, an arrow pointing right.

The car drove slowly round the corner.

—See? All fine. It's a thingy… filter light. OK? I use that junction all the time. It's fine.

—Shut up.

They went round a few more corners, Tattoo directing.

—This is me. He said, and they stopped at a block of flats. He reached into the bag and pulled out one of the cling-film wrapped packages. —And I got a present for you. He said, reaching into his jacket pocket, leaning over, flicking a knife out at Shell Suit's neck.

—If you ever piss me off again, I will fucking kill you: understand?

Years later, sat in the canteen, Peter could still see the knife: a curved blade with a pale, wooden handle. The pivot was a bright button, winking just above Tattoo's index knuckle. He held it tight at Shell's neck, staring deep into his eyes, as though he was looking for something there. Shell's hands were off the steering wheel, finger's spread wide, head lifted high, larynx bobbing.

Peter sat in the back, trying not to laugh.

Tattoo folded the knife away and lurched out of the car, jogging up the steps into the building. Shell put the engine into gear and they drove off slowly down the street.

—And that, said Shell Suit, his voice hoarse. —Is why I always ask people to pay upfront.

—You alright?

Shell waved a hand and dabbed at his throat, looking at his fingers in the darkness.

They parked up by Peter's bedsit.

—You want to come in for a bit of this?

—No, I… no, I think I might just head home.

Peter got out and opened the front door to get his package from the plastic bag.

—Couldn't believe you just wandered around with all this lot in a fucking carrier bag!

He looked up to see that Shell's neck was bleeding quite heavily, staining his purple jacket.

—Best way to hide: not look out of place.

—Jesus, man! You OK?

—I've had worse. Say hello to Scott when you see him, alright?

—Yeah… do you want a tissue or…?

—Nah, man. See you around.

Peter closed the door and watched the car drive away.

The screen flickered to the desktop, icons blinking into place. Peter watched it all appear, stutter to white and then settle, the bottom right a cluster of symbols changing and connecting. He clicked on the On-Boarding file, and the spreadsheet slowly opened. The window divided, a message appearing to announce the existence of the auto-recover version. Did he wish to load this? He clicked 'yes' and scrolled down. He breathed, finally. Not much lost, he thought.

He opened up the database, scrolling down through to where he had left off. Back to the same list of numbers, the names, dates, policy details, stretching down forever…

He thought of a woman at home in bed and a knife at a throat and his mother looking up at him from the sofa saying 'It's your father…' and a voice from the doorway 'you filthy fucks' and a girl screaming and 'Don't you know?'

He looked over at Martin, still staring smugly at his phone.

Peter imagined a dark-haired girl walking home, upset, angry, alone, scared.

Clicking open the company R-drive, he found the broker database and did a search for 'Shrimpton'. He selected and copied the email address into the composing screen.

He glanced sideways at Martin.

DEAR MR COCKFACE SHRIMP-TON
FUCK YOU YOU FUCKING TROGLADITE CUNT YELLING AT FUCKING WOMEN BET YOU NEVER FUCKED A WOMAN THATS WHY YOURE SO FUCKING ANGRY TRY YELLING AT ME YOU FUCKER AND ILL GET YOU FUCKING SACKED YOUYELL AT A WOMAN HERE AGAIN AND I WILL HUNT YOUDOWN AND SLUGHTER YOU LIKE THE PIECE OF SHIT COWARD YOU ARE DONT DESERVE MONEY BECAUSE YOU THINK IT IS POWER AND YOU HAVENT GOT ANY POWER AT ALL YOU ARE JUST TINY LIKE EVERYONE ELSE EXCEPT YOU CANT SEE YOU SO YOU MUCT BE BLIND AND FCKING STUPID SO EVERYONE IS POLITE AND TRYS TO TAKE YOUR BUSINESS BUT I SAY WHY BOTHER? WHAT'S THE POINT OF YOU? WHAT IS THE FUCKING POINT OF YOU? YOU DO NOTHING BUT REDUCE EVERYSINGLE ONE OF US. FUCK YOU. WE ARE NOT LIKE YOU. WE ARE BETTER.
We are better, than you will ever be.
Yours,
Peter Simpson.

The screen flickered. The email page froze. He swiped and jabbed at the touch pad, but nothing happened, the pointer did not move. He stared at it, waiting, eyes widening. Has the power gone again? He tensed his hands, out-stretched. The screen stayed exactly as it was. He read through the email. He shook his head and leant back in the sofa, fingers back to drumming on the arm.

Beside him, Martin sighed and slid his phone back into his trousers.

—Have to get me nose back to that grindstone! Eh?

He stood and shuffled out from behind the coffee table, holding his tray. Across the room there was a general rising clatter as the evening shift of telephony ended their meal and began preparing for work. The scraping of chairs echoed around the canteen: the eerie, keening sound a rising up, a call to prayer. The smell of the food was still in the air: the spicy, sweet notes of the carrot and coriander soup, the grease of the meats. There was a bitterness coming from the coffee machine. Peter watched Martin deposit his tray and walk out of the double doors to the office, picking his nose.

He looked back down at the laptop.

'Message Sent'.

The pointer was on the 'send' icon.

The email text had disappeared from the screen.

He stared, his breathing becoming shallow.

He opened the 'sent mail' tab, and saw, there at the top: Eighteen-twelve, Tenth of the eleventh, twenty eleven. To: Shrimpton, Derek. 'DEAR MR COCKFACE...'

Peter clicked through the menu system, desperately looking for an 'undo' button. He imagined the email on a long stretch of elastic, tight, and waiting for him to hit a particular button to bring it flying back.

He slowly lowered his head into his hands, pressing the heels of his thumbs into his eye sockets and pressing, pressing, pressing, till the pain became too much, and he pulled back, opening his eyes to purple swirls and blotches.

He'll take it as a joke! All part of the banter of business! Men, ribbing each other... All in a day's... fun. Him and Roddy must say much the same to each other. —Alright you old cunt? —Hello yourself, you fucking bellend!

Dave Carter, Roddy's boss: Shrimpton will forward the email to him.

Peter remembered Dave Carter. A large, bullish man with a balding pate and too much aftershave. He's bound to like a bit of banter! Thought Peter. Wanders through life calling everyone he meets fucking-this and fucking-that! Broker accounts: air is blue. Everyone swears. Just a joke, isn't it? Yeah. Read it in a cockney accent... —Dear Mr 'Cockface' Shrimpton... Fuck you! Eh? You fucking troglodyte cunt! Yeah? Classic!

He stared at the laptop, seeing himself write the email, watching his snarling, gurning face as his fingers jabbed away. Why didn't I just wait? Why did I even get involved? No. It was the right thing. Catherine. Yes. The fault... yes, lies with the laptop. Yes. It had been too long in loading because the battery had been run down... because he had been forced to work in the toilets... because of... No.

Shit!

Dave Carter will pass on the complaint and the original email to Geoff. What will Geoff do? He could picture Geoff, sat in his darkened office, about to go home, when... ping! Up popped the email. Leaning forward in the light of a single desk-lamp, Geoff would open it and begin reading. His normally calm face crumpling inwards to a frown. Sighing, he reached for the phone. —Janice? Sorry to bother you, can you draft a letter of dismissal for me? Tonight please. Thank you. The phone went down with a click.

Peter clenched and unclenched his fists. Geoff would have to. It was serious. There was no way round it, no denying it, no escape.

He ran his hands down his face, feeling cold and dizzy. Looking out over the top of the laptop screen, he saw someone reading their phone. They appeared down a long tube, everything around them swirling and spiralling away. They glanced up at him. Do they know?! Have they just had a text from Geoff? He sank down, face close against the keyboard, smelling the ionised, dusty heat, the hum of the fan loud in his ear.

He jerked upright and opened the menu system again. Could he set up another email account? He searched through... No. They were assigned by IT.

Could he tell them his account had been hacked?

He paused, hands above his keyboard.

He had never done anything like this before. It was totally out of character.

The side door banged open and three men walked in,

laughing. In the middle was the red-haired man with thick-framed glasses.

Peter watched him walk across the canteen, smiling with the other two, swinging a plastic folder by one corner, tossing it up into the air, spinning it around.

Clicking the screen to lock, Peter got up and quickly made his way across the canteen, bumping into other diners, holding up trembling, sweaty hands in apology. He skipped over a handbag to get across the path of the three, and then out of the tables and through the main door leading to reception. There he stopped, and looked back, watching the men continue across and out to the offices. Peter turned and went across the corridor to the toilets, walking in and standing, staring down at a sweet wrapper on the tiled floor.

He imagined the red-head sneaking over to the laptop, smiling in the screen light as he settled himself on the sofa. His eyes glinted as he loaded up the email, and then, with a faint, faraway look, he began frantically typing, his grin growing wider, a chuckle shaking him. He hit 'send' and got up, glancing around guiltily.

Peter smiled, but then saw himself at the laptop, typing away. He shook his head. No, no. It was him, and they'll punish him for it.

The red-head was sat at the table upstairs on the balcony, laughing with his two mates; a wild, cackling hooting. There was a tramping across the floorboards, shuddering their tea, silencing them. Up walked Geoff with two burly security guards. Looking down at the red-head, they ordered him up. When he protested, looking confused, they grabbed his arms and hauled him out of his chair, dragging him across the balcony and down the stairs while he screamed for clemency, for an explanation. He was hauled out of the main doors, into the rain, and thrown onto the wet tarmac. A print of the email was tossed onto him and, lying there, he read it, pleading with Geoff that he had never seen this, never written it! Come back! Please!

That's just how it is, thought Peter.

—No way! Said the girl, eyes big with chemicals, eyebrows puckered up in sympathy.

—Straight up. It was very traumatic. I was only a child and seeing those terrapins... their tiny teeth tearing it apart... I couldn't help but feel... like it was me in there, somehow.

—Oh God! That is so... so... like, really tragic! Y'know?

—Yeah. He handed her the joint. —I've had trouble sleeping ever since. I just lie awake, watching it happen, again and again, feeling so alone.

—Yeah?... She chewed her gum. The kitchen was dark, music thumped through from the living room, people went back and forth, carrying bottles and bongs. She sucked at the joint with pale lips. As she blew out, she added to the haze of smoke hanging under the ceiling. She frowned. —What are terrapins, exactly?

He sighed. —Well... they're freshwater turtles. Bit smaller than turtles, actually. His mind flickered. He had taken one of his own pills, those that he had come to sell. He felt like he had missed a chunk of time. The joint was now in his hand and someone was stood between him and the girl.

—They're vicious little bastards. Said the older man, his head shaved, a little goatee on his chin.

Peter looked at him, cross.

—Really? Said the girl, suddenly invigorated.

—Yeah. Diamondbacks? They'll attack anything that moves. Renowned for it. You don't go swimming in North American lakes unless you're prepared to lose a finger or two to a Diamondback. I've swum in a few of the great lakes. Caught one clamped onto my little toe. Kicked him off. Toe went with him. He was only little. Needed fattening up!

Peter looked at the girl. Her eyes were locked onto the

older man's, her mouth slightly open. He realised he could not remember her name. The room span slightly, lights too bright.

—They're very territorial though. Continued the man. —If they'd bred and there wasn't anywhere for them to go, then... Well, the biggest will pick off the smallest. Competition over resources. They stop seeing each other as their own kind, just see the weakest as being lunch, but in a familiar container.

—Oh my God! That's... so disgusting!

—Yeah. Don't get that on most nature documentaries, do you?

Peter walked over to the sinks and looked in the mirror. His skin looked grey, wrinkled. He ran his hands under the tap, rubbing the water over his face.

What else could I do? Go trudging up to Geoff's office and confess? He could hear the tap of his shoes on the stairs, slowly trudging up to the fifth floor, then down the corridor, his mouth dry, sweat dribbling down his sides. He stopped, slowing his breathing. Could he really go through with this? Yes, of course, he must: it was the right and moral thing to do. He knocked, and a muffled voice called him in.

Behind his desk, arms folded, sat Geoff, a sheet of paper in front of him.

—Geoff? We both know why I'm here.

Geoff nodded and pointed to the corner, where a sword lay upon plastic sheeting. Peter nodded and walked over, unbuttoning his shirt. Kneeling, he grasped the sword and unsheathed it, slowly turning the blade towards himself.

Afterwards, when his body had been dumped round the back with the kitchen scraps, rats crawled over him, chewing on his face, burrowing inside his stomach.

Peter shook his head and grimaced.

He tried again.

—Geoff? You wanted to see me?

—Sit down, Peter.

—What's up? You look serious. Don't tell me the coffee machine has run out of cappuccino sachets again?

—Damn it Peter! This is... important. We've had a complaint from a broker named 'Derek Shrimpton'. Ring a bell?

—No. Oh, wait... Martin from telephony may have mentioned him. Nasty piece of work. Something about abusing our staff? Trying to get them fired? I think Martin logged the complaint himself.

—Well, this is direct from the horse's mouth. Geoff leaned forward, putting his hands together, pursing his lips.
—Peter? Tell me honestly: did you email Derek Shrimpton?

—No. Why would I? Don't get me wrong, I think what he did was utterly reprehensible, as would any decent, upstanding citizen. But you know me... I wouldn't have seen fit to tackle the little blighter there and then, not without going through the correct channels.

—He says you emailed him. And I've got the printout here.

—Really? Hmm... I'm sure I would of remembered.

—It's a semi-coherent rant, littered with 'fuck', and 'cunt'.

—That... that really isn't me.

—I said it didn't sound like you.

—No... I would never...

—Well, it appears to have come from your email account. Any idea how that could have happened?

—Really? That's terrible! Could... Could I have been hacked? Just a thought... When was the email sent?

—Eighteen-twelve. Wednesday the tenth.

—Last night? What was I doing at six-twelve last night? I had worked in the canteen all day. No other choice now we've lost the office. I had dinner with Martin, then went home. That was... it. Oh! Yes! I went to the loo! That must have been just after six! Yes! So you see: someone must have seen my laptop, there in the canteen, unguarded, gotten lucky with my password, and... sent off this appalling message!

—For Christ's sake!

—I know! I'm as angry as you! It's my name on the email, my account that's been hacked! How am I going to live this down? The damage done to my reputation!

—This is ridiculous. We can't have members of Change running around, having their laptops hacked into!

—I'm afraid this is just a consequence of your grand plan for 'mobile working'. I mean, Geoff, don't get me wrong: you know I'm strongly in favour... but it does leave us rather... exposed.

—Well... Yes. Geoff sighed. —You're absolutely right. I should have thought of this...

—Come now Geoff, don't be so hard on yourself: we ought to be able to trust every employee of Safe Atoll, shouldn't we?

—Clearly we can't! I may have to reassess how you lot work, maybe find you an office, if only for security.

—That's... a shame, obviously, but you're the boss.

—Hopefully we can get away with just an earnest apology to Derek Shrimpton. He's small-fry, so no big loss if he decides to go elsewhere. And you need to get your password changed! Alright?

—Absolutely, boss!

—OK. Now be on your way, you little scamp.

—Cheers boss.

—Just one more thing, before you go...

—Yes?

—The email... it was very specific...

—What?

—Whoever wrote it obviously knew a lot about the situation between Derek and Catherine. What was it that you and Martin were discussing?

—Err...

—It's just that... if this were merely a random hack, I'd

expect it to be shorter, mere simple profanity: 'You're a cock', that type of thing. But this is very specific, addressing the exact issues in telephony which Martin says he talked to you about. Funny that, isn't it?

—Shit... I...

—Don't bother. Hand over your pass and your laptop. Any paperwork at home? Anything confidential down the back of the sofa? No? Good. Simon here will escort you from the building.

A big security guard appeared, filling the door frame.

Peter leaned on the sink. A single drip hung at the end of his nose. What next? How do I tell Louise?

Stepping inside the house, he breathed slowly and shut the door. The house was silent. She's probably asleep, he thought. He went into the kitchen and boiled water for tea, trying to think what to say. After flinging the tea bags into the bin, he carried them slowly upstairs and pushed open the bedroom door.

—Louise? Dear? I've made tea.

She woke, rolling over, peering up at him from under the duvet. He put her cup down on the bedside table while she stretched and pushed herself upright, painfully. He sat on the edge of the bed and looked down into his mug.

—I... I've got some news. I... I'm sorry: I've been fired.

—What? Why?

—I... accidently sent an offensive email to a broker.

—An 'offensive email'?

—Yes.

—'Accidentally'?

—Well... yes.

—What kind of knuckle-headed fuck-berk are you? I'm on sick pay, and now you're unemployed? How do you expect us to pay the mortgage when you can't even communicate safely with people? And how do you 'accidentally' send an offensive email? Either you wrote it, or you didn't?

—Well... I wrote it. I just didn't mean to send it...

—Good God, Peter! You really are a fucking cretin! A ham-fisted, dribbling ectoplasm of a moron! The idiot that all the other squinting retards look down on as being barely sentient! Christ!

—I... I'm sorry...

—Don't fucking say you're 'sorry'! What are we going to do for money? Or did you spend the last of our savings on some magic fucking beans?

—Look...

—No, you fucked up: don't expect sympathy!

—Well, you're the one who's been fucking everyone else behind my fucking back for... how many years? So don't... don't... He shook slightly, feeling a knot gather in his throat.

—Of course I have! I had to get a fucking orgasm somewhere!

Peter stared at her, mouth open.

—And, now, on top of being shit in bed, I find out you're mind-numbingly irresponsible as well.

Peter dropped his head, looking into his cup.

—What? Did you expect me to be impressed? How much of a child are you?

She leaned over and tipped his cup over, spilling hot tea into his lap.

—Woah! What the...? He jumped up, pulling the scalding cloth away from his thigh.

She looked sternly up at him and, turning, swept her own mug off the side. It tumbled in the air, releasing the tea in a looping brown tongue that slapped on the carpet while the cup clunked over and over up to the wall. She stared at him, bloodshot eyes wide.

Peter smoothed his hair in the mirror and straightened his tie, his hands still shaking. Sighing, he walked back through to the canteen.

One person looked up as he walked through the doors. A woman with her hair tied up. He smiled nervously at her.

Oh Christ, he thought as he walked through the tables. What am I doing? This is so...

He sat down, and swiped a finger over the touchpad, tapping in the password. There was the email system, still showing the same 'sent' list. There, at the top...

He felt himself sink, weighed down, unable to hold himself up.

He looked over the laptop screen at the few scant people still in the canteen. Who of these could I ask to be a witness? He thought. Remember what they look like, give a description. They were there! They saw me leave! Did they see the red-head write the email? No, of course they didn't! But they might remember him walking though.

Then he saw Jane, walking towards him from the side entrance, wrapped up in a winter coat. She was frowning, looking serious.

Oh no, he thought. They've sent her...

She came to a stop on the other side of the coffee table, twisting her fingers round the lanyard for her security pass.

She pointed at the seat next to him.

—Do you mind if I...?

—No... He shook his head and moved over slightly, closing the laptop, hiding the screen.

Has to be someone from management. Email pinged straight to the right people. They rang her up: —You going to the canteen? Tell Peter Simpson to get out and not come back. Cheers!

—I'm glad I caught you. She said, settling down. Her coat was black wool. It smelt bitter and earthy from the rain outside. —Do you mind if we talk?

He nodded.

Should I mention the red-head? How do I drop that in? No! Wait! I'm not even supposed to know the email has been sent! Utter innocence.

—That's... yes. I've just been to the... He nodded to

the main entrance and the toilets, feeling his cheeks flush.

She looked over, then back at him.

—I've heard the bad news…

I can argue. Protest. Make it loud. People here will notice. Make them remember. She can't reverse the decision, but… tribunal. Not my fault!

—And I wanted to see you in person.

He nodded. Got to. Dismissal requires a face-to-face.

—You probably already know… You're all connected and everything, see the news coming in, all digital and in-the-know. She waved a hand at his laptop.

He frowned. Was there doubt over his guilt? Maybe it was going to be gardening leave? Suspension pending an investigation? But still full pay!

—I found out when Dave called. He saw it on the local news.

Dave? Who the hell is Dave? Why the fuck am I on the news?

—The police found a… body.

A body?

Derek? Has he…?

That was…

He stopped.

He stared at Jane.

Louise…?

A panic to get home washed over him, pulling him up and towards the door, his palms itched, making him press them into his knees.

—It's Arthur. Arthur Finchley. I'm so sorry.

Peter breathed out, and felt himself sag downwards, the lump in his chest sinking, pulling hard.

—He was in a doorway by the car park, near the canal. They announced it late this afternoon.

He scratched the back of his head. A scruffy man, stood on the deck of a ship, swimming with a whale shark, pointing out at a polar bear.

—It sounds like, well… She leaned in. —They're not

looking for anyone in connection, if you know what I mean.

He nodded very slowly.

Grinning at an attacking snake, swimming through coral, holding scorpions and spiders, dangling bait before jaws bristling with teeth.

—Are you going to be OK?

—Hmm? Yeah.

She nodded.

—I'm so, so sorry. I know he was a... a bit of a hero.

—Yeah. But... I suppose... He looked at her then down at his laptop. —Thank you, but... I've got loads of work to be getting on with, so...

—God, yes. Sorry! Sorry. I'll let you get on.

—Thank you. Thank you for letting me know.

She waved her hand. —No problem! She stood. —And if you need to talk then... y'know, call me. She turned, edging out from behind the coffee table. —Don't work too late!

He watched her walk through the tables, over to the main entrance, her shoes tapping clearly on the polished floor.

five

—So... Arthur, tell me: what's it like to swim with a Great. White. Shark?

The audience murmured. Arthur looked down and smiled to himself, adjusting his tie.

—They're deeply misunderstood creatures, Des. They are beautiful and elegant. They're only scary if you are a seal! He said, turning to the audience. —And you do NOT want to be a seal with a Great White around!

Laughter rippled round the studio.

—They eat seals, then?

—Oh yes! They only ever attack humans if they confuse us for seals. Why do you think they usually spit us out? We're too bony, not enough blubber! You don't survive a Great White attack! You survive a Great White's mistake!

—Are they really...? How can you describe them as... beautiful though?

—They're very well-designed animals. Perfectly streamlined. When you see them glide through the water... oh, it's like a ballerina, or a sports car. And they are deeply fascinating! Said Arthur, leaning forward. —They can smell one tiny drop of blood in several thousand gallons of seawater! And they have strings of jelly-filled pores, called Ampullae of Lorenzini, which can detect tiny fluctuations in voltage, such as would be found in the flutter of a shrimp's heart beat! Arthur spread his hands and leant back. —They are remarkable animals, which we ought to respect and revere. But… instead, we hunt them, because we fear them. We create myths about sharks, and believe them. But, let me tell you this: the shark is more humane than humans. With all our high-handed imaginings of morality and philosophy, we still kill each other over pettiness like money, jealousy, religion, political ideology, history, greed, fanaticism, or abstract lines drawn on a map. We persuade ourselves it is necessary and right… Arthur pressed a finger into the arm of his chair. —Our big evolutionary advantage, Des, and might I say, the reason for this show! Is that we can talk. We can exchange ideas with each other, explain our point of view, persuade others of our reasons for existing. But, too often, we don't listen, or we use language to promote hate, to delude ourselves into violence or aggression. Arthur leaned forward again, opening up his hands. —At least when the shark kills, it's merely to eat!

Peter sat on the sofa in the darkened canteen, huddled under his waterproof, watching the internet video, blurred with lines and crackle from VHS tape. Glancing out over the screen, across the moonlit tables, he thought he saw a red jacket sitting by the double doors. Something hunched over, brown hair fallen down in front of its face.

—But you get in the water with them! What if they decide to eat you!

—I've had a few near misses, but… I'm still here.

—Near misses? Didn't you once have to fight off a shark?

—Err, no. No. There was a Shortfinned Mako that we managed to distract with a shiny camera case! We would have lost in a…err… punch-up! Arthur put his fists up, jabbing towards Des O'Conner.

There was a giggle from the audience.

—Really? You distracted it? That's quite... incredible! But do you not... worry? Because you are married? Are you not?

—Yes.

—With a son?

—Yes. He turned sixteen only last week.

—Really? Well happy birthday... err? He looked at Arthur.

—Rupert.

—Happy birthday Rupert!

—Yes, he's finally old enough to come out to sea with me. We're flying out to Micronesia very soon.

—He's going to be swimming with sharks as well is he?

—No, of course not! But I promised he could come out on a research vessel with me when he got old enough... So... Yes.

—You sound a little nervous?

—Ha! Yes, I suppose I am!

—Does your wife not fret at the idea of you... out amongst all the sharks? And now her son as well?

—Oh she's never worried about me! I've done far more dangerous things than swimming with sharks!

The audience burst into laughter.

As the clip ended, a mosaic of similar videos appeared in its place, all linked with Arthur, or Des O'Conner. Peter clicked back to his search results. Scrolling through the list, he looked at the thumbnails of Arthur: against a black background, stood on a boat deck, underwater, on a desert dune, or a bright suburban garden. They were all better than the image he had in his head.

A doorway.

A knife.

Blood.

Peter clicked on the image of Arthur sitting alone, beside a green pot-plant.

—Tell me, where were you born? Said the interviewer,

off camera. —Because there's an interesting story about that, isn't there?

Arthur arched an eyebrow.

—Really? I was born in Coventry... Is that an unusual place to be born?

—No... I was...

—Do you mean the rumour about the Isle of Man? Is that what you're referring to?

—The Alien Internment Camp, yes. Is that not true?

—No, I'm afraid not. My father was in that camp, just outside Douglas during the war, but he was released in forty-one. I was born in forty-three. You know... I'd like to find whoever started that little rumour and thank them for making me sound much more interesting than I really am!

—But your father was...?

—My father was German, yes. He came over in nineteen thirty-six. He was Jewish. I'm sure you'll agree it was a very prudent thing to do. He got a job with Standard Motor Company at Canley, in Coventry, making the drive shafts and chassis mounting for their cars. He was a German-trained mechanical engineer: they were lucky to have him. He worked immensely hard, and he tried desperately to become a good 'Britisher': he even changed his surname to a place he saw on the map. Imagine that! Severing that link with your father, your grandfather, the men who made you what you are!

—But then the war started...

—Yes. And he, along with all foreign nationals, had to report to the police. But they could still work, still... live. Then Norway and Quisling happened and Churchill, the oh-so-wonderful Churchill, was elected.

—You sound scathing?

—Churchill is more myth than man these days. What seems to have been forgotten is that the first thing he did after coming to power was to lock up all the alien civilians. 'Collar the lot' he said. As though they were guilty already.

—Was your father…?

—Well, he was 'of fighting age', as they called it, even though he was in his late thirties by then. First, he was fired. Standard said they couldn't employ foreign nationals. He got a job working in a garage. That only lasted a few weeks before the police turned up, on the orders of the Home Office. For all the suspicion by politicians, the local bobbies were far more relaxed. He was taken to a police station along with two other men who lived in the same area. At the time, the Local Defence Volunteer force was being set up, what would become known as 'Dads' Army', and the cell they put these men in was being used to store donated weapons and munitions! The police knew these men weren't really dangerous. Why put them in a room with a dozen rifles if they thought they were?

—Where did they go from there?

—They were collected by a large, open-top truck and driven through the streets, a nervous-looking soldier in the back with them. Everybody was freezing, and people stared! The Nazi fifth column going past, made up of men they'd known, and trusted, for years. They went out into the countryside, to an RAF field. There they erected tents, were assigned blankets, tin cups and bowls. He said it was quite fun for the first couple of nights. They sang songs between the tents. Then the boredom settled in. A few of the inmates were university professors, lecturers. They started teaching. But my father wasn't one for books. He had gotten his hands dirty ever since he was a child. Others were the same. And then they put genuine Nazi sympathisers in with Jews who had escaped concentration camps. Fights broke out. The authorities should have seen it coming.

—How did your father end up on the Isle of Man?

—I think it may have been a typing error. He should have been released as part of the category Bs, but instead was shipped off to Liverpool with the category As . When they arrived in Douglas, they found that the guards there had been told that they were all German parachutists, a first wave invasion. They were treated as enemy combatants. It was a much harsher regime than before.

—Forgive me... But did he not work for the Nazis? Before he came to Britain?

Arthur sighed and spread his hands. —He was a Jewish engineer in an increasingly anti-Semitic country. If he wanted to eat, he had to accept what work there was. And from thirty-three onwards there was a lot of work in the re-arming process. He got work, really very minor work, in a factory producing tank parts. Ironically, the Nazi's didn't seem that bothered by his being Jewish.

—Your father helped build Panzer tanks? To arm Hitler?

—He had a job in a factory making spare parts. He always said he had no idea what they were for, not until later.

—But still, that must have led to tremendous feelings of... guilt for him?

—Of course! He was a Jew who helped arm the Nazis! I don't suppose it mattered that if he hadn't, he would have starved... Those few Marks kept a roof over his head and food in his belly. That was the reality. But it still tore him apart for the rest of his life. When I was very young, just a few years after the end of the war, I remember my father and I met our neighbour's son, a young man who had fought in Germany. He was swinging down the street, one trouser leg flapping empty. My father got talking to the neighbour, his friend, who said it had been a panzer shell which crippled his son. My father made his apologies and took me home where he vomited in the kitchen sink.

—How was he released?

—There was pressure from the public, and from a few notable celebrities, to release those who were merely 'foreign'. All bar the genuine combatants.

—Did he contribute to the war effort?

—Well... I don't think he was allowed to fight. And

there was still a bit of suspicion. He worked in a garage, until Standard relented and allowed him back. He worked on the 'Tilly' cars. There was also a short stint in a food distribution centre, but… the organisers asked him to leave after it became clear he was courting one of the young women there. She quickly became my mother. I was born in the war. It shaped who I became.

Peter clicked back onto the database, where he selected text and pasted it into the project spreadsheet. He delved into another account and scanned through the activity log, selecting and pasting, working quickly, filling in the spreadsheet as fast as possible, one eye on the amount left to analyse.

He clicked onto the next account, imagining the sound of the completed project hitting Geoff's desk. —Email? To who? Shrimpton? Maybe, Geoff, I don't know: I've been too busy coming up with a further few hundred thousand pounds worth of savings…

The clicking of keys sounded like footsteps running down a street. Urgent feet taking a desperate man to a lonely cement-lined doorway, smelling of piss and petrol.

He switched back to the list of videos, pausing before starting the next one. There was an image he wanted to retain.

—Yes, I went to University here, back in the sixties.

Arthur and a man in a long coat were walking slowly down a busy town street, the clouds grey, the pavement wet.

—It was the start of the sixties, when they were still the fifties really. I spent my days in the libraries and the labs, picking over species classifications, anatomy jars and habitat maps. I had digs out in the suburbs, with the landladies and the net curtains. It was a… happy time for me, I suppose, looking back. Yes.

—Did you not see it that way at the time?

—No-one ever does, do they, Derek? My life was very… simple back then, just the science, not much else.

Well, there were girls, of course, but... But I didn't do terribly well with them! And I was considered a very mediocre biologist. So... I found myself... well... not a failure, but a bit... rudderless, to be honest.

—Is that why you went into the army?

—Well... yes... Partly. The recruitment office used to be here in town, just across the road from my bus stop. I kept seeing all the signs in the windows, promising action, adventure... honour! So after I'd handed in my dissertation, which was dreadful! I... I handed myself over to the army.

—It sounds almost... religious.

—Ha! No! Not quite! Not with their language! No, it was... refreshingly real. Practical. Straightforward. At first.

—So what was it like? Making the leap from Cambridge academia to... Was it the East Anglian Regiment?

—Yes. The newly-formed East Anglian. It was certainly a shock. There was the physical side of things of course, having to complete assault courses, run with heavy packs. And the weapons training: that was certainly jarring to the system! But I went through officer training as well, being a Cambridge graduate, so I had that extra burden of tactics and command. There was one tactics exercise in which the only way to achieve the objective was to sacrifice men. How do you deal with that? Twenty-one years old and being told that you have to send your own men to their deaths? I struggled, if I'm honest. I still do. But there was... Tell me, Derek, do you know the story behind the drums of the Cambridge Regiment?

—No, I'm afraid I don't.

—The Cambridge Regiment defended Singapore in nineteen forty-one. When it fell, they had lost seven hundred and eighty-four men. The survivors, as an act of remembrance and... guilt, buried the regiment's drums in the jungle. When Singapore was recaptured in forty-five, they dug them up. They still carry the drums in parades today, but never play them, to remember the seven hundred and eighty-four. Being in a parade with the Cambridge drums made me realise that the past is not a foreign place, more of a scar, there forever, either to be hidden or flashed proudly, but indelible; permanent. Army life, Derek, carries with it an inherent sadness, an obligatory sense of loss and... anger. The drums also made me realise that one word from a politician could condemn me to death.

—That's really... interesting. Now, I believe we're outside the Cambridge Centre of Marine Biology, where you taught. Can you show us around?

—Certainly.

Ahead of Peter, a few tables closer, the red jacket rustled, turning the pages of a discarded newspaper. The brown hair shook mournfully. Peter tried not to look at it, but he could hear the paper crumpling.

He clicked back to the spreadsheet and stared at the numbers for a while, before switching back to the web page of videos and starting the next one.

—I'm sorry, but I have to disagree, said Arthur, strongly. —Politicians rarely have any concept of what the armed forces are facing. Their decisions, in my experience, are just dangerous soap-box claptrap!

He was leaning forward on a sofa, facing another settee across a coffee table. Armchairs completed the rectangle. The background was pitch black. Several people were around him, drinking wine, one of them had been speaking, their finger still in the air.

—In sixty-four, said Arthur. —I went to Aden, in Yemen, straight from officer training. Given command of men in that chaos, the heat and the dust. The fine sand, getting in your eyes. Tight, narrow streets in the old town, smell lingering from rotting vegetables and night soil. Drinking vast amounts of tea, talking with the locals, all of us knowing that the date for independence was set, waiting, looming ahead of us. Do you know what we saw every day, right in front of us? The Liberation Front sitting back, and waiting for us to leave. The locals, the administration, the British forces, we could all see what was going to happen: everyone except the politicians back in Westminster. They preferred to listen to their own delusions than hear the reality. It was the same in Northern Ireland...

—Sorry! A man opposite Arthur held up a hand, a lit cigarette wafting grey lines in the air. —I really don't see... what you...? How could they...?

—It was the same in Northern Ireland. The streets may have been wet and cold, the houses endless rows of terraces. There was no date for independence, no consensus; virtually civil war...

—Exactly! Cried the man opposite.

—But the politicians did the same big gesture, irrespective of the situation on the streets. The Maze prison. The internments. They told themselves that by locking up militants it would make everything go away, that things would settle down. Funnily enough, taking away the liberty of angry people does not make them any more peaceful. Only an idiot would think that. Of course... we weren't just locking up the terrorists and the agitators: we were locking up anyone accused of being a terrorist, so any grudge that one drug dealer had with another... they could get the RUC to take them off the streets for free. It was ridiculous, anyone there with open eyes could see it as such. And I had to be on the streets, watching people stare, jump out of our way, shout's from the end of the road, the rattle of thrown stones and bottles.

—With respect, said a woman on one of the armchairs. —It sounds like your ego suffered when you sensed the failure of a difficult job...

Arthur shook his head. —They tortured people in the Maze...

Many voices rose at once, clamouring.

Arthur raised a hand, frowning. —Sleep deprivation, starvation, hooding, being blasted with all sorts of music…

—No, no! The European Court of Human Rights said it wasn't…!

—They said it didn't meet their definition. And if what I saw didn't meet their definition, then their definition was wrong! Even the men who were locked up for the right reasons, the intended reasons, were only there because, fundamentally, they disagreed with the way their country was being run. They went about it in the wrong way, but…

—Can you really be so naïve?

—Were you there?

—Well… no, but…

—Then which one of us is deluded?

There was silence.

—You're very political, aren't you? For a wildlife presenter… Said a woman on the opposite sofa.

—I… I feel a lot of responsibility for what I did, what those under my command did. What the army as a whole did. We have a duty to feel guilty, as a country, for what was done in our name. But I was there: I had a chance to stop what happened, prevent some of the awful things that took place. Northern Ireland… I still lose sleep over that… I see myself stood there, not… I'm watching, not moving. I just… It… It haunts me. The politicians keep it all at arm's length. They have no idea. And we, the public, the forces, are the ones that pay for their mistakes.

Peter stopped the video and clicked back to the spreadsheet. He scanned through a few more accounts, switching between screens to complete the cells, moving ever downwards. As he did so, he heard the sobbing of a lonely man, now besieged by guilt and pain, huddled in the corner of a doorway, pulling out a rusty blade. Peter kept his eyes on the screen, brightness blinding him to the darkness of the canteen, where a red coat rustled and an old man moaned.

He clicked on another video.

—Well... Hello Michael, said Arthur, holding a brightly-coloured phone to his ear. Beside him, also on a tall stool, was a spiky-haired presenter in a baggy, multi-coloured shirt. Behind them were several children, all with worried looks on their faces. —It sounds like you're going through a very difficult time at the moment, Michael. I remember when my father died: I was considerably older than you are now and was serving in the army. I got a phone call in the night to say that my father had been rushed into hospital back in Coventry. Now, I was in Northern Ireland, and I expect you know, Michael, that the Irish Sea, North Wales and a considerable bit of the Midlands are in-between Ulster and Coventry, so getting over there was a little tricky, but the stripes on my uniform helped, as did the reason why. But it meant I got a chance to hold his hand and speak to him. He was very weak and the painkillers they gave him... it... it was morphine, Michael, which can make people a little woozy, a little dreamy, a bit like they're drunk. And he looked me up and down and asked me why I was all dressed up. Did I not have homework to do? And I had to explain, again, that I was in the army. And he looked away in disgust, saying that he hated the army. It was an argument we'd had many times. And I thought he'd accepted it, but... he had just been polite. Now that he was dying, and the morphine had made him forget what year he was in, he let his guard slip: he revealed his honesty. When he fell asleep, I slipped off the cap and jacket and sat with him, waiting. When he woke, I told him I'd just got there, and we talked about our old house, where he still lived, and about my mum. He said how much he missed her, and how he wished he could have taken her to see his parents, but that they'd died in the war. Then he began singing, in Yiddish, a song I'd not heard since I was tiny. I held his hand and watched and when he stopped he was smiling and still, and I knew he was finally back with my mother, his wife, and he would be happy, free of all his suffering in this world. That's what you have to remember, Michael: when someone dies, they are freed from all the pain, all the hurt. They are gone from us, but never forgotten. I never forget my dad, and you shouldn't forget yours. You obviously loved him very much.

———Thank you. Came a little voice over the phone line.

—Thank you Michael. Said the presenter. —Thank you for your call. Well! That was a sad call, wasn't it? Arthur nodded, raising his eyebrows. —But… Thank you. I think we have a call now from Mandy in Chichester with a question about Octopuses. Octopi? What is the plural…?

—It's Octopuses.

—Thank you, Arthur! What's your question, Mandy?

Peter looked up. Ben was sat at a table close by, tapping his long fingernails, staring off to one side, bored. Peter clicked back to the spreadsheet, flicking numbers onto it, running down the accounts. Two or three times he switched to the wrong window, seeing Arthur's face look at him from the bright children's show. He saw it age, saw the face puff up and redden with drink, the hair become matted and long. He began to smell a musty, meaty odour, of an old man unwashed for many days. Heaviness pulled at the limbs and bent the spine, turning the face downwards. He clicked onto the next video.

—I suppose… I suppose it came to a natural conclusion. Said Arthur, walking down a pale-green corridor, lined with notice boards between wooden doors. —Soldiers only have a certain… shelf-life, you know. Once you get into your thirties, and the knees start going, well… He smiled, shrugging.

—You must have experienced some dreadful things.

—I… That was the nature of the work. It was… Yes.

—And so you ended up back here.

—Not straight away, but… yes. I was accepted, eventually, onto the Doctoral Research Course. It was odd…

—Moving from the battlefield to...?

—It had been about ten years, and then I was back. I felt like a young man again. Like I'd just... wiped away the past decade and begun again. A very odd sensation. Liberating. I could re-write the past, make it... better.

—And while you were here, you got picked up by the BBC...

—Well, yes and no. The story goes that Barry Fortiscue of BBC Bristol saw my Phd thesis and sought me out. The truth is, that it was a little while afterwards, when I had begun teaching, that I got their attention, and it was, well, because of a mistake, really. I did my doctoral work on coral reef ecosystems, on coral growth patterns following Parrotfish grazing. Parrotfish eat the coral, crunching up the calcium structure, but only digest the polyps, the organisms. Which means that when you are on holiday, lying on a white, sandy beach, sipping your cocktail, you are lying on what is, basically, accumulated parrotfish poo.

—What was it that got you onto corals and parrotfish?

—They were beautiful. I'd always stared at the photographs as an undergraduate, and after being in the army... I wanted to see as much beauty as possible. I made up a research proposal while I was stood in the college office. First thing that came to mind. The iridescent, shining parrotfish and the bejewelled, glittering coral, in the warm, dappled blue waters of the South Pacific. Perfect. My idea of heaven.

—It does... does sound rather lovely! Even if the beach is...

—Quite! As soon as I began teaching, I started fundraising for a field trip, a chance to take students out to a reef system and have them dive, to see, first hand, how tightly woven the ecology is down there. We took a camera and, well, while filming, I nearly got bitten by a Moray Eel. They're vicious things that lurk in crevices: ambush hunters. In the film, it looks as though I'm waggling my fingers around by its cave to attract it, to lure it out. In reality I had just brushed an anemone, numbing my hand. I was trying to get some sensation back. I had no idea the eel was there. Barry saw the footage and offered me a job on the spot, doing films for the Open University.

—Sorry, but that film, your accidental big break, so to speak, it was a bit more special than that, wasn't it?

—Oh. Do you mean about the Moray's second jaw? Another myth, I'm afraid! Moray Eels only use their pharyngeal jaw when swallowing. We used the footage to exemplify their strike attack, and then went on to describe the second set of teeth that hinge out from inside their throats. You need a slow-motion, studio set-up to film the way they swallow. It is fascinating, but no, we didn't film it on that occasion.

—Oh, that's a shame. But working with the BBC meant you could spend much more time among the coral and the fish!

—Not really! The first assignment I was sent on was to swim with Basking Sharks just off the Isle of Man!

—Really? That must have been… dangerous!

—Only in terms of the cold, and the traffic. Basking Sharks are plankton feeders.

—You're from the Isle of Man, are you not?

—I… Yes. Yes, I am.

—It must have been nice being back.

—It… Yes. Would you like to see some preserved parrotfish? Not as good as live versions, but…?

The video ended, Arthur looking left, eyebrows raised, one arm coming up, blurred, maybe a finger pointing, the inside of the wrist exposed.

Peter again saw him slowly shrink over, ageing, darkening, turning and walking away. Arthur's breathing hoarsened as he tried to run, shambling to the doors at the end of the corridor.

Bursting through, he was out and into the damp November night, scuttling away from the restaurant. Peter saw him huffing and wheezing along the wet street, the smell of spilt wine and stale sweat following in his wake. He staggered round the corner of the multi-story car-park and fell against the wall. He gasped and swallowed, then leaned forward and vomited on the pavement, wet liquid slapping down. He coughed, eyes watering, throat retching. Wiping his mouth, he peered back round the corner, up the street to the restaurant. No-one was coming after him. He pushed himself upright on the wall and swayed into the deep, dark doorway of a letting agency, sitting down heavily.

Across the wet road, the occasional car rumbling past, was a canal wharf, redeveloped into boutique shops and café bars. From where Arthur sat he could see down through a gap in the buildings to the glittering open water, bright lights reflected, rippling and bending, twisting neon signs in the wind-blown waves. A few common Mallards bobbed blackly on the water, their bills tucked backwards under wings in sleep. One unfolded itself and stretched, flapping, seeming to stand on the water.

Arthur pulled out a pad and pen, and started to write. He wanted to say exactly why he was doing this, but he could not think how. Stating the facts seemed too blunt, too cruel on the others. There was context. There were reasons. But no words stood up to the awful reality of what he had done: the unliveable truth of his actions. They were just sounds, empty and meaningless. He screwed up the paper. Maybe it would be best if the truth died with him, he thought.

In his trouser pocket was his old army-issue penknife, now nearly fifty years old. He unfolded the large blade and held it over his wrist. The skin was old, turned pale till it was near translucent. Where's best? He thought. Lengthways? Across the top? Lower down? He gritted his teeth and pressed the blade across, at the juncture between wrist and palm. He started to drag it back and forth, the pain sharp and fiery, the skin moving, bunching and stretching, until suddenly it slackened as he sliced through.

The pain lost its sting and became a deep ache. Blood wept out and trickled away down into his lap, warming his thigh. Moving his hand became difficult as the blade cut into the rubbery tendons. He felt tears and sweat run down his face. His fist, so tensely clenched, fell slack as the knife scraped on bone.

He stopped and looked at what he had done: his hand bloody and useless, his trousers soaked. Blood still dripped from him, but as he watched, it slowed and began to congeal, crusting up around the edges. He stared at it. Pointing the knife into the wrist, he drove it hard through, feeling the skin stretch, then pop open on the other side. He tried to twist the blade, but it was stuck between the tightly meshed bones. Wrenching it round, pain shot up through his forearm, his bones bulging out from the sides of his wrist. The blood began flowing freely, and when he pulled the knife out, with the sound of a wet kiss, the blood gushed with a steady, pulsing swell. He looked at his mutilated wrist, twisting it in the orange street lights, watching the blood run quickly down his arm.

A couple, walking hand in hand, passed his doorway. The man looked down at him in the darkness and they continued on their way.

Hefting the knife, Arthur tilted his head back and pressed around on his neck with wet, sticky fingers, looking for the artery beneath the beard. Pressing the knife upwards made him cough. Clenching his teeth, he dragged the blade across, feeling the point tear the skin apart, popping glands and tendons underneath. Blood began to gush over his hand, and when he flicked the knife out, he nicked his voice box, making him cough again, which gurgled as the blood ran down his throat, into his lungs. As he looked down at his blood-splattered shirt, he smiled.

Feeling sleepy, he leant over, the world sliding sideways to him, his head hitting the paving slab with an echo from far away. The canal quay, the ducks and the lights, all were now stood up on end: a twinkling, rippling wall that he was leant against. He could smell the petrol and the musty dirt of the road; the brackish metal of the cold water; and faintly, on the wind, the allure of tobacco and alcohol. On his other side was a million twinkling points of light, all scattered out on a deep, dark carpet. He felt cold and the ground started to swell and drop, slowly lifting him and lulling him, the waves ebbing beneath him as he drifted off to sleep. It occurred to him that should he live his life again and face the same disasters that brought him to that doorway, he would still arrive at the same decisions. What he had done had been forced on him by circumstance and nothing else. But the smell of salt was in his nostrils, and he could hear a gull calling. Waves broke over him and he sank deep into the water, his body floating, limbs free. The light and the sounds of the city faded away as Arthur sank to the bottom of the ocean, his body still and peaceful and cold.

Peter pulled his coat closer to him, still seeing the old man on the stone step, a dark puddle dripping down into the street. Old fingers had dropped the battered penknife, a relic from another life, roughly inscribed with a name and serial number. Peter sat in the canteen, eyes elsewhere, the chill seeping into him, making his bones ache.

An old man dead. Lonely and beset by guilt. Yellow face and whisky fingers, shaking.

—You look as old as I was when I started earning these. Said the old man, pointing at his medals, the bright sun dazzling from their shine. Peter looked sideways at him, unsure, surprised. —It's the greatest thing a man can do: serve his nation. Makes a proper man of you. Trains you to be fit in body and mind... and spirit.

Peter stood in the pub garden, looking through the open door to the bar, where his father was ordering drinks, and his mother watched food be laid out on a long table.

The old man sucked on his cigarette with fingers whose nails had been bitten down to half-moon stubs. —Ah, but I expect you have a very low opinion of the army, don't you? Well... not your fault. It's the teachers these days, all on drugs. Or communists. And if you've heard anything from your dad then it'll be nothing but the negative, making out we're the bad guys. He bad-mouths the bravery of us that sacrificed everything in order that him and his could have a free country. Free to hate whoever they like, to disagree and not get chucked in a camp for it.

Peter shifted his face away from the blue tobacco smoke.

—Your grandfather was a very brave man. Bet you only heard that in the eulogy today, didn't you? You should be very proud of him. He did some incredible things in the war.

The old man shifted the cigarette to the hand holding his pint and took a grip on Peter's upper arm.

—War can do odd things to a man...

—Please... I've... My dad is...

His father was still at the bar, resentfully nodding to the landlord while old men wearing medals gathered around him, waiting.

—Look, look... Look. Said the old man, keeping hold of Peter. —I know what your dad thinks of the forces: doesn't like them. Blames them for all sorts of problems. And he has his reasons... But you have to make your own mind up, don't you? Hmm?

Peter stopped struggling.

—Look, lad. All I'm saying is... you should know what happened, what really happened. Not the rubbish your father and all the other lefties have been feeding you. Because I bet he's been trotting out that line of Russell's: 'war doesn't determine who is right, only who is left'. As though war was simply a philosophical debate! An argument on morals! And that we that fought were out to prove a point! Lay out a thesis in bullets and bombs! The old man leaned back. —We fought because we had to: we were up against someone who would not listen to reason. There was no debate, no arguing, no persuading Hitler. We could only thump him as hard as we could and hope to hell. He looked over at the open door to the bar. —War covers nobody in glory. It covers you in blood. And whoever's still standing when the smoke clears has won. And you know what they've won? The rest of their lives. And when you're under fire, running up the beach, morals don't cross your mind! You shrink back to being an animal, fighting just to stay alive, to be the bloke still standing. You react! You lash out! Politeness and philosophy be damned! With all the explosions around you, bullets whizzing past, you can barely remember your name! Let alone the principle tenets of Stoicism, or what Wittgenstein would have said of it all! The man's voice was rising, his eyes widening. —You ever been to a fireworks party? November the fifth? Well, imagine all those fireworks exploding really close to you. One of them will eventually hit you: law of chance. And the only way to stop that is to stop the person firing them.

Peter looked to his father's back, where sweat had darkened the jacket. His head was down, nodding slightly, as the landlord talked.

—But you don't mind shooting them, in fact you really want to, because their rockets have just killed your mate. He was right beside you, then there was a 'tock', and he's crumpled to the ground with a big hole in his head, and his blood is all over you. And you find yourself up and running, yelling, firing, blood and brains dripping off you. And you don't stop until you've killed them. He took another drag on his cigarette. —War is terrifying. Not simply for the imminence of death, but from what it can make you do and feel.

Peter stared at the old man, eyes wide.

—There was none of this 'honour and glory' codswallop in the fields. That came later, when it was over, and mostly from, I have to say, the politicians, who weren't bloody there. No, at the time, we all just did what we could to stay alive.

I met your grandfather on the boats waiting to go over to Normandy. John Flinn, Daffy Podmore and I, we were new recruits, young and scared, sitting on our crammed-together bunk beds, playing cards and covering up our fear with bravado and bragging. Your grandad, George, he had seen fighting already, nearly been killed in North Africa, seen men die, roasted like chickens in their tanks, seen the maimed in the Egyptian hospitals, heard the sound of the bone saws and muffled screams. He spent months in some special hospital. He lay in his bunk, listening to us talk. Then he chipped in, telling us what it was really like. And we sat there, in silence, listening.

When our CO came round, handing out our anti-sea-sickness pills, we knew what it meant.

—Means we're sailing. George said. —Soon be amongst it.

I lay on my bunk, right up against the ceiling, trying to write a letter home. I thought I was going to die. I wanted to say everything that mattered, that it was all OK and that I would die for a good reason. But try as I might, the words just weren't forthcoming. I stared up at the iron ceiling, where all the sweat and breath and fear had condensed and dripped on me. And I thought, is this the last thing I'll remember? These rusty rivets? Forty-odd years later, I can still see them.

Below me, I could hear John ask George: —What's it like in France?

—You'll see it soon enough. Be grateful it ain't Libya, that's all I'll say.

—Wonder what them French girls are like?

—None too fussy! Said Daffy. —Seeing as how they jump into bed with Frenchmen!

I rolled over and looked down at them. —I just hope I survive the beach.

George looked up at me, then across at John and Daffy. He nodded. —You mark my words: stick by me and you'll see Paris.

We looked at him, at his fierce eyes.

—And what we do in Paris? He continued. —No one mentions to my missus! Alright?

We all laughed.

And then we waited.

In the night there was a tramping of boots on the deck above. The motors rumbled and everyone lay there on their bunks, silent, listening. There was a whistle and we cast off, us and seventy-thousand other vessels, into a force-five wind, whipping the sea into troughs and swells, our boat sinking and swaying, rising and falling, all of us heaving up our dinner into paper bags, the smell of vomit burning your nostrils.

At five-thirty AM we heard the booming of the warships, big guns pounding the French coast. Bang! Crump! On and on...

Then our CO was down amongst us, yelling, and we were grabbing our kit from the racks and running up the stairs onto deck. It was a cold, grey, blustery morning, black smoke trailing from the French coast. We could see tanks roaring up the sand, the marines just specks around them. The sea air was laced with cordite and smoke. Machine guns rattled and the boom of heavy guns still echoed up and down the coast.

Then it was our turn, the gangway splashing down, and we were charging into the surf, legs heavy and freezing, shaking, knuckles white round rifles. Everyone was quiet, head down, fighting through, up onto the sand. Wasn't long before I heard a whiz, something small flying past me. Someone next to me jerked, staggered, and fell. I just kept running, making for the clumps of dune grass.

There were two men ahead of me, and John was beside me. When we got to the lip of the hill, and started over it, one of the men fell backwards, his pack and rifle clattering onto me, knocking me over, his body on top of me. Then there was a noise so loud it made everything jump into the air. Sand and stones rained silently down around me. I tried yelling but couldn't make any sound. I felt my hand grabbed and pulled, the dead soldier pushed off me. And we were running again, through the valleys of dunes, men everywhere, dark shapes, flash of fire, chasing tank tracks. I never did thank the man who pulled me out. It was your grandfather.

We ran house to house through the town. I saw shops shattered, a box of tin-openers scattered on the street before a tank, like some sort of joke. We ran into a building, needing cover to fire on a German position. In the back bedroom, huddled under the bed, I saw a French family looking out. They were so still, staring, that in the glimpse I got of them, I didn't know if they were alive or dead. George knelt by the window, firing, firing. When he'd finished there was nothing left to shoot at. We were alive.

John was dead. He didn't make it off the beach. He got hit in the same explosion that I did. But I was protected, he wasn't. He was eighteen. Had a girlfriend back home. Lots of men didn't make it off the beaches. He was just one of many. We saw hundreds of dead. Thousands. You could get lost among all the girls back home, the parents, receiving the telegram, the favourite football team, their hopes and dreams, all of what might have been, what they could have become. John loved fishing. I remember him asking if he could fish when we were on the boat. I always think of him whenever I see someone by the side of a canal. A huddled shape, thin rod and draping line. Could have been John. Your grandfather told me what he looked like when he died: his front peppered with shrapnel, skin blasted away with burning sand. I didn't see him like that. George saved me from that, as well.

Months later, in the depths of winter, we were marching through the silent, snow-covered fields of Belgium, heading south, mopping up after the tanks had rumbled through. The German counter-offensive had stalled, failed. We were re-taking land that had, just a month before, been allied territory. We kept passing bits of Nazi machinery, artillery guns, trucks, wagons, a tank, all sunk in the mud, which had frozen solid around them. They were black shapes, looming out of the mist, angular and dead. Each one threatening, potential. A statue to the horrors that awaited us.

A shot cracked and we all dived to the floor, apart from your grandad. He stood there, swaying slightly. He thought none of us knew about the brandy he stole back in Saint-Quentin. And then he was running, and Daffy and I were running after him, bent double while George was running full upright, making for a little cottage among the trees. There was a whistle and the snow kicked up by my boot, then came the crack of the gun. I looked up and saw your grandfather pull his pistol and fire off a few shots before jumping over the wall, into the cottage garden. Daffy and I ran in and slumped up against the stones, breathing hard. The cottage window was open and not far. We could hear clattering and banging from inside, French being shouted. I peeked up over the wall, in through the window. I saw George, bent, elbow rising, fist falling, rising and falling.

When he came out he was carrying an ornate hunting rifle and some bread. There was blood smeared up his cuff, but wiped from his fist.

—Got the bastard Kraut. He muttered, chewing on the bread.

The rest of the men had gathered around.

—Any more food in there? Asked Harold.

George shook his head. —They cleaned the place out.

—Maybe… Said Harold, stepping forward.

—NO! Yelled George, putting the rifle up against Harold's face. —Don't! Nothing in there! Just… just leave it, alright? The bastard was shooting at us… and now he isn't. What more do you want?

——Food. I was going to check for food… stammered Harold, looking down at the muzzle of the gun.

—None. Come on. Gotta… gotta find beds for the

night. And the rifle was flung into the garden, your grandfather staggering back out into the field.

Days later we reached Houffalize, or what was left of Houffalize. A few streets with bombed out, shattered houses. We couldn't believe people were still living in them. We were assigned billets in an abandoned house on Rue Ville Basse. Daffy, George and I took the attic room, where we smashed up the bed and chair for fire wood, shovelling it into the grate and lying on the floor with matches and cold, damp fingers.

The house had been occupied before. There was a German poster on the sloping ceiling opposite the fireplace. 'Kampf für die Sach' it read, and a girl, all long legs, saluted in front of a parade of Nazi flags and the Iron Eagle. I turned from the fire and saw George staring up at it. He was hollow-eyed from lack of sleep and cold. Too much death, too much fear. He stepped forward, reached up and tore down the German poster. Behind it was a cheap newspaper print of Betty Grable, glancing over her shoulder. Your grandfather, he stared at it, then down at the German poster. Looking out of the cracked window, he started muttering to himself.

—You alright George? I asked.

—Tides. He said. —Enormous tides: crashing in, then rumbling back out again. Impossible… Endless.

It was a few days later that George packed his stuff and set off into Germany on his own. Last thing he said to me was strange: he told me to look after myself, Daffy… and John. But he was drunk… maybe he forgot. He was found a couple of months later, holed up in a house in Giessen, just outside Frankfurt, near dead from starvation. He'd slipped behind German lines, maybe trying to make his way to Berlin, I don't know, he never said. The Americans who found him thought he'd been trapped in there for weeks, with no food, and no ammunition, listening to the German army walking right past his window. He was shipped home, spent a while in hospital, but… there are some things that even the best doctors can't fix. And no-one came back from the war unscathed.

Daffy never made it back. He died in August, forty-five, months after the surrender. He was an idiot. Your grandad had promised us we'd see Paris. Poor Daffy, he saw it, saw the Eiffel Tower, but not the furniture van coming round the corner.

The old man sniffed and crushed the stub of cigarette underfoot.

—So, your grandad: think kindly of him, alright? He was brave, he threw himself into war, put himself in danger to save his fellows. But that does stuff to a man's mind: fractures it, makes it see danger where there is none, makes them always live in the terror, makes them doubt what's really around them. Don't judge him for being scared, alright? That's what your father did, only ever saw the injuries, never the sacrifice that caused them. Very selfish man, your father, but… I expect you knew that already, didn't you? Eh? Now, how do you fancy a drink? A proper drink?

Harry put a hand on Peter's back and gently took him into the shade of the building, towards the open door, where Peter could see his father, head bent, shoulders hunched. An old man with glints of metal at his chest was leaning in, finger pointing, his mouth curled up into a sneer. His mother, down the angle of the bar, was watching his father's face, frowning. The landlord was watching as well.

—Dad…? Peter asked, as Harry led him up behind.

His father swung about, one fist catching Peter sideways in the chest, like a hammer, knocking the breath from him.

—Christ! He whispered.

Peter staggered backwards into Harry, clasping his hands to his chest. He heard his mother cry and footsteps running over.

—What the bloody hell did you do that for! Shouted

Harry.

—I.. I'm so sorry!

—There's no need for that now, is there?

—Peter? Asked his mother.

—I'm okay. Said Peter, blinking back tears.

—You came running…! I… I turned and…

—You ought to be bloody ashamed of yourself, mate! Hitting a kid!

Sylvia led Peter away, quietly.

—I didn't… I didn't hit him, he just came running up, and I turned… and he was right… there…

—No. I saw you! Your own kid? You don't bloody change, do you?

—I didn't… it was an accident! There was a pause, while Jim stared at Harry. —Hang on… I know you… You're… Harry Stannington. PC Harry Stannington.

Jim looked down at all the medals.

—You were with him in the war… weren't you?

—What? Well… yes…

Jim stared at him.

—You… you covered up for him, didn't you?

—What?

—You made the story up.

—I don't know what you're talking about.

—You saw exactly what had happened, what he'd done, and you lied about it, didn't you?

—No!

—Yes, you did, you knew he was guilty, you knew what had happened and you let him get away with it!

—Now, now! Harry held up his hands. —Calm down! Are you absolutely sure about this? Because you're accusing me of some pretty serious stuff! What actual evidence have you got? Barring the purely circumstantial…

—You haven't fucking changed, have you?

—And you're still flinging accusations about! Never learn, do you? Didn't work the first time.

Jim leaned in. —I knew I was right! And now… You

gave it away by coming here, to your old mates funeral!

—Oh give it up! You're like a stuck record! Always the same thing! You're crazy! Cracked in the head! What've you been smoking out in China?

—I'll prove it. I'll see you in prison! I'll make sure the truth comes out!

—The truth? The truth is what you've been running away from for all these years! She died because you left. You broke her heart!

—No...

—You hit him, beat him up, and left. It killed her. Face up to it, son.

But Jim had turned and was walking away, heading to the side door, pushing through, into the blazing sunshine, igniting everything around him. Peter felt himself led out into the heat and the blinding light.

—Yeah? Running away again? It's what you're best at, isn't it? Harry called from the darkened bar.

Peter huddled into his jacket, blowing into his hands. Scrolling down through accounts still to read, he sighed, and looked at his watch. Too many for tonight, he thought. I can't... I can't get all these done.

He imagined the next morning, the sky still a grey smear, as he strode down the corridor to Geoff's office, and rapped on the door.

—Ah! Peter! I was just going to... Have you come to...?

—I've just emailed you the graphs for the On-Boarding project. In them I detail how it has led to a five-point-three day decrease in the pending period, leading to a four hundred thousand pound saving. I've also identified a further two hundred and fifty thousand pound saving through a refinement of the procedure for accounts coming through from brokers.

—Really? And this is... err... the work you began yesterday morning?

—Yes sir.

—Well... that is impressive. I... err... Look there's...
—Yes?

Geoff stared at his computer screen, drumming his fingers on the desk.

—This whole Shrimpton business... How about you stick to emailing internal people from now on, OK?

Peter clicked to the next account, quickly reading through the notes and pasting the relevant passage into the spreadsheet.

His fingers and knees ached with the cold. He shook himself, trying to get warmth into his limbs. Again he scrolled down through the accounts, imagining the chill increasing as the list descended. He tried to pull the cuffs of his coat down over his hands, leaving just the tips of his fingers. He rubbed his knees with the covered palms of his hands.

What I need is some sort of fan heater, he thought. Something to blow hot air at me, stinking of burning dust and cobwebs. Keep me going till I'm finished.

The image of a white plastic pillar, waist high, one side riddled by a black grill, swam into his mind. Yes, that. There's one of them in the building somewhere. It was in the corner of a room, discarded, out of sight of the conference camera. Which is in...

He clicked control-s, and closed the laptop. He could see it: decent chairs to sit in, the computer on the conference table, the heater warming him. Maybe he could watch a film or TV show on the projector. He unplugged the laptop and wound the cord round the adapter. He could get a cup of tea from the vending machine, maybe some chocolate too, a late-night snack to give him that last spark of energy for the final few accounts. He opened the case and slipped the laptop and the plug inside. The final accounts will fly by, he thought.

He slipped the case over his shoulder and walked gently out into the low forest of chairs, silent and still in the moonlight, table tops like the calm surface of a pond, chromed legs the weeds to be picked carefully through.

The smell of rotting, decomposing flesh drifted up to him. Of animals dead beneath the water, their skin flaking away, meat like cotton wool.

A sound behind him made him turn.

Ben.

He was stood beyond a long line of tables. Peter looked at him, waiting. Then he turned back, continuing to the door.

Another sound made him glance round.

Ben was slowly walking towards him, legs pushing past tables and chairs, which swayed and rocked in his wake. Bubbles streamed up from his mouth, rising, glinting in the pale, white light.

Peter shook his head, looking down.

It's not… It isn't… he said to himself.

Slowly, not looking up, he walked to the door and pulled it, opening the dark hole of the corridor.

Peter stood there for a second, imagining a security guard in the blackness, Alsatian on a tight leash.

Do we have security guards at night? Maybe cameras?

There was the note; the post-it on Alistair's desk. The security guard had noticed he'd left his window open overnight. Left a note. Uniformed officer, wandering around, keeping an eye on things. If they can see an open window, they'll see a man still working. Keep it down. Silent running. Stealth mode. Can't add further misdemeanours to the… Called in by Geoff for this, rather than that. —Thrown out at midnight? Creeping around? What's wrong with you, Peter?

Going quietly across the darkened corridor, slowly, carefully, hearing only his breathing, he felt for the conference door, eased down the handle and slipped inside.

The large, oval table and padded chairs were bathed in orange from the lights of the car park. Around the walls there were bland, abstract paintings, and, in the corner, beside a potted plant, there was a door to a store cupboard. Crossing to the windows, he found the cord to pull the vertical blinds shut, plunging the room into near blackness. He turned on a single spotlight above the table, walked over and carefully, quietly, placed the laptop case within the circle of light. Turning, he found the tall heater standing in a corner. He pulled it to the table and clicked it on. It whirred noisily up to speed, loud in the silent building. Peter breathed in the dusty air and coughed, but warmth buffeted him, seeping through his clothes and soaking into his body.

He opened up the laptop, the screen flickering back into light. Glancing over the top of it, he saw Ben, now sat at the other end of the long table, his head lowered, pale eyes looking straight at Peter, grey lips curled in a grin. Peter stared, mouth open.

After a while, Ben looked around, nodding slightly.

Peter tried to smile. He swallowed. —Yeah, nice, isn't it? He said, in a breathy whisper. —But of a leap from that flea pit we used to live in. Do you remember? That shithole on Brompton Street? Mould on the walls, the shower that leaked through into the kitchen?

Ben frowned, looking away, shaking his head.

—It was awful… muttered Peter, embarrassed.

Ben lifted a forkful of food up to his mouth. On the plate in front of him was a large, plump section of steaming cottage pie: a dark ooze of rich beef gravy beneath browned potato mash. His blue plastic beaker was full of red wine, and was by the plate of their housemate Mickey, who was eating his own portion of the pie.

—It never fails to fucking astonish me, Mickey, said Irvine, sitting between Peter and Mickey. —How your deeply-held Buddhist beliefs somehow fall away when presented with a plate of dead cow.

—That, said Mickey, swallowing. —Would be a fundamental misunderstanding of the basic Principle of: 'Thou shalt not kill'. I've not killed this cow, have I? It was already dead. If I don't eat it, then this animal's death will have been in vain. Which would be terrible. He stuffed another fork-load into his mouth. —And, Mickey continued, mouth full. ——A waste of your most excellent cooking.

—Piss off! Said Claire, the other side of Ben. —By eating this you create demand from suppliers, who will then butcher more cows!

Peter stared at her: pale, thin, dark-eyed from too many amphetamines, jet black hair tied up.

—This cow might already be dead, but the next several hundred thousand or so will only die if they think there's a reason to kill them! She frowned at Peter—What are you looking at me like that for?

He shook his head and looked down at the laptop.

—Ah, Mzz Claire, you raise an interesting point, said Mickey. —Allow me to refer you to my own guideline, which I call the Principle of Useless Protest. Do you really think that if I, on my own, did not buy this beef, which I didn't, by the way, my learned colleague to the left of me did.

Irvine raised a fork.

—Then that cow, or any cow, wouldn't get slaughtered? Mickey continued. —Vegetarianism has been around for thousands of years and yet animals are still killed for meat. Even if every human quit meat tonight and never ate it again. Many thousands, if not millions of animals would still be killed, either in the belief that it's a passing fad, or because there's simply no point in keeping them anymore. So... If I don't eat this most excellent pie...

—Ta. Said Irvine.

——then the animal that went into it will still have died, but for less of a reason. If I do eat it, then there is at least some use in their death and they will attain another life, of sorts, as their proteins become a part of my own body, as biology has so designed. If you want to reduce animal suffering, buy quality meat from supplies who look after their livestock. You did that, right?

Irvine shrugged. —But what about the other commandment, eh? The one about not taking intoxicating substances? You get pished all the time! You fucking drink, and you consume more bastard drugs than the rest of us!

—Yeah, said Claire, pointing her fork at Mickey.

—Again, I have to refer you to the wording and how you interpret it…

There was a collective groan and Claire slammed her fork down onto the table.

—No, no, wait… hear me out.

—Aye, go on, this'll be good, said Irvine.

—The Principle states that a person should not seek out oblivion, which not only covers intoxication, but also suicide. It is a warning against trying to remove oneself from reality, to descend into delusion and darkness, further and further away from the enlightenment that all Buddhists attempt to achieve.

—Sounds like a fucking brilliant night in… doesn't it? Said Irvine to Peter, who smiled and shrugged.

—However… continued Mickey. —Certain tantric meditations and rituals are designed to induce a state of altered consciousness, something which can also be brought about by chemical means. Indeed, it could even be argued that the very act of enlightenment is, in itself, a form of removing oneself from the accepted delusion of reality that dominates our everyday consciousnesses. Thus, the Principle is really only warning against the intention of the drug-user, not the drug itself.

—So, last Saturday…when you were puking your guts up round at Frankie's house, that was part of your path to enlightenment?

—Yes. And it is a road I travel diligently and consistently. And I will be proceeding along it tonight, whilst watching Ben's pirated copy of Terminator Two. If anyone would like to join me?

—I'm sorry, I'm gonna have to disappoint you. Said Irvine. —I have business matters to attend to in my attic boardroom. The packaging department are doing overtime tonight. He smiled. —Need to do my bit to help others achieve the blissful state of Nirvana!

—And I have a date with an Iain Banks book. Said Claire, looking over at Peter.

—Oh? Really? Reading in bed again are we? Said Irvine. —Brilliant! You can keep an eye out for the po-lice.

—Why do you…? She held her hands up. —Even if they did find a reason to raid this house, they have two flights of stairs to run up before they get to your room! They won't do it quietly, will they?

—Oh come on! If I get busted again, especially with the stuff I've got upstairs, I'm going down proper. It'll be fucking Strangeways or some other Victorian dungeon, full of ponces and psychopaths, wanting to fuck me or fillet me. Besides, what else you gonna be doing? Hmm? Your boyfriend here will be watching the film, ain't that right, Ben?

The dead man, forking the last clump of mashed potato and minced beef into his grey mouth, shook his head and started to stand.

—You working tonight? Asked Claire, all innocent.

Ben nodded, wiping his mouth with the back of his hand.

—Aye, well, I suppose someone's got to earn an honest fucking penny round here, eh? Said Irvine. —How about you, Pete?

They all looked at him, waiting: Mickey chewing, Irvine with an eyebrow raised, Claire glancing casually sideways, Ben stood with his wine, not drinking.

—I… He pointed down at the laptop. —I've got to finish this.

—Fair enough. Said Irvine. —It was your fuck-up, at the end of the day. Looks like you're on your own, Mickey! Don't get lost on those transcendental planes!

Ben tilted his head back, gulping down his wine. He put the beaker down, staring at Peter. He glanced at Claire, then back at Peter. He winked and walked over to the conference room door, opened it and walked out.

—Wait! Wait... Ben? It's not...! I...! I'm sorry! Called Peter, getting up and running to the door. But outside there was nothing, just the dark corridor. Remembering the security guard, he pulled back sharply and gently shut the door. Turning round, he found the room empty, nothing but the hum of the heater.

He looked down at the floor, his hands trembling, clenching and unclenching.

This... this is... fucking... No. Come on. Just need to pull myself together. Get a cup of tea. Wake me up. Nice cup of tea. Maybe that chocolate. Have a bit of a break. Not been sleeping too well. Lucid dreaming. All just my... Only in my... Yeah, nice cup of tea.

He opened the door again and listened. Not hearing anything, he leaned out and looked into the black.

The darkness swam and shifted, shapes moving and twisting, alien tentacles wrapped around themselves, hovering blotches ballooned and collapsed, noiselessly. He pulled back in, shaking his head.

Just... in my... It's all fine. Absolutely fine. Nothing there.

He stepped out, looking up and down, listening for the heavy thud of footsteps, his fingertips skirting the wall. He crept down to the vending machines near the corner by the toilets. He paused, listening. Nothing. He fumbled in his pocket for change, trying to feel for what the coins were in the utter darkness.

The first coin dropped with a loud clang, and rattled down through the vending machine. Peter stepped back, still clutching other coins. He tried to punch the coin-return button, as the coin dropped again and again, clanging louder still, but it only shook the whole machine, creaking and glooping. He gave up and ran quickly back to the conference room, heart thumping, the sound of tinkling and crashing following him: metal keys and feet chasing close behind.

Inside, he clicked off the light and the heater, and snatched up the laptop and coat. He opened the door to the storage cupboard and dropped the computer and coat inside, shutting the door and kneeling behind it, trying to breathe quietly, a pounding in his ears.

He listened, and waited.

There was nothing from the room.

—You always were an inept fool. Said Louise, somewhere in the blackness of the cupboard. —Never got anything right. Putting money into a machine that's turned off? What an idiot...

Peter's eyes adjusted to the gloom. He turned and saw that the cupboard stretched out into the entrance corridor of a three-story house. To his right was the door to the living room, a flickering blue light came from underneath, the sound of gunfire, and the sweet, herby smell of Mickey's cannabis. In front of him was the stairs, leading up into deeper darkness. He cautiously took a step up onto the first tread, remembering that the stairs did not creak if you put your feet close to the wall. He climbed slowly, carefully, one step at a time.

At the top was first the bathroom, then, to his right, Ben and Claire's room. As he climbed, their door was slowly revealed through the banisters: a big, dark rectangle, brass handle glinting in the darkness. He crept along, hand outstretched, trying desperately to breath quietly. His fingers closed around the handle, and he gently turned.

Inside, there was nothing but darkness. He heard a rustle, as someone under bed-sheets moved around. Carefully and quietly closing the door, he patted the wall for the light switch. Clicking it on, he found himself in a stationary cupboard, the walls lined with deep, metal shelves.

Peter stood there, the laptop at his feet, covered by his

coat. There was another rustle and a mewling: a faint murmur of a cry, muffled. Peter looked around, confused, becoming frantic as the crying got louder and louder, edging into ear-splitting screams. He could feel the heavy boots thudding towards the cupboard, trembling the metal shelves. He lifted his coat and the sound got louder

Of course, he thought, it's the laptop: the browser is still open and it's started playing some weird video of a crying baby.

He tugged at the jacket, finding it stuck on something.

As the coat came away, the noise got suddenly sharper. Tumbling from the folds of the black waterproof came a small foetus, the size of his fist, covered with blood. It tumbled onto the carpet and lay there, tiny fists clenched tightly as its face wrinkled up into a scream. Peter stumbled backwards away from it, crashing into the metal shelves.

It lay there, howling, vibrating with the noise.

Peter covered his ears and sank to the floor, staring at the blooded thing.

With his foot, he flicked the coat back over the foetus, muffling the noise. Peter stared, not knowing what else to do.

A boot came suddenly crashing down on the screaming lump in the coat. There was an abrupt silence in the cupboard. Peter looked up the leg to Ben, staring down at Peter. Ben shook his head, reached over to the light switch, and clicked it off.

six

Within the pleated, dusty folds of an old set of curtains, Peter tapped away at the project, bathed in the shifting bright white of the screen, like moonlight reflected in water. His coat had been kicked to the opposite end of the cupboard, and every now and then he would glance nervously over at it.

All I have to do, he kept telling himself, is to finish this project. Once all the information is in, and the graph has been built from it, then I can... I can say what the problem is. Then I can say what they need to solve. Then I can present the whole thing finished and complete. Costs and savings. Yes. Facts and figures.

He frowned and felt the up-swell of sobbing in his chest. He hit alt-tab to flick between windows, but left his finger on tab and watched as the selection cycled quickly through the icons. He watched it going round and round, all the files and folders and databases and spreadsheets and PDFs and access portals and browser tabs, round and round, trying to release it at the database icon. But it was too fast, too much of a blur, and so he shut his eyes and took his finger off slowly. When he looked again, he was back on the desktop.

—If you get a dog, dickhead, you'd have to take it for walks, and pick up its shit, and feed it, and all that.

He was walking down an over-grown road behind a housing estate, lined with piles of rubbish and old sofas dumped in back gardens: children's plastic play-sets sprouted weeds from among car tyres and milk cartons. Beside him walked Jonjo and Chris, both newly shaven-headed and, feeling the chill of the autumn air, they kept rubbing their scalps.

—Yeah, but it would be dead fierce, like, and could attack people who had a go at me!

—How'd you train it to do that?

—Well… y'know, wrap someone up in something tough, get the dog to attack them.

—Eh?

—Like what the police guys wear. They came to our school once, got their dog to leap at them, bite them, get them to the ground. So I'd get someone to, like, dress up like them policemen and pretend to attack me, and, when the dog has got them on the ground and they're like, rolling around, screaming and shit, I'll give the dog a biscuit. Fuck, man, it'll be easy! Basic reward and reinforcement, ain't it? Plus, all dogs bark at shit and want to protect their owners. Piece of piss!

—Who the fuck are you going to get to stand there and get bitten by a dog? Who? Mind you… if they get the chance to kick the shite out of you, they'll be fucking queuing up!

—Yeah, said Chris. —But anyone who's prepared to kick the shit out of a human, isn't going to fucking blink when it comes to putting the boot into a dog. Especially the kind of cunts who don't like you.

—Besides, you'd need to have the dog from a puppy to have that kind of bond, so that it sees you as pack leader, y'know? So it'll be a year or so before it's big enough to attack people properly.

—Can't I just get a fucking dog?

—Sorry, Jonjo, but Pete and I have known you for too long: you aren't the dog-owning kind.

—You have a habit of getting bored. And wasted.

—Fuck off.

The three men reached Meadow Head Garage, a broken brick shed with a peeling white sign outside. They wandered in, stepping over broken plastic milk crates and buckets of sump oil. A rusted car, wheel hubs resting on blocks, sat in the centre of the workshop.

—Hallo! Oie, oie! Federico!

Jonjo kicked a rusted tin can and it skipped and clattered into the shed.

—Christ Almighty! A short, thickset man, wearing greasy overalls climbed out of the rusted car. He scratched his stubble and stared at the three. —What the fuck? You kicking my shit for fun?

—You sleeping in your car again, Federico?

—No I'm bloody not, you cheeky little shit! He pulled out a packet of cigarettes and lit one. —What do you fucking want?

—We're here for a… packet?

—Eh?

—Irvine said…

—Irvine? That scheming little shit!

—Well, he said you were looking to get rid of… something. For Spencer?

—Oh, yeah: that… I fucking hate it. Stupid idea. Make's me fucking nervous it does. He started slowly walking over to an office in the corner. —Why I took it in the first fucking place I have no idea. Stupid. So stupid. But I'd already done the work… He went in, and there was thumping, clattering, as something fell to the floor. He emerged with a cardboard box. —Here. They said someone would pay me in exchange for this? Yeah?

—How much?

—Five hundred.

Chris weighed the box. —What? Pounds? Or packets?

—Eh? What? Pounds! Jesus! I ain't looked inside. I want nothing to do with it…

Jonjo opened the box.

—Hmm. Look here, Pete.

Peter looked into the box and saw five large bags full of small, brown pills.

—Wow! He mouthed, his back to the garage owner. Looking at the other two, they nodded, eyes wide.

—Well, see, the thing is, Federico, said Chris, —This is medical-grade morphine. This stuff is really hard to shift. Your average morphine addict is a fucking Victorian, y'know? The only people into morphine these days are the ones who can't get hold of the real shit, the Big Brown: Heroin. And these pills will only take the edge off, like. I think, between you and me, it's because jacking up with a needle is all part of the high. Very psychological, y'know? How about we say… two-fifty?

—What? Seriously? No, no, no… He slowly shook his head. —Five hundred. This is payment on work, my friends, and that work cost five hundred pounds. I had to replace the exhaust, engine manifold, sparks, head gasket and distributer. Really, I'm only charging for parts. Two-fifty…? He shook his head. —Five hundred.

—Three-fifty?

There was silence.

—Are you fucking deaf? It's five hundred! That's the price. There's no fucking haggling here!

—Look, Federico, you've maybe got around two hundred in each bag, and four bags. This sort of shit, you're only looking at around fifty pence per pill. So there's only about four hundred pounds here. Max.

The mechanic stared down into the box. —I fucking knew he'd rip me off.

—How about we say four hundred? We won't be making any money, but it's the best you'll get. And then it's off the premises. Stop you feeling nervous, eh?

Federico rubbed a grimy hand round the back of his neck and sighed. —Fine. Fine then. Take it. Look around you: I'll add another wing to the mansion, buy another fucking yacht, how about that? Yeah?

—Come on lads, pay the man. Said Chris, putting the box down. The three went into a huddle, getting wads of cash out of their pockets.

—How much is it each?

—A hundred and… thirty… three? Thirty three? Wait… what the fuck?

—Fuck that. Have you got…? Put all that in. I'll put in the forty. Have you got thirty?

—Right. Said Chris, turning, cradling a pile of notes and a few coins. —There we go, my good sir! Pleasure doing business and all that…

—OK. Well, fucking-whatever, my friend. Said Federico, taking the money and thumbing through it. He turned and shuffled back into his office. —But… if I find out that you've taken me for ride? That you've royally fucked me up the shitter? Then I'll be fucking coming for you, alright? Watch your fucking backs!

He went into the office and shut the door while Jonjo, Chris and Peter walked out from the workshop and back down the overgrown road, looking behind them, hurrying along. When they were out of sight of the garage, they broke apart, looking open-mouthed at each other.

—Fuck me. FUCK me. Fuck ME.

—Shut up shut up shut up, he'll fucking hear!

—What do you reckon? At least a thousand of these little fuckers, sell them for a couple of quid each? Deano sells this sort of shit for a fucking fiver a pop! Doesn't he?

—Shit me, we have fucking scored! We have fucking scoooooorrrred!

—Yeah, yeah, yeah, but gentlemen, please: to business. Pete, do you mind doing the usual and bagging this lot up into, what do you reckon? Ten to a bag? The other men nodded. —I'll get talking to a few people, like Wilson over at the Arrow's Head, see if I can get a few buyers, maybe shift a few bulk orders. Jonjo, can you see if Mouse and the rest of his cheese-eating, veggy, heroin-addict mates want some downers?

—Really? Why do I have to go hang out with them? All they do is sit around and fucking fart. Don't dare smoke in case the fucking house explodes!

—Because Pete is doing the baggies, because he's the baggie king, and Mouse still wants to tear me a new anus for that dodgy, knock-off methadone, doesn't he?

—Jesus… Fine! But it'll fucking kill me, it really will.

At the end of the road they walked down the hill to a crossroads. There they split, with Peter and the box of morphine getting on the bus into town, where he pressed through the rush-hour crowd to catch the bus to Brompton Street.

When he got to the stop, still hugging the box to his stomach, Claire was stood there, hunched over, her hair tied back, her face pale, thin, looking up at him.

His fingers curled protectively round the edges of the laptop, hugging it to him, still seeing those black eyes, ringed red, staring into him.

Could I have said sorry? Then? Would that have changed things? No. No, of course not. Shouldn't have done what we did. Killed a man. Stay with me forever. Looming over me, what we did. We did it. Us. Him dead because of us.

Could I have changed things?

Yes. If I knew then what I know now. Lots of things I would change. Do things differently. Undo many things.

There was a crash of metal, loud.

—Jim? Jim! What are you doing out there?

His mother was calling from the kitchen, her voice coming up the stairs to Peter's room. There was a deep, rumble of reply from his father.

—Come inside, come on, have a cup of tea. Please? Come on in.

Another reply, louder, angrier.

—Just... Jim! Jim, be careful!

There was another crash of metal, a clang and a tinkle of glass. Peter went over to his bedroom door and peaked out, down the stairs.

His father darkened the bottom of the stairwell, coming in from outside, thumping up the stairs with heavy, unsteady footsteps. Peter jumped back, swinging the door shut. The thumps got closer and closer, Peter took another step backwards, before shaking his head. I'm sixteen now, he thought. I can stand up to him. But the feet clumped past his door, down the corridor to his parents' bedroom. There was a heavy thump, making the floor shake. Peter stepped forward and carefully looked round his door, down the corridor, to see his father lying face down, half under his bed, wriggling and twitching. The smell of whisky still lingered in his father's wake.

Peter froze, staring at the legs as they kicked and shuffled. He thought of how his grandfather had been found, dead in his armchair, alone for a week. But still he stayed by his door, watching.

—What is your father up to? Said his mother, making Peter look sharply down the stairs. He caught the faint smell of smoke coming from the open door to the back yard

—Err? Said Peter, as his dad shuffled and wriggled back out from under the bed, red-faced, holding a taped-together jigsaw-puzzle box.

—Leave me alone, woman! He shouted, sitting upright, staring at the box.

Peter ducked back behind his door and listened as his father stumbled past and down the stairs.

—What are you going to do with that? Said his mother. The feet went outside. There was a loud clang of metal on metal and then heavy footsteps coming back in.

—What the bloody hell did you do that for? Jim? Jim!

They went into the lounge, the door slamming.

Peter crept out and down the stairs, looking carefully round the corner to check. Whispering, tense and angry, came from the living room. Through the open backdoor, he saw the metal dustbin, surrounded by rubbish, a faint wisp of smoke curling out from under the lid.

—Why can't you just talk to me? Said his mother.

—Why should I…? All you ever do is… bloody whinge… and blame ME!

—Blame? What for? Specifically. Tell me. Come on! What have I blamed you for? Hmm? Or have you just made it up? Again!

Peter stepped outside and gently swung the back door shut. He walked over to the bin and lifted the warm lid. A brief puff of grey smoke drifted out. Inside, he saw that the jigsaw box had been dumped on top of some smouldering old newspapers and rubbish. It looked dirty, but intact. He pulled it out and brushed it off, blackening his hands. Turning, he went quietly back inside the house and up the stairs, carrying the box.

—Really? Said his mum. —Who keeps things together whenever you go away on one of your little trips? Hmm? I'm expected to just put up with you leaving at a moment's…

—This is my house! I earned it! I paid for it! Me! I can do whatever the hell I like in my own fucking house!

Peter closed his bedroom door and put the box on the floor. Opening it, he looked down at sheets of typed paper. He read a few lines from the top sheet.

—Jim! Just… calm down and tell me…?

—Nothing! No! … useless…

He pulled the paper out and put it down beside the box, then reached into a drawer and pulled out a pad of paper and put that inside the box and took it back downstairs. He took matches from beside the gas hob and went to the bin in the back yard. Striking a match, he held it to the edge of the blank pad, the paper blackening and curling, faint orange flames flickering in the daylight. He half-closed the lid and laid the box back inside the bin. The flames grew and grew, reaching up over the lip, straining to get higher, fierce within their drum. He picked up the bin lid and dropped it on top, the heat scorching his arm.

Stepping back, rubbing the skin on his elbow, he heard the latch on the backdoor, and he turned to see his father stood in the doorway, his face blank and drained. Peter edged backwards, watching his father, the fire crackling away. Jim marched over to the bin and pulled the lid off, releasing a flurry of embers, floating up like insects into the sky. His father stared down into the flames, his mouth open.

—Fuck, fuck, FUCK! He yelled. —FUCK! He reached down into the bin, the flames licking up around his hand. —Jesus! He said, pulling back, shaking his arm. —Shit! Shit, shit, shit!.

—What are you doing? Said Peter's mother, at the back door. Jim ran back inside the house, barging past her, returning with a plastic broom, which he stuck, handle first, into the fire.

—Oh Jim! No! That's... Oh for God's sake!

He prodded and levered, face crinkled up by concentration and effort. Peter watched as the burning box slid up the wall of the bin before crumpling into a shower of burning ash and sparks. His father slumped, pulling out the blackened, slightly-melted broom handle and dropped it beside the bin, where it smouldered. —Fuck, he muttered, stamping on it. He sighed, staring into the bin, lips pursed. Finally, he turned and walked slowly back into the house, leaving a sooty handprint on the door frame.

—Jim? Look, you can write it all again, can't you?

Peter watched them go, staying quietly still. He breathed out and walked up to the door. Looking round, he saw Jim sitting on the sofa, his head in his hands, Sylvia stood by him, looking down. Peter ran quickly up the stairs and shut his door, leaning against it. Low voices came from the living room.

The smell of smoke was everywhere, filling up his room. He looked down at the pile of papers on the floor, unsure of what to do. He looked back to his door, imagining the stairs beyond, the man sat in the living room, bereft and grieving. Eventually, Peter lay down and started reading, the pile of papers ready to be shoved under his bed at any second.

As he followed the words, he tried to imagine his father speaking them, but could not. These were from another person, someone Peter had never met. A stranger's voice, telling him of distant lands and strange sights.

—Christ, Jim, look at that! Said John, pointing off the starboard bow.

—What? What am I looking at?

—There! Can't you see them?

Before me, beyond the rails of the cargo ship, *Cygnus*, the water was a pure, iridescent blue, reflecting the sky. I looked at where John was pointing, at a few small figures, walking on the waves, nearly a mile out to sea.

We were entering the narrow Sangian Strait between the southern end of Sumatra and the north-western point of Java. The journey had been steady over the previous week or more, coming south down from Sri Lanka, which was then still called Ceylon, heading for Jakarta. The night before, we had been awoken by loud rumblings and booms, the very sea beneath us seemed to tremble and vibrate with every crash. Those that went out on deck, expecting to see a tremendous thunder storm on the horizon, were greeted with a clear sky, except a single column of dark cloud ahead of them, boiling with red and yellow light. It was the third mate who connected the cloud with the Karang Volcano, at the northern end of Java. —We'll be passing much closer tomorrow, he said.

When the sun rose, it was a bright, clear day. Ahead of us was a thin column of smoke, drifting vertically up till it flicked away in the upper atmosphere. We could now see it came from a blackened mountain to our starboard. As we motored through the straight, John had seen the people standing on the surface of the water as though it was a path or playground.

—Bugger me... Look at them, Jim! People walking on the sea!

—Christ alive...

—Talking of which... what do you think our reverend father will make of this?

Edward Mitchell was the ship's purser and self-appointed chaplain, leading grace every meal-time and a service every Sunday, in which he gave lengthy sermons on such subjects as the trinity, the transubstantiation, and personal hygiene.

We looked along the deck, now crowded by crew standing at the railings, and saw the purser stood on a capstan, straining to see over their heads. His brow was furrowed, mouth open, and his fingers twitched.

—Oh good God... look at that. Said John, pointing further along the coast to where a fishing boat was unloading its catch into a waiting cart, pulled by a pair of oxen, stood idly, tails flicking, upon the gently lapping waves. —If we tell anyone about this, they will laugh us out of the southern hemisphere!

All the crew stared at the cattle and the wooden cart, being loaded with basket after basket of fish.

When the ship docked in Jakarta, the Indonesian deck crew unloaded the cargo alongside the local stevedores. They laughed and joked together, just as they always did.

—Look at them. Said Daniels, the third engineer. —Do you think these darkies understand what we just saw?

I shrugged. —They saw it the same as us.

—Yes, but... how can they act like nothing happened? I mean, are they simple? It was...!

——It was what?

—Christ, man! I don't bloody know!

I turned and looked at Daniels, watching him fidget and frown. He looked at me, smiled awkwardly, and walked away, tapping his fingers on the railing.

That night, John found me stood at the back of a bar filled with cigarette smoke and British crewmen, drinking cold, pale, European lager.

—Hi there! What's the beer like?
—Cold.
—My favourite. He held up two fingers to the barman. —Two more, please.
—Thanks.
—I've just been talking to Wilkins over at the India Line offices.
—That's a shame.
—Hmm, yes, normally. But he'd heard of our 'witnessing a most-blessed miracle'.
—That must have been great sport for him.
—Especially as he only found out because one of our first-trippers, inspired somewhat by our esteemed purser, had taken it as a sign to start trying to convert the local populace. He's been going round the bars where the Indonesians drink, spreading the 'good news'.
—What a fool. There's a church or tabernacle on nearly every corner.
—Ahh, but his skills of observation are of more particular amusement to the indigenous population than that!
—How so?
—Seems our little miracle was nothing of the sort. Fairly common occurrence in fact. And, might I add, perfectly well-known by our own second officer.
—Really?
—Apparently so. Seems the volcano we saw erupting has, over the years, sent lava down into the strait, forming a shelf right out to sea. The locals use it all the time. It's a bit like Morecambe Bay, but made of rock. Marked quite clearly on navigational charts.
—Ha! And all the locals know about it?
—Do you know about Morecombe Bay?

—They'll find him hilarious…

—Yes, they did, which is why, at some point, Wilkins would like us to go and get him out of the clink. He's been arrested. Seems he didn't quite get what they were laughing at, thought they were laughing at Jesus. He thumped a few of them and the police took rather a dim view.

I shook my head and smiled into my beer.

—Poor chap. Hear the gaols around here are pretty horrendous.

John nodded.

—Another? I asked, waggling my empty glass.

Peter clicked between windows, and pasted a short section of text into the spreadsheet. He uncrossed his legs, stretching them out underneath the curtain, feeling a cool flush as blood flowed properly again.

He stared over at his coat, lying crumpled up in the corner. It did not move. Around him, no matter how many times he looked, everything stayed the same.

—You alright? He asked Claire, hugging herself at the bus stop.

She flashed a sarcastic smile, and continued to look down the road for the bus. The rush hour crowd hurried round them, urgently pushing past. Voices shrieked to be heard, or muttered low to stay private. People in the queue were bunched together, heads down, gathered into their own little worlds. The crush of people pressed Peter's box into Claire.

—Rough weekend? He asked. —Not seen you for a few days.

She frowned, looking away, across the road to the shops selling holidays.

—You heading back to Brompton Street?

She nodded, looking down at her trainers.

—Yeah. Got a busy night ahead. He nodded down at the box.

—Look… Pete. She turned to him. —I think we need to talk.

—What? Yeah? Alright, sure, if you…

Claire looked around at the crowd, sighed, and pulled him across the pavement, through the flow of people, to an alleyway behind some shops. Around them were dustbins and black sacks, boxes and litter. There were voices at the other end of the alley, then a shower of sparks as someone flicked out their cigarette, the door banging behind them as they went back to work.

Claire leant against a wall. —I… I've… She said, folding her arms. She was trembling.

—What? What the fuck's the matter?

—It's just… I don't know if… Fuck… She shook her head. —It was easier to tell Ben.

—Tell Ben what?

—I had to tell him, and you. I'm telling you… She chewed her lip. —I've had an abortion.

She looked down the alley, fingers up to her mouth.

—Oh…

—Have you got a cig?

—No. I don't…

—Fuck. She grimaced.

—What do you mean? Were you pregnant?

She turned and looked at him.

—Yes. Yes, I was fucking pregnant! Why would they shove a fucking… vacuum cleaner up me if I… Jesus! She looked away, folding her arms, hunching up against the wall. —'Were you pregnant?' She mocked.

—Fuck off! Alright? I… I didn't know! This is… It's a… It's a lot to take in, alright? He stared at her. —Fuck me. He ran a hand through his hair.

—Oh? Well, I am sorry. Maybe I should have broken it to you more gently? Given you time? She sneered. —Not like this was happening inside you, to your own body, and the doctor wanted a decision there and then. Judgemental bitch. Toxicology reports don't come back that quick. Should've known. Kicked up a fuss. Asked for a second opinion.

Peter stared down the alley at the crowds hurrying past, all busy, with jobs and families and friends, laughing and vibrant and alive.

—But we used protection. He said, quietly.

—Doesn't always work though, does it?

—Yeah? But what about you and Ben?

—Same. We always used rubbers.

—Always?

She said nothing, chewing her fingernail.

—You said... you said you told him?

She nodded.

—How did he take it?

Looking down the alley, she said nothing for a long time.

—Not great. She shrugged. —Hard to tell. He sat there. He listened. He muttered something. He went away. Not seen him since.

—Was he angry?

Claire sighed, sagging, leaning her head against the bricks. —Yes. No. I think... I think he knows. She looked at Peter. —About us.

Peter stared. —Fuck.

—He didn't... He didn't say anything, but he asked... he asked if he was the father. Why would he say that? Why would he ask if he didn't think...?

Peter shifted the weight of the box. —Maybe...

—Yes?

—Maybe he just... hoped it wasn't his. Not his problem.

She stared at him. —Maybe, she said, looking out at the hustle of pedestrians. —We couldn't have brought up a kid anyway.

Peter nodded, looking down at his box. —Yeah.

Rain started to fall, rattling on the bins around them.

The end of the alley darkened as their bus came in, hissing to a stop. The doors creaked open and the queue shuffled on. Claire and Peter watched as it drove off, the rain falling, drumming on their skulls.

Peter ran a hand over his head, feeling the cold wind of the alleyway whistle past him. He looked down, into the bright screen and clicked through several more accounts.

Something so big. How could I miss it? How could I have not seen it coming? Shouldn't be possible for it to sneak up on you.

Depends on the route you took, I suppose. Sometimes, if you're looking the other way, anything can creep up and shock you.

—Bit of shore-leave lads! Bit of time to go out and catch the clap! Come on! Line up! Easy there, plenty to go round!

I had been serving aboard the *Dionysus*, a Greek-owned vessel, when we docked in Hong Kong for urgent repairs to the propeller shaft, shaken loose by unbalanced blades. All the crew, except for the engineers, were given five nights shore leave. When the purser was handing out wages, he warned us about attempting to travel into China. —Them that have tried it, get arrested pretty sharpish, know what I mean? He said, pulling his eyes back into slits and projecting his upper teeth. —You lot don't look yellow enough!

But after hours of walking amongst the clacking mah-jong players, the rattle of wooden sandals, and the continual calls of the street stalls and the markets, some of us felt that we had experienced most of what Hong Kong had to offer.

—I've always fancied seeing the Great Wall. Said Glenn, a seventeen-year-old second-tripper, nursing his pale, warm lager.

—Go to Mongolia, see it from there. I told him.

—Nah… You seen a picture of the Wall? Ain't much more to it than that. Said McClinery, the third-mate's assistant.

—You've been? Asked Glenn, wide-eyed.

—Course I have. Been all round China. They don't

'arrest' you. That's all bollocks. They just stare at you.

—I can believe that. I said. —You're taller than I am. And ginger.

—They'll arrest you if you're breaking the law, or promoting capitalism, or bad-mouthing the state. But being foreign ain't itself specifically illegal.

—I'm finding the idea of you wandering around the People's Republic quite hard to swallow. I told him.

—You don't believe me? Well, how about we go for a little ride? Hmm? Go see China?

—Great Wall? Or Forbidden City? Go on, McClinery, get us into the Forbidden City, you big ginger bastard!

—Oh, there's something much better than that: something huge, enormous, and that no bloody westerner has ever set eyes on!

Glenn and I looked at each other.

—Don't get your hopes up, kid. I said. —He's going to blindfold you and then show you some Chinky's dick, I'll bet.

McClinery led us down to the corrugated warehouses on the northern end of the island, rapping on a few doors till he found a lorry driver prepared to carry us. He turned to me and Glenn.

—Right, wages: give 'em.

—What?

—Money, now. It costs to get across the border. Quickly, before he changes his mind!

We reluctantly handed over our pay packets, and were lead up to the rear of a tarpaulin-covered truck, the inside dusty with bags of grain and rice. McClinery held the flap open, looking around. —Go on, in yer pop. Quickly now!

—I thought you said it wasn't illegal?

—Well, it isn't, if you have all the right visas and everything, which can take months! So... this is the quick route, yeah?

—Wait! Hold on! Doesn't that... well, we'll get arrested for sure, won't we?

—Nah! China's a bit like a bee hive: once you're in, everyone will assume you're supposed to be there. Don't worry!

We all climbed up and the sheeting was tied down behind us.

—Best get comfy lads. It's a two day ride to get where we're going!

—What! You bastard, McClinery!

The wagon jolted and rolled out of the warehouse, into the honking, roaring, screaming streets of Hong Kong. I found a crevice in amongst the sacks of grain and lay down, my sailor's stomach allowing me to sleep quite peacefully.

I woke several hours later, when we stopped by a quiet roadside. We were given food and beer by the driver and sat looking out at the Chinese countryside. Glenn was looking pale and it was decided that he should ride in the front, along with McClinery. I went back to my nook and lay down, but didn't feel like sleeping. We stopped a few more times, and I swapped with McClinery once, just to see the scenery. Mile after mile of rough, broken roads stretched out ahead of us: everything drab and worn and bleak. Everyone wore the same utilitarian clothes, in greys and browns, patched up and frayed. After a while, I wished I was back among the bags of rice.

Late on the second night, we pulled up onto the verge of the road and stopped. —We're here. Said McClinery, sticking his head under the tarpaulin. —We'll rest up tonight, then go take a look tomorrow.

I nodded. —Where are we?

—Leshan. Szechuan province.

—Where the hell's that? Isn't it halfway to Russia?

—No, no. Said McClinery, smiling. —It's much closer to Russia than that. See you in the morning.

When the sun was barely up, we were woken and led up the hill, through a dark forest, by the driver.

—Isn't someone going to want all that grain? I asked.

—People look pretty hungry around here. The driver just smiled at me, nodding.

The trees were dense and thickly leaved, blocking out the sky. Other people were also going up the steep hill: I noticed saffron-robed, shaven-headed Buddhist monks; women and children carrying baskets of flowers; and an old man clutching a single, green apple.

—Be careful! Called McClinery. —Mind your step!

—What? Jesus!

The hill dropped away right before me, down many hundreds of feet into a canyon and a choppy yellow river. Across from us, on the other side, was an opposing yellow cliff and more trees. I noticed people knelt along the top, looking towards us. McClinery pulled me back and held my arm.

—Careful now! The path goes this way! You wanting to take the quick way down?

We walked along the canyon edge, to where a square bite had been taken out of the cliff top. Over the lip, into this hole, descended the pilgrims, turning carefully, climbing down sideways. When we came to it, the driver went first, stepping down onto steep steps carved into the cliff face. I stood at the top and stared into the gap where the cliff had evidently once been. At first I thought that in the gap, near the top, was just an immense boulder, topped with innumerable, regular knots of stone. But then a line became an eyebrow and a split bulge a half-closed eye and an angled protuberance the nose. I gawped, looking down at the vast sculpture.

—Come on, you're holding up the queue! Said McClinery, behind me.

I climbed carefully down the zig-zagging staircase, trying to look only at the cliff beside me, dust and soil making each step slippery, the switch-backs crumbling away. At the bottom was a large stone platform where monks knelt in meditation. The four of us stood there, staring up at the immense seated figure of the Buddha, soaring above us, hundreds of feet high.

Without turning his gaze, McClinery patted me on the back.

—Told you, didn't I? He said.

We watched a continual procession of people coming past the feet, bowing and laying flowers and fruit. Some would sit and chant, others just bobbed backwards and forwards, hands together at their foreheads.

—I thought Communists hated religion? I asked.

—Chairman Mao. He sometimes decides not to look, you know? Just lets them do whatever makes them happy. They come here, they give presents, hoping for luck, hoping for the harvest to come, for sickness to be taken away, all the usual shit. You ever been to Lourdes? Same thing. Besides... He leaned in, whispering. —Round here? Party officials make the biggest offerings. Their necks are on the line more than most. And you see how hungry everyone is? How thin? The Party plan went wrong. Their own people are starving because they messed up.

—So the grain... in the truck...? I asked.

McClinery nodded, pointing at the monks. —For them. They'll give it out as fairly as they can. He winked. —See? The Buddha does bring good luck!

As we were leaving, I patted one of the three-foot-high toes and felt, perhaps, a little tingle of something like static. I felt the stone was simultaneously a part of the cliff and a tender spot on a kind and gentle person. As I climbed up the steps, I felt a lump rising unexpectedly in my throat, threatening to burst forth as tears. I've never been able to understand why.

Peter clicked onto the next account. A letter had gone out, requesting more information about the current medical status of the wife of the main member. He clicked on the link to the scanned correspondence, bringing up a letter from her oncologist, describing a malignant tumour in the lower intestine.

Peter stopped and stared at the glowing screen.

—I've been for a colposcopy. Said Louise, three months ago.

Peter looked up from his dinner. —A what?

—A colposcopy. I was referred by Dr Sallis.

—Ah.

—Yes. I went because… I'd been… bleeding. A lot. There were other… pains. I was tired a lot. Dr Sallis thought it best to get it checked out.

—With a…

—Colposcopy.

—Yes. Sorry… What's a 'colposcopy'?

—They examined my cervix.

—Oh…

—The gynaecologist saw something. He took a biopsy.

Peter stopped. —Did they… find anything?

—I don't know. The results should be in next week.

He looked at her. She pressed her lips together, fork hanging above her plate. She stared back.

—OK. He said. —Well… I suppose… till next week, then.

Louise got a phone call five days later, asking her to come in straight away. Peter drove over from work and met her in the reception of the hospital. She nodded towards the gynaecology department and they walked quickly through polished corridors, the bitter, sterile smell of the alcohol gel at every doorway.

They waited on the row of chairs outside the specialist's office, opposite a notice board covered with posters and pamphlets about cervical cancer. Peter stared at the floor.

When they were called through, they found a large man, smelling faintly of aftershave, sitting behind a desk, clicking through notes on a computer.

He stood to shake their hands and introduce himself. Dr Neelkanth Bankar. Peter saw it written on his badge, and on a sign on his desk. Peter looked at Louise as they sat down, pulling the chairs up close to the desk.

Dr Bankar looked at the screen for a long time. —I'm sorry... He said, and Peter heard the rest of his words drift away into a loud buzz, a meaningless drone, a flurry of images drowning out the information. —So... The doctor pulled a pad of paper out. —We'll get you booked in for an MRI tomorrow morning, and we'll see what that reveals. OK?

—Another scan? Asked Peter, outsde. —So they're not sure?

Louise said nothing.

The scan revealed a stage three cancer, centred around her cervix, but which had spread to her pelvic wall. The consultant in Oncology, Dr Deasy, brought the scan up on the monitor.

—Let me show you the growth, what we're talking about here.

They looked at the black and white slices of Louise's body.

—Here you see your spine? This white space here is your bladder? The grey here and here are your vaginal walls. And here at the top is the tumour. He pointed at a large grey bulge where the walls turned and swept up into the womb. —And it extends out from here, to here, and... here.

He clicked off the screen and turned to them. —This is a very advanced stage of cancer, I won't lie to you. We're going to use a form of radiotherapy called brachytherapy, which is a more invasive procedure, but very focused. I'm also going to book you in for chemotherapy, starting as soon as possible.

He pulled a pad of paper out from his top desk drawer. —You're going to need some time off work. I'm writing you a note for eight weeks sick leave, but you'll need more than that. He began writing. —What is it that you do?

—I work in HR.

—Oh? You must be quite used to these things then? He said, pointing at the pad.

—No, not really. I'm the bitch who gets to fire people.
He looked up at her.
She smiled.
He turned to his computer. —Is… ten o'clock alright?
Louise pulled out her diary. —What day?
He shook his head. —Ten every day.

Peter went with her for the first course of radiotherapy, carrying her bag into Oncology. She was shown to a changing room, but Peter was told to wait: the young nurse smiled at him, shaking her head.

—But I have her… He said, holding up the bag.

Still the nurse shook her head.

When Louise came back, barely half an hour later, she was buttoning up her shirt.

—Are you OK?

She nodded.

—Do you… want to get a coffee?

—Can do. I think.

In the café, over white porcelain, she told him what it was like.

—It looks like one of those seaside telescopes, the ten-penny ones, but with a bright orange radiation warning on the side. Where the eyepiece should be, there's a long flexible tube, which they put up, y'know, into me, and a small sliver of radioactive metal goes down the tube, so that it sits right within the tumour. She smiled. —It was easy. Fine. Lie back and stare at the ceiling.

He watched her. —So, why do you…? Look so… drained? Low?

She shrugged. —It's a huge room. Bigger than the ground floor of our house. And… there's just a single bed in the middle of it. Makes it feel… I don't know. Overwhelming. Lonely. The technician is behind a screen all the time it's happening…

The next day, he sat beside her as the chemotherapy drip was inserted into her arm. She was sat in an armchair in a sunny out-patient ward, surrounded by others hooked up to similar drips. Specialist nurses flitted here and there, checking and reading, chatting and laughing.

Louise looked at him. —Not quite what we thought, is it?

Afterwards, a nurse asked if she felt alright. —Any nausea? Cramps? Diarrhoea?

Louse shook her head.

—You look worried! He was looking through her notes. —Ah! It's your first time! That explains it. Don't worry: you'll be fine.

In the car on the way home, Louise sat upright in the passenger seat, one hand laid over the catheter in her forearm.

—You're very quiet. She said.

Peter stared at the car in front, the traffic at a standstill. He shook his head. —Just... thinking. That's all. He turned and smiled.

—What about?

He sighed. He had been thinking about work, about why Alistair had been given the Foreign Investments Project and not him. —Oh... nothing.

—Fairly serious 'nothing'.

—I was thinking about... the word 'tumour'.

—Hmm?

—When you first mentioned going to the doctors, that you'd gone for the... what-d'ya-call-it...

—Colposcopy.

—That. It was the word that leapt up, straight away. And when the guy said it, said you had 'a tumour', it wasn't as though I experienced a moment of relief, after the anticipation, the not-knowing. I'd thought that once we knew, then it would be as though a weight was lifted from us. No. It was just worse, heavier. I felt as though he had given you cancer, just by naming it. Which is stupid, I know, as the growth was already there, already inside you, all he did was identify it and prescribe treatment. But... when he said it, it's as though he created it, as though before, it was just a... a cloud, an idea, a horrible fantasy. And then he said it, and suddenly it was a solid weight, slapping us into the ground. It was defined. It was definite. I...

The traffic crawled forward.

—I don't know. That. I was thinking that.

She did not reply.

He turned and saw her leaning against the window, eyes shut. For a moment, just a moment, he thought she had died.

Peter typed: 'incomplete application' into the spreadsheet, then deleted it.

No. Not right. Everything is always incomplete. Best not to try, sometimes.

He typed: 'On-boarded with care and attention paid to ongoing medical situation'. And deleted it straight away.

Too... informal. Too sensitive. Wishy-washy, airy-fairy, touchy-feely. Twaddle. Besides, they didn't care. They would have been pissed off and then suspicious.

Finally, he typed: 'Medical notes requested'.

Makes far more sense. Sensible. Formal. Straightforward. Can't be tip-toeing around people in such a situation. Shit happens.

—Are you awake yet? I brought you up some dinner.

He stood by the bed, holding the tray. The shape under the covers, still dressed, rolled over.

—I... I don't... I don't want it. She said.

—You need to eat. Keep your strength up.

—No. It's OK. I'm fine.

—Rubbish. You've not eaten since breakfast. I can tell. He put the tray on the edge of the bedside and turned on the lamp, sitting down beside her.

—I had something at the hospital.

—Come on...

—I can't. No. Get me some chocolate. Or toast.

—What's wrong with this?

There was a sigh. —Garlic. You put garlic in it, didn't

you?

—Well, just a little…

—It… it turns my stomach.

—You're just hungry… Come on. Try some. Please?

He sat there with the tray.

She looked out from under the duvet. —Seriously, it makes me want to vomit. Take it away.

He shook his head. —Please… for me. Just eat something. Garlic isn't poison. It's just… just an empty stomach. This is light. Just some stir-fried veg and rice. Pak choi, cabbage, red onion, broccoli, carrot. Lovely stuff. Easily digested. Please, just try it.

She heaved herself upright and he put the tray onto her lap. She picked up the fork and stared down at the plate, sighing.

Peter watched, sitting on the bed.

—So… I asked Geoff today if the plan was for me and Alistair to liaise on the Foreign Investments Project, or would I be brought in at another part of the project? And he said that Alistair should be alright and I should get on with the Dispatch Processing thing we've… You alright?

She thrust the tray at him, clumsily, pulling herself out of bed and running down the hall to the bathroom, heels thumping. He sat there, holding the tray, rice spilt all over it, listening to her vomit loudly. He felt his own mouth get slick with saliva. Eventually the toilet flushed and she came thumping back along the corridor.

—Please, no more garlic. Or oil. Or bloody pak choi.

Sat in the cupboard, wrapped in the curtains, nose full of dust, Peter could see her climbing into bed, wrapping herself up the duvet, and facing away from him.

He clicked through a few more accounts, filling up the spreadsheet, trying to ignore the faint smell of vomit drifting down the corridor from the bathroom.

Could I have changed things? Could I have done better? Blood on our hands. He was found in the gutter, round the back of the pub. Should have run away. Avoided the bitch as best I could. Lives ruined. Leave her alone. Die alone. He died. She killed him. Didn't intend to. Just happened like that. But there are always consequences.

—What you have to realise is… He said. —Life is a progression, a chain… a sequence of cause and effect. He was stood at the bar with his foot resting on the box of morphine tablets, crushing it slightly.

—That's a bit… patronising, isn't it? I mean… it's utterly fucking obvious. Said Claire, frowning. She turned to the man who kept elbowing her in the back. —Oy! Mate? Stop it, alright? Please?

The man glanced over his shoulder at her, but made no effort to move.

—Fucking dickhead… She muttered, turning back to Peter. —Yeah, everything is cause and effect, action leads to reaction, etcetera. But… have you never thought that, well… Have you never thought…?

Peter saw her frowning, and grinned as he drained the last of his pint of cider, his hand already holding the precise money for two more drinks.

—What? What you thinking? he said, waving the coins at the barman, who was chatting to someone at the end of the bar.

—Cause and effect, right? One thing leads to another. Basic, core, fundamental principle of the universe, right? Except the reality is that things are never that simple: there's never a straightforward, neat, closed progression of just one, unconnected action leading to only one outcome which doesn't, in turn, lead to something else. It's never that. It's always a chain of one action leading to another action leading to another action, etcetera. It's more like cause and cause and cause and cause again, y'know?

The drinks were slopped down on the tray in front of them, the money taken. Peter nodded his thanks.

—But this is the really interesting bit! She continued. —If every event can be linked back through this chain of causes, you can, I suppose, follow it all the way back to the

Big Bang, the start of the universe itself. Every decision, every cause or effect right now can be traced back to that. Everything leading back and back and back, all the way to the start of the universe! Where it all began!

Peter looked at her over the top of his glass, the yellow liquid draining away. He stopped and wiped his mouth with the back of his hand.

—Yeah… I get it. Kind of like a reverse domino effect. If you pick over the wreckage, it'll form a trail right back to where it all… Yeah. Cool, I like it.

He sniffed and hiccupped slightly, putting a hand to his stomach.

—Shit. You alright? She asked, leaning back.

He nodded and held up a finger.

Claire stepped backwards, watching Peter, colliding with the man behind her. Peter sniffed again, and let out a long, rippling burp, straightening his neck. The man behind Claire pushed back, shoving her away. Peter closed off the burp suddenly, feeling an uprush of liquid. Opening his eyes wide, he leaned forward and grabbed Claire's wrist as she pulled a plastic Stanley knife from her jacket pocket.

—I FUCKING told you to FUCK OFF! She yelled at the man, struggling to pull her hand free, to bring the knife up to his face.

People around them started to move away, clutching pints to their chests. The barman stepped forward, frowning, trying to look over the bar without getting too close.

—You have really been pissing me, CUNT! So just fucking back off, or I'll fucking cut you! Understand?

The man looked at her, chin jutting forward. He looked at Peter, then slowly down at what Peter was preventing Claire from using.

—C'mon. Said Peter, pulling her wrist towards the door. —Let's get out of here…

—You're a fucking… Fucking CUNT! Claire shouted

as she stepped away, putting the knife back in her pocket and striding out of the door. Peter watched her go while picking up his box. He grabbed her still full pint and glugged down as much as he could. He raised a hand to the open-mouthed barman. —Much obliged.

Outside, he jogged up the road to catch Claire. —What the fuck was that all about? Eh? She stared straight ahead. —Why are you carrying a fucking knife around?

She stopped and looked at him. He stepped back, surprised. Years later, sat in the cupboard, he would remember that look. It was not anger, nor fear. It was an absence, a blankness, as though she had become a plastic mannequin, a wax model of Claire. He looked back down the road, to where a few men had just emerged from the pub and were looking their way.

—Come on. Keep walking.

She shrugged his hand off. —No! Don't fucking tell me what to do. She folded her arms, leaning against the wall.

—Alright, alright. But…

—You want to know why I have this? She held up the knife, still in her pocket. —I… I thought at first I'd kill myself if they aborted it. That losing it would… But then I decided that I'd kill myself if they didn't. She was looking away, off into the middle distance.

The group of men were walking towards them.

—Please, we need to go!

—I don't know what… I… I think I fucking might have, if they'd said 'no', I still might… She turned her face away, into the darkness.

The men were five metres away. —Yeah… Claire, we…

—Look at me! How could I bring up a fucking child?

As the men got within reach, Peter pushed her up against the wall, shielding her, and the box, with his back. He shut his eyes.

The footsteps kept going behind them.

He felt her crying, softly, her face resting against his neck. Around them, the night was a black emptiness: hollow and lurking.

He stepped back, looking down at her. She was sniffing, wiping her face.

—Come on. He said, taking her arm and leading her back down to the bus stop.

When they were aboard and the bus was roaring round the corner, he turned to her: —You said you told Ben...

She looked up, straight ahead.

—Were you going to tell me? He asked, quietly. —I mean, if we hadn't bumped into each other?

She looked out of the window, at the lights and darkness streaming past.

He looked down at his box of pills, noticing the big, wet, dirty shoe print on the top.

—It's OK. He said, after a while. —I understand.

She plucked at a loose thread on her cuff, pulling it out, and twisting it round her finger.

The streets and the houses rumbled past. Lights and shops dotted the way, an orange glow always sliding through the inside of the bus.

Claire leaned forward, pushing the bell. Peter stood, still clutching the box. They swayed down the bus, staggering as it stopped, and got off, back into the cool night air.

They walked slowly down the street.

—So... what's going to happen?

She did not reply.

—I mean... are you going to... move out? Stay with Ben? Stay...?

—I don't know. I don't think I can...

—Oh. OK. Do you...? Do you think I should...

She waited. —Should what?

—Stay? Would it be better if... if I went?

—Do what... do what you want. See how Ben is. He might move on himself... I mean...

They got closer to the house.

—Is he going to be home?

—I don't know. Probably.

They stood in front of the door. Peter looked at her, holding his key.

Claire shrugged.

He opened the door and stepped in.

—Where the fuck have you been? Said Irvine, sat with Mickey on the stairs.

Peter held up the box. —I went...

—Not you! You! He jabbed a finger at Claire.

—What? Come on! I'm tired, I'm not in the mood for this shit...

—Shut up! Shut the fuck up! We've had the fucking po-lice round because of you! Because of both of you!

—What...? Why? What's going on?

—It's Ben. Said Mickey, quietly. —They found his body.

Peter leaned forward, over the laptop, bringing his hands up to his face.

Can't take anymore of this. Going insane. Why am I...?

He brought his hands down, knocking against the keyboard. The browser opened, reloading the page of videos.

He stared.

There was a new one.

'Police Interview with Arthur Finchley RIP'.

He clicked on it.

It was poor quality video from a camera high up in the corner of a sparse and pale room. In the centre of the screen, sat at a table, was a thin man, his dark clothes baggy. Beside him was a woman in a suit jacket, a large file in front of her. Across the table was a big man in a dark suit, papers arranged in front of him. Another figure, clutching a notepad, sat by the door. The sound was distorted and scratchy.

—Interview commencing, ten AM Tuesday the twenty-fifth of January, nineteen ninety-five. Present are: myself, DS Martin Kilbride, DC Henry Fossdyke, Doctor Arthur Finchley, and Mrs Abigail Wilson who is... Dr Finchley's solicitor.

The policeman read through some of the paperwork in front of him.

—Have I been arrested? Asked Arthur.

The detective carried on reading. —No, Mr Finchley, you have not. As has already been explained. Several times. You are here to assist in the investigation into your son's whereabouts and the accident which led to it.

—So I could leave? At any time?

—You are being held under caution. Which means you are required to attend this interview and are advised to have legal counsel with you.

—You need to stay, Arthur. Said the woman.

—Dr Finchley... Said the detective, laying down the papers. —What can you tell me about the night of the nineteenth, September, nineteen ninety-four?

—It happened in Micronesian waters.

The solicitor leaned towards Arthur. —I think, as Rupert was a British subject, they have a duty to investigate what happened.

—But... there's already been an investigation! I've already bloody done this! Hours and hours of interviews, sat in a bloody hospital! Micronesians, Australians, even the Americans tried to accuse me of...! Ridiculous! Can't you just use their...!

—Dr Finchley? Please...! Can you just tell me about the run-up to the accident, to the capsizing?

—Christ. She put you up to this? Didn't she?

—Who?

—My wife. She's... She blames me. My fault. She doesn't say it, but...

—No, Dr Finchley, you're here as a follow up to the investigation by the Australian and Micronesian authorities. There hasn't been a complaint received from within this country. No-one has 'set you up'. Please, just… tell me about the boat. Who was on board?

—It was called *The Ammit*. It is, or was, a twenty-berth research vessel. Owned by me, as part of a… consortium. The crew was, well… there was… Sam. Sam Daleshire. Australian. Captain. Worked with him many times. Always went well. He helped out on several ships round there.

—So he knew the area well?

—Detective, we're talking about nearly three million square miles of ocean…

—Tricky to navigate?

—I… I don't know. Yes. But we had Li. Li? I can't remember his second name. Chow? Chue?

—Clow.

—He was second mate. Navigation. Taiwanese. I think.

—Who else?

Arthur sighed. —There was Ting, the cook; Derby, the engineer; and Richard, a camera man.

The detective looked up. —You had a camera on board?

—Frazzled in the capsizing. Tape ruined. Couldn't even use the batteries.

—There was also…?

Arthur looked at the policeman.

—Your son? Said Kilbride.

—Yes. Yes, he was aboard. Arthur took a deep breath, spreading his palms out on the table. —Rupert loved that boat. It wasn't his first time on board, but it was his first time diving. Diving out in the open ocean.

—Did he enjoy it?

—Very much so.

—No problems between you two?

—No. None.

—Relationship always been good?

—I… I maybe wasn't there for him as much as I should have been, growing up. But… We were… Yes. Things were… well, between us.

—OK. Did you trust the crew?

Arthur remained silent.

—Did you have doubts about them? Do you think they could have... been involved... in some way?

—Detective? Said the solicitor. —He can refuse to answer, if he wishes.

—How about you start from the beginning. Where did you set off from? Where did you go?

—We sailed out of Kolonia, on the island of Pohnpei. It's part of the Federated States of Micronesia. We went on a... westerly heading for about three hundred miles, to some reefs off Tol and Fefan islands. We did some diving there. Filmed a bit. We were there for... five days, I think. Then we came back, following the same route. There was a storm, which pushed us off course. And...

—Go on.

—The seas were rough that night. Very choppy. The boat slung itself around. We went below decks to play cards and drink tea. I went to bed around eleven, I think. Li took the night shift. There was always someone at the helm. Always. We made sure we did things properly.

The detective nodded.

—I... I woke to the alarm bell, and a terrible... grinding noise. I remember falling out of bed, things falling with me, banging into me. Something hard hit my head. I think it was my computer. A laptop. I was unconscious for a short time. I woke with Richard shaking me. I couldn't work out what was going on. I was confused. I thought, for some reason, I was in the garrison camp at Arden. Such dark nights we had there. I had the sense I was being woken by the NCO's attaché. But... I was wet. Water was getting in. Everything was on the floor. No. Ceiling. I was lying on the ceiling. Richard woke me. Footsteps banged in the boat. Hollow sounding. Richard said Rupert had gone overboard.

—Did he explain what had happened? There and then?

—Several people did. They stood around me, leant in

through the door. Li was gabbling away. Sam could translate bits. Seems Li, stood on the bridge, saw Rupert out on deck, just before we capsized. Then a wave came, knocking us over, putting us onto some sort of sandbank, they thought. And no-one could find Rupert.

—Why would he have gone out on deck?

—I don't know. Seasickness? Insomnia? He was young! He probably didn't think it was as dangerous as it really was. He was brought up in Bristol and Cambridge. Even the worst storms there aren't... aren't life threatening!

—Could you search the deck? Where you in a position to...?

—Not easily. We were upside down, completely. The bridge and the mast had been crushed, mangled. They said the storm surge was too great. We did look, when it was calm.

—And there was no way of calling for help...?

—Radio gear was on the bridge.

—So... The policeman held up a pen. —If Li was on the bridge... and the bridge was flattened...? How did he...?

—Yes... I know. He said he went to get a waterproof to get Rupert.

—So he left the wheel?

Arthur scratched the back of his neck. —Yes. Or... I think there was some sort of wedge which locked off the steering.

—OK... How did you react? How did you feel on being told you were trapped? And your son was missing?

—I... I was desperate. I fought. I accused. I... think I tried to... I didn't know what I was doing. I was concussed. Everything tumbled about in my head. It was... awful. They gave me a sedative. I slept. When I woke, he was still gone.

—OK. The policeman turned to another page of notes. —How did life progress?

—Oh... At first we... had lots of ideas. We...

—What sort of ideas?
—Survival ideas. Escaping ideas. We had no food left. We needed fresh water. We started ripping the ship apart to make a raft. But... well, there was just nothing buoyant enough.
—Were there not life boats?
—They were on deck.
—All this activity. Must have kept your mind off things.

Arthur was silent, looking down at his hands.
—I wanted to search for Rupert. But...
—The others didn't want to?
Arthur shook his head. —No. It was me. Army training. Stay with the wreck. Best chance of being spotted.
—What else? What did you do all day?
Arthur sighed, looking up at the ceiling, glancing at the camera. —I slept. Found a little corner. Wrapped myself up in blankets. Another army trick. Saves energy. Passes time. Useful.
—What did the others do?
Arthur shrugged. —Much the same, I suppose... We stopped talking.
—You stopped talking? Do you mean you fell out?
—There were tensions...
The policeman looked at Arthur.
—Can you tell me what those tensions were?
—Sam and Ting. They... they kept... whispering. They would crawl down to the other end of the boat to do it, but their voices would carry. I'd hear them: talking about me, saying it was my fault. It wasn't. It wasn't my fault. I'd tell them. Scream at them till the hull vibrated. Li was on my side. He agreed with me. But then, he was guilty. He should have known. He caused that crash. And they knew it, which was why they didn't pay him any notice. They just kept plotting, muttering about me, looking at me...
—In the dark?
Arthur stopped and stared at the policeman.

—There was enough light. You could see faces. White faces. Eyes black. See them gawping back at you... mouths open.

—Tell me how you survived. What were conditions like? Did you find food?

—Yes. Fish. They caught fish.

—What kind of fish?

—Bloody disgusting ones.

The policeman looked at Arthur, then back down at his notes.

—When you ate, did you eat together?

——Yes. We all went to engineering... and... ate.

—That must have been nice.

——Where are you going with all this?

The detective looked at him.

—With everything that had happened, it must have been nice to maintain a sense of... ordinariness.

—It wasn't...! It wasn't... It was bloody horrible! I had to listen to them! Slobbering and chewing! Christ! It was... I lie awake...! Even now! I can still...

Arthur had put his face in his hands, his voice muffled.

The policeman looked at the solicitor, who shrugged.

—And then, after six weeks, a plane dropped out of the sky, carrying the Micronesian minister for International Trade, four businessmen and a pilot. And crashed right beside your upturned boat. Their deaths saved you. They died, and you were rescued.

—Yes... I remember. The sound of its engine. I got... excited. And then, louder and louder, the whine. And... the crash. An extra wave slapped our hull. I... I wasn't surprised. I didn't think... didn't join the dots.

—That they'd come searching for the plane?

—I envied them. Quick death. Plummet into the sea. Bang. All over. Lucky bastards...

The policeman looked down at the papers on the table.
—Hmm. Maybe. He gathered up the sheets. —Well, Dr Finchley, is there anything else you wish to tell us?

Anything you think may be pertinent?

—They said it was fish.

—Excuse me?

—A big fish, they said. A Parrot Fish. They… they caught it while I was sleeping, they said. Just after we'd crashed. I was sedated. I didn't see the fish. I only saw it when… when they served it up. We ate it. I ate it. There was no other food. We were lucky to have it… Ting made a broth. That's how I saw it. Already cooked. I never saw it whole. I had no idea… They said it was a Parrot Fish. But it… it made me ill. Right from the first mouthful, I swear! I couldn't stomach it! It made me want to vomit. Richard couldn't. He'd seen. He knew. Poor Richard. God rest his soul.

—You…? Ate…? What?

—The flesh was… We caught other fish. Never one so big. And the meat was… It was… It made me sick, but… it tasted… You have to understand, we had nothing else, even if they had… if they'd done the unthinkable… it still saved our lives. Just that small amount. Without it… we wouldn't have made it…

—Right…

—I just wanted to explain why we…

—Why you what?

—You don't…? That's not why…?

—What did you do?

—We… we ate… Parrot Fish.

—Doctor Finchley: Thank you. Said the Detective, standing. —Your version of events tallies with the Micronesian and Australian investigations. I think, possibly, that our involvement is at an end. Thank you for your time.

—That's it? That's all you brought me here for?

—Yes. What else would we have been asking you about?

—There was… the Parrot Fish.

—Dr Finchley, I neither care, nor see any reason to

care, about whether your fishing catches in the Pacific are, or are not, a matter for Her Majesty's Constabulary.

—So I can go?

—Of course.

There was a cough from the corner.

—Oh, wait! There's one more thing…

—Yes?

—Detective Fossdyke would like an autograph. For his son.

—What?

The second policeman stood and held out the notebook and pen he'd been holding on his lap throughout. With shaky hands, Arthur signed it.

—Thank you very much, sir. Said Kilbride. —Madam. He nodded at the solicitor.

Arthur looked at the policemen, and slowly began to stand.

—Interview terminated ten-thirty AM.

The video stopped and went to the mosaic screen of similar clips.

Peter leaned back against the shelving, resting his head against the hard metal edge.

This… this is too… Wow. He can't have? Can he? That explains… it. The blade and the blood. Carrying that around.

But why now?

Peter scrolled down through the videos, looking for any that he might have missed. He recognised all of them.

That's the end of that then. All gone. Over.

Say goodbye and…

—Hear that, Jim? Soon be home!

My bunk mate, Mark, slapped the side of my bunk as the crackling sound of British radio came from one of the other cabins. We had entered waters just past the Iberian peninsula, skirting the bay of Biscay, where shipping lines clustered together, narrowing into the English channel

—When I get home, I'm going to go straight round to

me mams, beg her for roast tattys and a bit of beef! Christ! I would kill for some of her cooking!

I listened. Every journey was the same. On the way out men talked with great passion of what they would do once they got into a foreign port, the whores they would fuck, the amount of liquor they would consume. And then, on the way home, their mother became a sainted presence, a figure of divine goodness, ladling out the best food and love a man could ever experience. Home became their Mecca, their place of spiritual fulfilment, calling them to return, opening up, warm and protecting. Crewmen would weep at the thought of going home.

—And I'll be going down the club. Meet up with Brian and the guys! Get a few bevies down us! You know what I mean, eh? Jim?

I would nod. Yes, I would tell them. Yes I know what you are trying to tell me. Your words are understood. But it was not a world I had ever inhabited. It was as alien and distant to me as the ports we had just left.

I nodded at Mark. He was an excitable scouser and there was still another couple of days or more of travelling. I lay back and thought of home, of what it really meant to me.

The first thing that floated to the surface was of being a small boy, sat on the cold, white, tiled floor of the bathroom, just below the little window, beside the enamel bath. It was a long, narrow room, stretching out before me to the white panelled door beyond the sink and the stinking toilet. There was a musty smell of cold, damp towels from the rail and a bitter smell of spilt mint tooth powder.

I sat on the floor, scared and crying. I know now why I was frightened, but did I then? There was always an atmosphere, a tenseness, when my father began drinking. At a certain point my mother would tell me to go up and lock myself in the bathroom. And I would sit there, assuming I had done something wrong, while beneath me the voices would murmur and rise, feet would stomp backwards and forwards, the kitchen door would slam, cupboards opened and closed. Pots and pans would crash and rattle. There would be heavy thumps that shook the walls.

Looking back, ignoring what came later, I realise that, for all I knew, they could have been making omelettes. My memory is coloured by what was to follow. But I still hear those sounds and cannot fail to imagine what might have been happening.

Sometimes, when things were really bad, my mother would come with me, and we would hide in the bathroom, huddled up together on the floor, waiting for my father to get bored or fall asleep. She would wrap me in a towel if it was cold, and we would play quiet card games.

My father wouldn't leave us alone.

BANG, BANG, BANG! —Come on! Open the door! Let me in! Why is it locked?

My mother put a blood-red finger nail to her lips and played another card.

The door crashed and rattled. —FOR GOD'S SAKE, OPEN THE DOOR!

She pointed at my cards, beckoning me to play another.

—Please! For pity's sake! Let me in! He pleaded. I could hear him leaning against the door, sliding down it. —I... I know there's someone in there! Came a quivering voice outside. —I can hear you... Please.

My mother looked at me, watching me. And I tentatively played the first card in my hand. She frowned, and played hers, completing her trick. I was too young to understand the game.

—There are... things... animals, filthy beasts, crawling around outside! I've heard them! Please! They'll eat me! Let me in!

Mother looked at me, shaking her head softly, half-shutting her eyes, pursing her lips. It was the same look, I later noticed, that she had when listening to beautiful music, or savouring her first glass of wine. It was the look of the connoisseur.

—They speak! They speak in German! They're all around me! Help... me!

And he howled, bashing and thumping against the door, making it bend and rattle, crack and splinter.

—LET ME IN! Damn you! They're... Oh God!

She turned to the door.

—Sergeant Simpson? Her voice was bold and loud, echoing round the bathroom.

—Yes...? Sir?

—Sergeant Simpson: you were given specific instructions to secure the lower floor of this house and guard against enemy incursion. Why are you upstairs, trying to get into my office?

She turned and winked at me.

—I... I'm sorry. Sir. Marm... I...

—Sergeant? Ill-discipline is not how we run this brigade, is it?

—No... no, Marm. Sir.

—I want you to go back to your position and maintain a watch until oh-four-hundred hours. Do you understand?

—But... Marm? The...

—I will NOT tolerate cowardice in my brigade, soldier! Now do your DUTY!

—Yes...yes, Marm...

There was a pause, then footsteps clomped unsteadily down the stairs. She turned and winked at me.

—He's a silly man, isn't he? She whispered.

But it did not take long before I began to see what life was like on the other side of the bathroom door, and there were many times I ended up back in there, stood in front of the mirror, examining the latest red mark, split lip or blackened eye.

Home was never a place of refuge or belonging for me, quite the opposite. Which was why I did not share my colleagues enthusiasm for the sound of British radio,

English pop tunes, ghostly sounds from over the waves.

I lay in my bunk and planned my next voyage out, the sooner the better, lest I ever run the risk of having to go home.

Peter clicked onto the spreadsheet.

Only a few more to do. Then it'll all be over. Then I can leave. Go home. Yes. Maybe. Find out what's waiting for me there.

—What do you mean 'found his body'? Claire asked.

—They've just been. They wanted someone to go identify him. Said Mike, shaking his head. —We… we gave them his parents' address.

—What? What the fuck are you fucking talking about? 'Body'? What's happened to him?

Irvine stepped forward. —He's dead. The police found his fucking body. Now, where have you fucking been? Off, fucking Peter again?

Claire slapped him. —You cheeky cunt! I'll…! I'll fucking…!

Peter watched her hand and the pocket the knife was in.

She turned to Mike. —How did he…? What the hell happened?

—We don't know. Said Mike. —They just asked if we knew him and then said they wanted someone to go identify the body. We were hoping you two might know…

—Us? Said Peter, as Claire turned slowly round and sat on the stairs, covering her face with her hands.

—For fuck's sake, Claire. Come on… Said Irvine, prodding her with a foot. She bucked, and vomit spurted out from between her hands. —Oh, fuck! Fuck, fuck… Have you been fucking drinking? Are you two pissed? Is that where you've been? Out on the raz?

—We… Said Peter —We had a couple…

Irvine bent over Claire. —You've been gone for four fucking days! And you roll up with him? When Ben's lying dead in a fucking back-alley in town?

Claire started howling, hands in front of her face, still dripping, face contorted, mouth open.

—What the…? What the fuck is wrong with you?

She stopped, looking up at him. She stood, clumsily pulling out the knife and slashing wildly. Mike grabbed her round the neck and pulled her backwards. Peter grabbed her arm, watching the knife, glinting in the hallway. Irvine stepped back, sucking at a cut on his hand.

—You crazy fucking BITCH! What the fuck did you do that for?

—Claire! Calm the fuck down! Drop the knife! Claire…? Come on!

She let out a gurgled, angry scream and struggled against Mike and Peter.

Watching, they saw her fingers uncurl and the knife drop to the carpet.

—Keep a hold of her, just for a mo. Said Irvine, walking over to the box by the door. —What have you got in there?

—What? It's… it's morphine. Morphine tablets…

Irvine looked at the other two with a raised an eyebrow. Peter and Mike looked at each other and nodded. Still clutching his bleeding hand, Irvine opened the box.

—Blimey. You know Deano sells this shit for a fiver a pill?

—Irvine!

—Yeah, yeah. He opened one of the bags. —How many do you think? Two? They look pretty small…

—Yes! Said Mike.

—And crush them! Said Peter. —Makes it quicker.

—She'll get them as they come. Said Irvine, holding two pills up to Claire. —Right, hold her steady boys. Come on, you fucking little psycho bitch, play along… He pulled her jaw open, smearing blood down her face, forcing the pills in-between her clenched teeth. —Calm you the fuck down.

She looked up at Irvine, her face furious.

He pinched her nose shut and pushed up against her jaw, forcing her head back. She shook and struggled, until finally her throat bobbed as she swallowed, and he released her. She took a deep gasp of air, her face streaked with Irvine's blood.

—Now… Are you going to behave? Said Irvine, as he bent down to pick up the knife.

Mike slowly released his hold around her neck.

Irvine clicked the blade shut. —What's a pretty girly like you doing with a nasty old thing like this? Hmm? Fending off all the dirty bastards who'd have their wicked way with you? He said, glancing at Peter.

Claire just stood there, looking down at the carpet.

—Look, said Mike. —Let's get you upstairs, eh? You've… you've had a shock.

She turned to Mike, her eyes unfocused, and nodded. Mike glanced at the other two men, then back at Claire.

—C'mon, Claire…

She burped as Mike took her shoulders gently and started to lead her up the stairs.

—Fuck me! Muttered Irvine, sucking at his cut, looking at the hallway floor. —Disgusting bitch!

—Irv! You're not helping!

—Nor do I fucking want to! You seen what she's done?

—It's fine. We can clean and you will heal.

—If you're… if you're going to be sick again… Said Mike. —Just, y'know, tell me… and I'll…

Peter stared at Irvine, then turned, picked up his box, and pulled himself up the stairs, feeling immensely tired. He heard Irvine stomp down the hall to the kitchen. At the top, Mike lead Claire round to her and Ben's room and went in, laying her down on the bed, still rumpled from when Ben had got up that morning.

From downstairs they could hear the sound of Irvine scrubbing at the carpet and sighing loudly.

—You wouldn't have thought the deposit was that

important to him. Said Mike.

Peter shook his head and sat down next to Claire, wiping her face and hands with the cuff of his coat.

—You just rest. Said Mike. —We'll see... we'll see how things pan out.

They watched her, lying there, her eyes shut.

Peter looked up and around the room.

—There's that guitar he never played.

—He had a book, it'll be round here somewhere: Learn to Play with The Stone Roses. He could play a few chords... not much more! He chuckled.

—And his tapedeck there.

—That fucking Bob Marley album he always put on when he was getting stoned.

—His videos... Bloody hell! Look! He's got 'Natural Born Killers'!

—Where did he get all the bootlegs from?

—Some old geezer down the market, he said... But I think they might have been payment... Bit of couriering here and there.

—And he got paid in pirate videos? That's a shit deal.

—Yeah, well, he wasn't really into that side of things: didn't like it, did he?

—Still took, still carried.

They were silent for a bit.

—Do you think someone...? That he was...?

—Naa... Not Ben. He wasn't in that deep.

—Someone broke his fingers once. He said he screwed them over.

Peter looked up at Mike and was quiet for a moment.
—Knowing Ben it was just for being a cheeky bastard. He can't have been into anything too... Y'know.

Mike nodded. Irvine ran up the stairs.

—Is that the stuff from old Federico? He asked, nodding at the box.

—Yeah.

—Hope you paid him properly, I told him it would pay

off Spencer's bill.

—We did. Don't worry.

They looked down at Claire.

—How's she doing?

—Seems pretty out of it. Do you think we ought to call an ambulance or something?

—Are you fucking nuts? Have them running around here? Tell them about the fucking morphine that is no doubt lifted from one of their bloody hospitals?

—One of us should stay with her. Y'know, to make sure she doesn't roll onto her back and puke.

They were silent. Irvine looked at Mike, Mike down to Claire.

—I'll sit with her. Said Peter.

—Yeah? Said Irvine —'sit'?

—Fuck off Irvine.

Mike looked down at Claire. —Sweet dreams, Claire. He turned to Peter. —Shout if you want anything. And he walked out, slowly clumping down the stairs.

Irvine stood there for a moment. —Don't… Don't do anything that'll… Don't be stupid. He pointed at the box, then at Claire. —Alright?

Peter nodded, and shut the door.

He looked down at Claire, lying on the bed, a dark shape in the gloom of the room. She looked small, the bed so big. Her side faintly rose and fell, reassuring him.

There was a smell in the room, a sweet, meaty odour that Peter supposed was Ben, his skin, his sweat, clinging to the sheets and clothes.

He opened the cardboard box and popped a couple of pills into his mouth, crunching them, running the bitter grains around his gums. He sat on the edge of the bed, putting his head in his hands, waiting for everything spinning around him to slowly settle. Through his fingers, he looked down at his shoes, still wet and gritty from the street. Underneath them was something white. He reached down and pulled out 'Play Guitar With The Stone Roses', a muddy heel print over the top half of the cover. He cradled it in his lap, then wiped it and slipped it back under the bed.

He sat there for a while longer, watching the car headlights streak by outside, the noise dipping as they passed, until the morphine kicked in, making him feel soft and disconnected.

He twisted round and stared again at Claire, at the way light from the hallway entered through a gap in the door frame and lit a perfect line over the wrinkled sheets, up across her side. Peter watched her breath, imagining the tightness of the tendons and the ribs.

Her body appeared like a landscape of rolling hills and rippling valleys. The web and weave of the fabrics were ploughed and furrowed fields, worked by thousands of miniscule people. Leaning in, he saw that one of the little people looked just like Ben, who waved up at him. And another was Ben, and another, and another. Peter leant back, frowning. He looked down at his own skin, looking for anyone to be there. All he saw was a dry and arid desert, with wind-swept stalks of trees. He touched it and saw it as just his skin, just his hand.

He shook his head, shutting his eyes, remembering a cartoon, or a film, and felt dizzy and seasick for it.

Looking back out of the window, he could see shadowed figures in the houses opposite, moving around behind colourfully lit curtains. The road in-between was a quiet, peaceful river. He could hear it trickling and gurgling, running over rocks and sand. He felt the house gently sway in the breeze, peaceful and rhythmic. He felt very tired, eyelids drooping. He looked up and saw the windows across became Chinese lanterns, glowing squares of colour that drifted softly up into the stars. Always moving, never leaving.

Something in the mirror caught his eye.

Claire's face.

Her eyes were staring at him.

He felt a sting of adrenaline, crackling like fireworks through his body. He tried to move but his body refused.

She started to slowly turn, rolling her body over incrementally, one vertebrae at a time, click, click, over she came, her head the last to roll over.

She stared at him through black holes, her face dark against the window. He backed away, slipping off the side of the bed, hitting the floor hard on his side. He looked up as her face slowly rose over the edge of the bed, looking down at him, lips pulled back, revealing teeth.

He smelt, in the back of his throat, her decaying flesh, heard the low moan that came from her. She opened her mouth, reaching out to him, gums shrunken, teeth yellowed. He tried to shuffle backwards, but she jumped down upon him, grabbing his head and shaking it, slapping and scratching him. He tried to pull away, hands flapping, trying to push her off. He wrenched away, pushing the computer off his lap, striking his head on a shelf, making his skull ring with the impact. He slumped down into morphine sleep, the laptop still open on the floor next to him, the curser blinking in an empty spreadsheet box.

seven

—Good morning, ladies, how are we all this morning? You alright, Mary?

Peter lay on the floor of the cupboard, listening to the meeting start. His mouth was dry, his sinuses ached. He carefully turned to the laptop and saw it was still plugged in, the light blinking for stand-by.

—Good, good. Doreen? Margaret? OK? Good. Look... I needed to get you all together before work this morning because there were some... rumours flying around yesterday. Completely unfounded, idle speculation: that's all. Nothing for you to worry about.

He had woken to noises from the conference room, feet thumping about, low murmurs, the door creaking and clunking shut. He had stayed silent, quiet, eyes locked on the cupboard door, trying to think what his story would be if they walked in.

—Karen? I'm sorry, I don't mean to interrupt, but how can you say there's nothing to it? The man who told us, I recognised him, he's a member of Change. Surely he would know, wouldn't he?

Peter frowned, pushing himself up on one elbow.

Shit. Are they...?

—I can assure you it... it isn't true. Who was this person?

Peter felt a cold wave seep through him.

—I don't know. He's in Change, that's all I know.

—Well, I called Chris Green, head of Site Operations and Corporate Holdings, and asked him, directly, and he denied the whole thing. They have no plans to replace the current canteen arrangement.

Peter sat up, rubbed his eyes free of dust and pushed the curtain off. He noticed the pressure of a full bladder.

—Is that it? That's your... 'assurance'? A bit of spin from management?

—Oh come now, it's nothing of the sort! I explained about the rumours and asked him if there were any plans and he said there was, quote, 'nothing like that in the pipeline.' Nothing at all! Who would know more? Hmm? Chris? Or this mystery, un-named member of Change?

—I'm sorry, but did he actually say 'nothing in the pipeline'? Those exact words?

—Yes, yes he did. What's your point?

—Phrases like 'in the pipeline', or 'planned' can refer only to measures which have been taken forward into costings exercises. IE: beyond the brainstorming meetings, the boardroom discussions, the managerial chats over coffee. They could still be doing cost-benefit analysis, looking at possible contractors, even sketching out the legal documents, all things they would need to do before getting permission to get quotes and enter into discussions with vendors. So he can quite legitimately say it isn't 'being planned', because in the language of business, it isn't. It's subtle, but significant.

—OK. But if they were thinking about any sort of change, then wouldn't they come to me? Wouldn't they involve me? Hmm? And besides... Come on! Change? Those guys talk an awful lot of... y'know... shit...

—All the figures are on the company R-Drive. How much we spend, how much we take. They're accessible from anywhere by anyone. They don't need you for that. And, besides, you're the last person they'd involve, if you think about it: if you knew what was going on, you'd have to lie to us, you'd have to be lying right now, and they couldn't make you do that, partly, I'd hope, for ethical reasons, but also because... well... your job would be going as well, and they need to make the canteen look like a really viable business when it goes out to tender, and if it all looks like crap then the bids will be too low. They have to make sure their apples are shiny.

There was silence in the conference room. Peter tried to breathe quietly.

She's right. Mostly. I think Alistair described it as being written on the back of a fag packet.

Fuck me I need a piss.

—I...

—Oh, and, sorry... but I think Change prefer to think of it as 'speculation' rather than 'shit'...

Peter was surprised.

Is she defending...?

—I spoke to Chris Green...

—And what he told you was designed to placate you. It was supposed to make you think nothing was happening. He said there were no plans, which officially there aren't, but we've both worked here long enough to not take that at face value! She paused. —What he told you was a kind of truth, depending on your interpretation of certain words.

—Look, this is... preposterous! It's silly! There is no plan to sell off the canteen! It's... it's just laughable! Why would they do that?

—I'm sorry Karen, but this guy from Change definitely knew something. He let it slip. He was angry and he muttered something unguarded. You know what? Because of that, I trust him. I think he accidentally told the truth.

—Really? This guy just 'muttered' something? Did he? You're reading a lot into what someone merely 'muttered', aren't you?

—It wasn't just that. I questioned him about it: he pretty much admitted it.

—Still fairly flimsy though, isn't it?

—He admitted it.

—Right. OK. What was he angry about?

—Ohh... He'd wanted some fish fingers, and they were still cooking... nothing really.

—Well... Sounds like he wanted to upset you. And it worked. You took it in the way he intended. He was probably cock-a-hoop that you questioned him! Meant he'd got you rattled, that his taunting had hit a nerve! If he knew we were having this meeting... he would probably die laughing!

—No... He said...

—He said something spiteful, something angry and ugly, to make you frightened. He knows that jobs are scarce out there for older people... the economy is tough, pensions being pushed later and later. He tried to tear out your foundations from under you! Make you scared for the future! He is clearly a very cruel man.

—No...! Look, when he first said something, he was... pissed off, I suppose, but when I questioned him, he was... he was anxious because he'd said something he shouldn't have! He knew he'd made a mistake!

—But everyone else involved is saying it isn't true! Where is the evidence? Hmm? Where is the proof that this plan even exists? It's simply all in your interpretation of angry words 'muttered' by a man who wanted to upset you!

—Have you spoken to Change?

—I tried. No-one in their office was picking up.

—So they haven't denied it?

——They didn't answer the phone! How could they deny it?

—But...

—But nothing! I'm sorry... This meeting is over! And I

want to hear no more of this scare-mongering, Mary!

—Wait, Karen, I'm not going back to work, none of us are, until you answer me one simple question.

——OK. What is it?

—Can you give me your absolute guarantee that the canteen won't be sold off?

—I will only say this one more time: there are no plans…

—You can't, can you? There's a little seed of doubt in your mind too. You know that there might be something, some 'speculation' out there, some unofficial idea that might, one day, get sanctioned. So you can't deny it, just in case.

—OK! OK! I guarantee it won't happen. Alright?

—You're lying. I don't believe you. Someone film her. Get your phone out, Margaret, film her saying it'll never happen. Then, when it does…

—No, now, come on… Give it up, Mary…

Another, slightly deeper voice spoke up.

—This is pointless. Utterly fucking pointless.

There was silence.

—Doreen? I think…

—Shut up. Just… stop talking.

There was another silence before Doreen continued.

—Have you listened to yourselves? Language is all we have. It makes us more than monkeys. And you two are mangling it beyond all comprehension. Just stop. Listen to each other. Listen to what the other is saying, what words they're using. Language is a code, it demands agreement from both sides for it to work. You're taking that code and only hearing what you want to hear. It's called 'confirmation bias'. You two may as well have heard 'La, la, la' from those guys. Except you didn't. You heard important information. And now you're arguing over what really happened, when, in reality, neither of you really know, because you weren't paying proper attention at the time, or your memories have twisted it into something it wasn't.

Peter put his head in his hands and concentrated on everything except the pain in his bladder.

—Listen. Believe it or not, you're both on the same side. The unfortunate reality is that whether they're planning something or not, both of you need to work together. We've all got eyes, we can see what the economy is like, and what companies are doing about it. So something will happen at some point, sooner rather than later. You have to stop picking holes in everything the other says and fucking pay attention!

There was another silence

—Thank you, Doreen, for that input. However... I think Site Management has been very clear with us: there are no plans for a sell-off.

—Which doesn't, said Mary. —Mean they're not thinking about it...

—Fuck this, said Doreen. —I'm going back to work.

—What? Wait! There was a clumping of feet. —I haven't ...!

The door creaked shut. Peter could hear footsteps out in the corridor.

—Well... Yes, Margaret?

—I... I just... I always do the... with Doreen. We cook the...

—Go on.

The floor shook quickly as she ran to the door.

Peter knelt by the door.

Come on: end the meeting, end the meeting, end the fucking meeting.

—She... she's got a point, Karen: we're on the same side. Neither of us want this to happen. But it will happen. Or something like it will. They'll want us to make cuts. We'll have to defend what we do.

—I came across your CV the other day. Someone in Risk was doing a clear out and came across it. You applied for a job. Business Assessor. Twenty years ago.

——Didn't get it though, did I?

    —I didn't know you had a business degree from Sheffield Polytechnic. More than I ever got. I started in Sales when I was seventeen. I was good. Top saleswoman three months in a row. I should have been made Team Leader, climbed the ladder, be on the Executive by now. But I was passed over, and after thirty years, I'm the manager of the bloody canteen.

    —Karen…

    —Sometimes I wonder if anyone would notice if I…

    —Karen!

    —What?

    —We'll… sort something out. Alright? Do you fancy a coffee? How about we go get a coffee? I've a few ideas… But… I think I'm going to need your help. Thirty years? You must know a lot of people round here then?

    —I suppose…

Two sets of feet thudded over the thick carpet.

    —Well, maybe it's time to use some of those connections. Show them something extra, eh?

The door clunked shut.

Peter shuffled forward on his knees and listened at the door. Hearing nothing, he slowly opened it, leaning out to look around. Outside, the room was empty and silent, the chairs pushed back from the table, the heater where he had left it the night before. He grabbed his coat and the laptop, shoving it into its case, and walked quickly out into the room, his eyes scrunched up against the bright sunlight. He opened the door a crack, looking out. There was no-one. He slipped out and down the corridor to the toilets.

Swinging through both doors, still clasping his coat and laptop to his chest, he went into the left cubicle and kicked the door shut. He dropped everything in his arms onto the floor and, with fluttering hands, still clenching a hidden muscle tight, he unzipped and fished about inside his trousers, firstly for the opening, and then for the anatomy, till finally, when he managed to fully extract himself, he could feel the dam beginning to break, the fluid starting to flow, coming swiftly, unstoppably, to the opening, where, spluttering through his wrinkled foreskin, it sprayed out over the toilet bowl.

He groaned and relaxed, feeling tension ease, pain subside.

So near, he thought, to pissing all over myself, like some baboon, huddled in straw, marking his territory.

Urine tinkled and splashed, staining the water yellow.

No, wait, that's not right. The ape would be doing it on purpose. I'd just be… losing control.

'More than monkeys'.

No, we're not. We prove it all the time. To our own families.

Peter pissed, feeling cold and bruised from the night in the cupboard. His left side ached, his eyes felt puffy and swollen.

—You're home early, Jim.

The voice came out of the darkened kitchen. I fumbled about on the wall for the light switch, clicking it on and off, but nothing happened.

—Been cut off. Said my father. —Not enough money coming into the house.

As my eyes adjusted, I could make out a shape sat at the kitchen table. A point of light shone from a whisky glass.

—Don't sigh at me, you petulant little shit! You don't pull your weight! That's why we're in this mess!

Not long now, I thought, walking to the stairs.

—Oie! Get back here and apologise!

I paused.

—Sorry father. I said, without turning.

—Ignorant bastard!

I leapt up the stairs as he stood, chair feet scraping.

—Go on! Run! She won't save you! Not after what you done!

At the top of the stairs I could see that my bedroom

door was open, the orange streetlight streaming through the window. On my bed, next to the bag I'd packed, sat my mother, holding the letter I'd received.

—Close the door. She said, quietly.

—I can explain…

—Shut up. Don't speak until I say you can. And when you do, whisper.

She was silent for a moment, staring at me. I stood there, the orange light giving the scene a surreal atmosphere, blurring the lines between what was real and what was not. I was reminded of the submarines in war films, of how they looked when they went to red alert.

—You… Why did you do this? She waved the letter, her voice still no more than a whisper.

—I…

—You have no right! You didn't even discuss it with me first!

—I thought you'd be pleased!

—Shh! Why would I be pleased? I'm not going to leave! I can't leave!

—You…

—What?

—You can't stay! He's getting worse!

She was silent. —Exactly. He needs me more.

—Please, mum. Come with me. They're prepared to offer both of us a job! Both of us! We can go and work on the shipping line together! Go and see the world!

—No! I can't leave him!

—Why not? Do you enjoy living like this? Getting beaten? Not having any food because he spends it all on drink?

—Shut up! Shut up! You selfish, selfish little boy! She hissed. —You have no idea what the war did to your father! I knew him before, and I saw him when he came back. The war broke him. He came back shattered and I'm still picking up the pieces. If I leave he'll fall to bits and I'll never be able to forgive myself. Do you understand?

I looked at her. —This... This isn't...

—No. She shook her head. —No, it isn't... But you have no right to...

She stopped and looked past me.

Stood in the doorway was my father. He raised his glass of whisky to her, smiling. He looked at me, the smile slipping.

—Seems your little scheme failed, didn't it? Stupid fucking idea anyway, taking her away from here. Do you think that would make her happy? We were happy. We were happy as Larry before you came along. You were born and that turned everything to shit. You ruined us, you did. If you leave, we'll be happier. Just me and your mother, nothing getting in our way...

—George...

I opened and closed my mouth. My mother was saying something else, but I couldn't hear it. My father sneered at me, a thin smile spreading across his orange, blotchy face, eyes soft and watery. I felt my hands clench. I'd be heading off in a day's time. I could even head off tomorrow. Tomorrow morning. First thing.

I stepped forward and grabbed the old man around the throat and pushed him backwards, out of the room.

—JIM! NO! Screamed my mother, suddenly loud in the silent house.

I pushed him, struggling and gasping, to the top of the stairs, his face an ugly, savage snarl. There, I held him, on the lip of the top step.

—Jim! Called my mother. —Leave him! He's... he's your father!

He stared at me, clutching my arm, trying to claw at my face.

—Go on then, you stupid little shit! Go on!

I pulled my free arm back, bunching up my fist.

—GO ON!

I stood there, fist tense, nails digging into my palm, muscles feeling like they'd snap.

Behind me, my mother walked barefoot along the corridor towards me.

—Jim... She said.

—You can't do it, can you? Said my father. —Pathetic little shit...

I twisted, punching him hard in the stomach. He gasped, winded, and crumpling forward, groaning. I let go, and he sank to the floor.

—JIM! You...! Screamed my mother. —How dare you!

I turned to her, fist clenched, as she stood there. There was a noise behind me, bumping and thumping in the darkness. I looked back to see my father slide gently down the stairs.

—GEORGE! George! Oh... Oh God, what have you done? Jim? What have you done?

I stared at her, incredulous. She pushed past me and tip-toed down the stairs.

—George? George? Are you... alright? She whispered.

I watched, wondering why she didn't just stamp on him, grind her heel into the side of his head.

She bent and touched her husband's face. —Oh George... There was a tremor in her voice that I will never forget.

I looked down at them and my eyes filled with tears. Why had I never seen this? I had only seen what I wanted to: never the horrible, unpalatable truth.

I shook my head and turned back to my room, shutting the door, pushing the chest of drawers up against it.

She had made her choice.

I did not know it then, but that was the last time I ever saw my mother, leaning over my father, gently stroking his forehead and cheek.

Five years later, aboard *The Trondheim*, moored in Singapore, I received a telegram from him. It said, bluntly: 'Your mother dead. Already buried.'

The unstated implication was clear: it was to undo the final ties that bound me to home, and the funeral had been held without me to remove any further reason to return. I was not wanted.

Over the course of any sea journey there is plenty of time to sit and think. During the return leg I went over all of my experiences with my parents, the first sixteen years of my life, and what little I knew of my father's time in the war.

When we docked in Britain, I had made up my mind.

I got a train to my home town and walked through it, feeling like a foreigner, nervous of looks and glances, seeing deception and threat everywhere. I was going to do something which I knew many would see as wrong on a more fundamental and deep-rooted level than mere law and justice. I was the worst of all men, guilty, walking through the crowds to the scaffold.

I walked slowly up the steps of the central police station and paused at the door. Was I really going to go through with this? I pushed my way in and went to the front desk, my mouth dry and sticky.

I told the sergeant on duty I had information about a murder.

—Murder? Really?

I nodded.

He looked at me, eyes furrowed. —I guess you ought to come with me then, son.

He lead me down a corridor to an office.

—This is our DCI's. He's off sick at the moment, so… Have a seat.

I sat. He stared at the chair behind the desk, pursing his lips, before shifting paperwork to perch on the desktop.

—Tell me what's happened then.

—It's… my mother. Gloria Simpson. My father is a violent man… I think he…

—Gloria Simpson? I remember that… We… We did look into it. An officer was first on the scene. Your father… yes. We… we know what he's like, believe me: we know. But… this? The sergeant shook his head. —Not him.

—It was. It must have been.

—Do you want to know the details? Of how she died? It ain't pretty, son. You're allowed to say no.

I nodded.

—She fell down the stairs.

A weight crushed my insides.

—She slipped at the top and… fell. It was nasty. Snapped her neck, broke both wrists, fingers, skull, hip. She was… unlucky, to say the least. But… it wasn't murder.

—Where was my father when she…?

—He was asleep upstairs. Found her in the morning. It wasn't… good.

—How do you know he didn't… push her?

The sergeant leaned back again. —You really going to do this? Are you? Accuse your own father? Do you think we made a mistake? I'm telling you: we had an officer there, he checked out the scene and made sure it was kosher, know what I mean? He looked at what was there and saw it was just a terrible, terrible accident. I know what your father is like. We've had to pull him out of a dozen pubs. He's seen the inside of our cells a good few times. But murdering his own wife? If he had, we would have spotted it.

—I think… I think you may have missed something.

The sergeant shook his head. —How about I go get the officer who was first on the scene? He can tell you what happened. Maybe show you some of the photographs, how about that?

I shuddered, wrinkling my face up in disgust.

—Thought you wouldn't. Wait here.

He got up and left the office, returning a short while later with the constable: an older man, face lined from cigarettes.

—This here is young master Simpson. He's accusing George Simpson of murdering his mother.

The other officer walked around me, staring at me, going behind the desk and sitting down, still looking at me. His hair was wrinkled and sweaty from his helmet. The smell of car exhausts and tobacco still hung on him.

—Yes. I can see a lot of your father in you, do you know that? He smiled. —It's OK to be angry. You've lost your mother. That will always have a devastating impact on any young lad. He coughed, fingers yellow, and pulled out a notebook, flicking through it. —I believe you were at sea when it happened? Must of been a horrible shock, I'm sure. And it must have given you lots of time to think. Come up with all sorts of ideas. All sorts of theories.

—I know it seems a bit...

—A bit ungrateful? Hmm? Maybe... But perhaps I know what your old fella is like. Maybe I took that into account? Did you think of that?

The policeman pulled out a packet of cigarettes and lit one. I noticed his hand was shaking slightly when he held the lighter.

—I've just got back from patrol. Saw a kid get hit by a car. Terrible accident. Driver was going far too fast, ran through a zebra crossing, caught the kid and dragged her a hundred yards up the road. He knew he was going too fast. He's been nicked for it in the past. And now he's killed a kid. It's crushed him, it really has. That man is an utter wreck. White as a sheet, shaking, crying, whimpering like a beaten dog. He saw what he'd done. The horror of it. I doubt he will ever drive again.

The constable ran a hand through his hair.

—Was it an accident? Yes. It was. Did your mother slip down the stairs? Yes, she did. I was first there. I saw your father. He wasn't guilt-ridden, wasn't beside himself with self-loathing and shock. No. He had just woken up, from a long, peaceful, night's sleep. He'd come down and found her, all bent and broken at the foot of the stairs. He did the right thing: called us. And he was just... sad. Mournful. He'd lost his wife. He'd found her body. He kept muttering about how he should have woken earlier, should have stopped her drinking…

He took a long drag on the cigarette. —Your father is not a perfect man, not by a long way. But he is not a murderer.

—But… I said, not wanting to say it out loud. —The stairs. I… before I left… me and him, we had a… fight. He slipped. I think… the stairs… it was a message. He did it to tell me…

—You pushed him down the stairs?

—No… I… punched him and he… slipped. He was alright. But don't you see? He was getting back at me. For that, for beating him.

—You punched your own father, pushed him down the stairs, and think that because you could do it, he could too?

—No! It's… He is a very violent man. He hit me. He hit my mother! He used to beat us black and blue! He broke her jaw once! This was… This was revenge!

—I hate to say it… but he didn't mention you at all. When your mother was lying dead on the kitchen floor, you were the last person on his mind. I get it: I was young once. And when I was, I thought the world revolved around me too.

He shook his head, slowly and sadly. —From where I'm sitting, I think you have more to answer for than he does. You confess to violent conduct, whereas the only evidence of your father's crime is your… theory, and, in light of your admission, it isn't worth much.

He ground out the cigarette in the DCI's ashtray and looked up at the Sergeant. —I think I'm done here, Fred. Best get back to that report. He stood, looking down at me. —Like I said, losing a mother can be devastating. Really rocks someone to their core. Maybe you just need time. Go and see your dad. Clear the air between you. Go see her grave, but… just don't go spreading malicious rumours, alright?

He walked out, whirling the wisps of hanging smoke as he went.

I felt a hand on my shoulder. —Come on, son. Said the sergeant. And he led me out through the building, telling me as we went: —He's a good copper is old Harry Stannington. I trust him. If he said the scene was kosher, then… I believe him. Maybe you just took her death a little too much to heart, want to blame someone. We've all been there.

He held open the door for me. —Just… just don't drink too much tonight, yeah? Keep your nose clean.

And with that, the door was politely, firmly, shut.

I looked out into the gathering dusk. Buildings loomed up against a sky the colour of a bruise. Dark figures scuttled between them.

I walked slowly down the steps and kept on, wandering into town, watching the streetlights switch on. People hurried home from work or shopping, carrying bags, smiling. As I moved, I felt as though a black wake was forming behind me: a wave of dark oil spreading out, washing over the good, innocent people of this world, polluting them, infecting them. So I walked out of the city centre, into the old streets, the poorest places, still bombed and broken from the war. Shells of houses watched me eyeless from behind chain-link fences.

I found myself on a patch of waste ground, trying to get near a bonfire. A few teenagers stood round it, throwing piles of wood on. I pressed forward as though dreaming, holding my hands up to the roaring flames, watching their silhouettes dance. I realise now that I was probably suffering from mild hypothermia. It reduced the world to a beautiful and peaceful place, seen only in snippets. At one point I was drinking brandy with someone, the next I was sat in their kitchen, wearing a thick duffel coat I'd never seen before, and a cup of tea was burning my hands. I tried to push the coat off me, convinced I was oozing dirty black oil, staining this person's clothes. But she pushed it back on me, this small slip of a girl, telling me to hush now and get warm. I looked up at her, wondering why on earth she would be nice to me.

Peter slowly picked up his coat and hung it on the back of the cubicle door.

Looking at it, it became Louise's dressing gown, hanging on the front of the wardrobe.

He leant forward and pressed the coat up to his face.

The dressing gown smelt of Louise. Her lived-in self. Her back, her neck, her shoulders, her sweat and shampoo. All within the cotton, kept there, held, softly, to be released for his nose.

He got only dust, the floor of the cupboard, and plastic.

One day, he thought, the gown will stop smelling of her. Then she'll be gone. Completely gone.

He sat on the toilet lid and put his head in his hands.

—I was just going off-duty. Said Mr Beaumont, smiling. —Call came in, thought I'd take it, be a friendly face.

Peter sat in the front, smelling the stale, musty smell of car seats, long seeped in stale sweat and aftershave. He felt sick. I've been caught, he thought. And all those faces staring at me from the classroom windows! Watching me be led away to a police car! Would they would think Mr Beaumont is CID?

The sunny streets drifted by. Bright colours under a clear sun, beaming down from a cloudless sky.

—How has your dad been?

Peter looked at Mr Beaumont, even in ordinary trousers and a shirt, with his short moustache and shiny, bald head, he was still very much a policeman.

—He's alright. Said Peter, unsure.

—Oh... Good. I was... just wondering... after the funeral and all...

Peter was trying to remember Mr Beaumont as the man

who had helped him when he fell off his bike, whose big, hairy hands had carefully brushed off bits of grit from Peter's knee, and had smiled and joked as he took him home. He could not imagine him to be like Harry Stannington, lying to conceal a murder.

—I know he and his father didn't really get on, did they? Mr Beaumont continued.

—No…

He had been told, before they got into the car, that it would be OK for him to be sad. He wondered what he meant. Maybe, he thought, this wasn't about the sweets.

—Still, must have… upset him? Made him act weird, eh? Sometimes death affects us in odd ways…

—He burnt some papers. Said Peter, as they turned into their road.

—He what?

—He tried to set fire to some stuff he'd written.

—Oh, Right… Mr Beaumont stopped the Sierra outside Peter's house, clicked the engine off and sat still for a moment, both hands on the steering wheel. Peter watched him, listening to the engine 'ping' as it cooled. Outside, the sunlight slanted down over their side of houses, carving the street into the dark and the bright. Peter looked around and saw the street differently, as though they were at the wrong address. They were in a street which looked exactly the same, down to every detail, but it was not his home, and he was trespassing. He was filled with a sudden, urgent desire to get away.

—Well… Come on! Said Mr Beaumont. —Let's get you inside. And… it'll be… OK… OK?

They got out into the blinding sunlight and walked slowly to the house.

Shortly after, Mr Beaumont left again with Sylvia, Peter's mother, returning forty minutes later, pale but composed. Mr Beaumont deposited Sylvia on the sofa and asked the policewoman to look after her. He looked at Peter and nodded towards the kitchen.

—Peter?

They went in and Mr Beaumont closed the door.

—Sit, please. He pointed at the dining table.

Peter pulled out the chair his mother usually sat in.

Mr Beaumont sat opposite him and pulled out a small, black notebook. —I've been asked by your mother to tell you that the early indications are that your father, I'm afraid, took his own life. There will be a coroner's inquest to determine the precise... but... from the description of the scene, and his injuries... I'm sorry.

Peter sat there, his fingers touching the grained wood on the sides of the seat. Outside, birds sang and traffic drove on the main road at the end of the street. There was a slam of an outside door from down the row of houses, and the faint cry of a baby. Peter could hear the crackle and rustle of the breeze moving through dry grass and trees.

—Peter, I know it's a lot to take in, but it would help a lot if you could answer a few questions.

Peter nodded.

—I was wondering... the papers you mentioned? the ones he tried to burn? What happened?

Peter felt a chill run through him, sweat standing out on his skin.

—He lit a fire and threw all these pages in. He'd been drinking.

—What was it? This stuff he'd written? Do you know?

—Stories from his life at sea. His whole life. Stuff about his childhood, about his dad... He thought he'd killed his mum.

—Important stuff...

—Yeah...

—And he tried to burn it.

—Yeah. Well, he thought he had. I rescued it.

—He thought he had?

—Yeah... I... pulled it out, then put a load of paper in, so he wouldn't notice. It worked: he didn't notice when he tried to rescue them.

The policeman paused in his writing and looked up.

—He tried to rescue them? To pull them out of the fire?

Peter thought back to how hot the fire had been, how his father had reached into it, his desperation. How silent he had been afterwards.

—Yes.

—So they were really important to him? And he knew he'd made a dreadful mistake? How did he react when you told him you'd saved them?

Peter was silent.

—Did you ever tell him?

—I… thought he'd be angry.

Mr Beaumont nodded and wrote in his notebook.

—He could get very angry. Said Peter. —He hit mum. Once. A few times.

—When was this?

—Every now and then.

—When was it most recently

—Couple of weeks back. Last week.

—After he thought he'd burnt his life's story?

——Yes.

—We may have to have a look at this biography, if you've still got it.

Peter nodded.

Mr Beaumont finished writing and closed his notebook.

—Still, I suppose you weren't to know how things would turn out.

—Do you… do you think it made him…?

—I don't know. And… even if you'd have told him… maybe it wouldn't have changed anything.

—But if I had?

—Peter… I don't know. What's done is done. He… did what he did, and there wasn't a note, so maybe we'll never know what the truth is, exactly.

The toilets were cold. A tap dripped. Peter leaned back on the toilet seat, rubbing his hands over his head.

I need to finish the spreadsheet, he thought. Still early. Email it to Geoff. Pray it arrives before the complaint.

He reached down, pulling out his laptop and opening it up.

Just need to put a graph together, attach it all and send it off. Easy. Quick. Get it done.

The screen flickered awake. He keyed in the password and it opened at the browser. The video of Finchley in the police interview was still open.

He stared at the intro screen, the small, emaciated figure sat behind the table. The same figure which was now lying on a steel table in a morgue.

Peter frowned, flexing and clenching his fingers above the keyboard. He rubbed a hand through his hair and looked at his watch. He stared at the grainy image, trying to imagine that person never moving, never thinking.

Opening another tab, he found the website for the restaurant. Clicking on their online menu, he scrolled through, looking at the broths and soups.

He stopped.

That was it. That was what he had. And it was why...

Cooked with ginger, onions, chayote squash and watercress, was their Polynesian Parrot Fish Stew.

Peter stared at it.

Arthur, stood in the living room of his council flat, stared down at the advert for a new restaurant. Books were piled up around him. Bottles and dirty plates covered a dark wood dining table. A fly buzzed at the window, knocking up against the glass. Outside, a lorry rumbled down the road, the tailgate clanking. Music played from the builders working three doors down.

He read again, and again, the list of exotic fish they served. He gently lowered the paper and sat down on the sofa. He started to smile, then stopped himself.

—There we go... He said to Rupert, his son, sitting on

the TV in the corner. —Soon know.

He lifted a glass to his lips, stale dregs from the night before, strands of fluff floating on the surface.

At the train station he found the bar and sat there, watching his train arrive, and leave. He ordered another drink. People around him sat, they laughed and joked. The TV showed the news, with subtitles. On the screen, people sat in tents in New York, hand-painted 'Occupy' signs around them, guitars and earthy colours. Silvio Berlusconi smiled and waved at cameras as he got into a plush car, surrounded by armed men in suits.

Arthur watched the next train leave as well.

On the bar was a collection box and a tray of paper poppies. He looked at them, then at the handful of change in the palm of his hand. Selecting several coins, he leaned forward and waved at the barman.

When he got off the train, he walked through the town. Had he been here before? There was a coffee shop he recognised... No. It was... They all look alike, he thought. Cities. Especially nowadays.

He walked up the hill, looking for the address. When he found it, he stood and stared for a while, unable to move. He heard footsteps behind him. He turned. A young man walked towards him, silhouetted against the car headlights. Arthur leaned and swayed, tripping up the slight step into the restaurant.

Everywhere was red and gold, seats, tables, wallpaper and plates. People turned and looked, chattering and clattering. Smells of rich sauces filled the air, unctuous plates and wafts of rice-flavoured steam were breezed along by serving staff in white shirts.

One of them looked at him.

Arthur coughed, wiping a hand across his mouth, a tickle in his throat. He held up a finger and the waiter pulled a menu from the rack and walked among the tables, selecting one near the middle. Arthur stumbled forward. Was it his? His hand brushed something that might have been hair, he flinched, and noticed there was a fish tank on one wall. He frowned at it, but then he was at the table and the waiter was handing him the menu.

Across from him sat Rupert, silent.

Arthur looked down at his hands, trembling, sweaty, holding the red and gold menu.

—You want food, Mr Finchley?

He looked up at Ting, holding a battered metal stewpot.

—Good food, Mr Finchley! Parrot fish. You like parrot fish?

Arthur looked around the table. Sam leaned forward, holding out a bowl and spoon to him.

—You've been asleep. Do you remember? You were upset. Screaming, shouting. You punched Li. We gave you a little something to help you sleep. You're still quite groggy, aren't you?

Arthur took the bowl with old, wrinkled hands. Sam looked no older.

Li sat on the other side, beside Richard. Above them were the entrance steps to the engine room. He could smell the metallic fug of dripping sump oil.

Ting slopped a ladle-full of chunky broth into Arthur's bowl. The white meat firm and solid. Pork, he thought. Nice pork stew. His stomach growled.

—You don't... said Richard, reaching for Arthur's hand holding the spoon, eyes close on his. Arthur frowned at him, then down at the stew.

—Please, Mr Finchley, eat! It's very nice! Said Ting.

—We caught it. Said Sam. —It was a whopper. Really was.

—Please... Arthur, don't. Said Richard.

Arthur looked down at the stew, his stomach rumbling and groaning. He smelt light saltiness, a metallic-tinged, meaty aroma. He dipped the spoon in and picked up a chunk of meat, raising it up to his mouth. His teeth bit down, finding it slightly stringy and fatty.

Richard shook his head and stood up from the table, walking away through the restaurant, towards his cabin.

—Don't worry about him, said Ting, slopping stew into the other bowls. —He just got cabin fever, y'know? He get banged on the head. Like you! But not as strong as you! He not eat, so he get weaker. Weaker and weaker. We get strong! Good stew! Keep us alive!

—We... we have no radio, no flares, nothing. Said Sam. —We barely have means of getting water and food. This... this could be our last proper meal.

They all started digging in, treating the dish with reverence. Arthur watched, still chewing. His head swam. He could hear the slap of the waves against the grounded hull, feel the stuffy heat as the sun shone down on the upturned boat, baking the exposed underside. But he was in the restaurant. Why was he there?

Rupert stared at him, then down at the bowl Arthur was eating from. Arthur looked down and saw there was nothing there.

—Are you ready to order, sir?

Arthur nodded and pointed in the menu to the parrot fish stew.

—Wine?

Arthur nodded. —Red. He rasped, his voice husky.

Moments later, the bottle was before him and poured into his glass. He drank, feeling the liquid sink down into him, calming him.

Left alone with the bottle, he looked at Rupert across the table.

—I was always proud of you. Immensely proud. Never told you that.

He rolled the wine around in the glass. —I liked you. Liked having you around. Used to look at you and see myself. Sort of. You looked like me. When I looked at you, I was proud, and I began to have a bit more pride in myself.

Rupert stared back, head down, hands placed on the

table.

—You made me feel better about myself. That's... what. I never felt worthy before you came along. I just felt... I don't know... Worthless. Unworthy.

Rupert rolled his eyes.

Arthur looked at him. He took another gulp of the wine and re-filled his glass.

—I remember when you were born. You were handed to me by the midwife. And I held you, this curled up, screaming thing, covered in blood and mucus, and I realised that... that one day I might drop you. It was terrifying.

He took a heavy swig of wine.

—When you died, it was awful, but, to be honest, it was also like a weight had been lifted. You were gone. I didn't have to look after you, to worry about you.

Rupert took a deep breath in, stretching out his fingers, growing them into the weave of the table cloth.

—The worry, the guilt, was always there! Did I spend enough time with you? Too much time? Did I buy you too many presents? Did I answer all your questions? Help you enough? Guide you? Being a father is hard. I didn't want to be like my dad, you see. Distant. Mournful of a place he hated, resentful of the place he lived. Always somewhere else, even when he was sat beside me.

Rupert laughed, throwing back his head.

—Yes, yes. You're right. I wasn't there. I was away, earning money. I got money from TV that I never would have made through academia. And I did that for you. I did all that for you.

Rupert put his head on one side, raising an eyebrow.

—So... really, I only had that boat because of you. If I'd not needed an expedition boat for filming, then...

Rupert shook his head.

—No. No. Arthur sighed. —I've been down this path before, haven't I?

Rupert nodded.

—We agreed, didn't we?

Rupert again nodded, closing his eyes.

—Your food, sir. Said the waiter presenting the bowl to Arthur.

Rupert was wide-eyed, staring at the bowl. The stew was grey in colour, lumps rising to the surface under a thick sauce. A sprig of herbs was set daintily to one side

Arthur stared down at it. He dipped the spoon in and lifted a portion of grey, flaky meat, crumbling under its own weight.

He looked at Rupert, who was shaking his head, mouth open.

—I've got to…

He lifted the meat to his mouth and bit down.

Rupert pointed, howling, his jaw stretched, teeth extended, tongue curled, eyes bulged out from his face.

Arthur held the meat in his mouth, unable to move. Finally, he chewed, gently, savouring the meat. As he swallowed, he felt his chest heave, the tears blur his vision.

Rupert tore at himself, screaming, purple, claws extended, ripping chunks from his chest, flinging them at Arthur as he writhed and screamed. Arthur ducked and swept the bowl aside, running for the door, knocking the table over. Rupert flailed after him, his hot breath and bone-raw fingers at Arthur's neck, clawing, clutching, out the door and down the street.

Peter stared at the menu.

To anyone else, he thought, it would stand out as beautiful and exotic. Something of wonder and excitement. But everyone's life was their own, a chain of events particular to just that individual. And to Arthur Finchley, it became something else. An answer. Of sorts.

He opened the spreadsheet again and scrolled to the bottom, highlighting the final figures.

He clicked on Create Graph.

The pie appeared within the box. He shifted it to the side.

Creating another box, he lined up the amount lost through late on-boarding, then divided it by the percentages for the causes.

Looking at the final figures, he breathed in, feeling suddenly very light, almost as though he would cry.

—Pete? Pete!

—What?

—PETE!

—Claire? What is it?

—Get them…! Get them off me! They're… all over me!

—What? What are?

—Insects! They're all over me! Scratching, biting! Little legs… pincers… scurrying…

—What? Really?

—Yes!

He heard the duvet be kicked around, the mattress above him rattling and shaking.

—I can't get them off me!

—Claire… there's nothing… You're just… just nodding! Just the pills, that's all. Go on, take another, get off to sleep.

—Don't… No! Peter? Get up here! She began crying. —Help me get rid of all these insects! Please? They're… biting and itching!

—Fuck's sake, Claire! There aren't any insects… it's just… He pushed himself up from the floor and got his elbows onto the bed, looking across at her as she scratched her naked body, clawing at the skin. —Why are you…?

—GOD! Get them off me!

He got up onto the bed and grabbed her hands, pinning them above her head.

—There aren't any insects! You'll scratch till you bleed! Stop it!

She wriggled and fought beneath him, trying to pull free.

—Get off! Get off me! Oh my God! Oh my God!

—Please! Claire! Stop it! You're going to…

There was a click and the door swung open, letting in cold air from the stairs, the smell of outside still there, lingering.

—You filthy fucks.

Peter looked up to see two men stood in the doorway, wearing balaclavas. He frowned. There was a third behind them, peering from the shadow of the hallway.

It was his father, grinning, holding up soot-covered hands: fingers burnt and blackened.

Peter shook his head. —I… I'm so sorry!

—Fucking too right you're sorry.

The taller man in the doorway swung something down onto his skull, knocking him sideways into darkness.

—Ben's barely fucking dead and you're doing this?

Claire screamed.

Peter reached out, trying to push her away. Something hard cracked down on his arm: a flash of pain and the pop of breaking bone. The bat come down on his side, his hip, his legs. Lying on the bed, he kicked out at the attacker, flailing with his bare feet. The body got onto the bed, making it spring beneath Peter, and began punching his stomach, his face.

—Come on, stop this man! Let's just get the gear and go, alright?

—You see what this sick little shit was doing?

—Just…

—With that skank! I'll fucking kill him!

—No man, just leave it!

Peter had pulled his good arm up over his head, curling up as much as he could.

—Get the FUCK off of him! Screamed Claire.

The weight lifted from the bed. Peter could hear heavy breathing, the rasping of lungs damaged by smoking and recurring bouts of pneumonia.

—Fuck you. He muttered.

—What did you fucking say?

—I said FUCK YOU!

The bat hit him round the head.

—Fuck you too.

Someone grabbed at his broken wrist and dragged him off the bed. He gasped at the pain, reaching up. The bat came down on him again. Boots kicked and stamped on him. He lay there, arms up over his head, smelling the iron of his blood, the soft smell of earth from the shoes, the dustiness of the carpet.

He could hear Claire screaming, hear the two men yelling something, but it sounded faint, distant. The kicks seemed softer, as though he was wearing thick padding.

He felt himself gradually falling through the floor, past the thin carpet and the hard floorboards, into soft, billowing nothingness.

Peter began to feel cold, frozen. His skin itched, his mouth was dry. There was some sort of rough blanket over him, and a weight holding down his face and head.

He could hear voices, a phone ringing. He opened his mouth to speak, but only a moan came out.

Someone beside his bed moved their chair.

They almost spoke. He heard them take a breath, their mouth opening. He felt them move closer, a small weight upon the bed, something clanking, then a cold, wet glass at his lips. He sipped, clumsily. The dribble was wiped away from his chin with thin, cold fingers.

He tried to smile, to say thank you to his mother, but felt himself falling, tipping backwards into soft cloud again.

Time blurred, slipping in and out of consciousness, seeing light and dark, day and night, the same doctor leaning over him, their tie a change of colour, the nagging sense of déjà vu in everything he saw and thought. The police came and went, the dreams swirled and swept through him. Time remained elusive, and his days were spent staring out at the same beds across the ward, the same huddled shapes, the same blue uniforms hurrying past, until he fell asleep again, and the dreams returned, of volcanoes and war, of beds and boats.

Then one day he heard the chair shift, and he opened his eye.

Looking back at him was Irvine.

—How you doing, tough guy?

Peter stared at him.

—They got you looking real pretty, don't they? Eh?

—Hello Irvine.

Irvine smiled. —Thought for a moment... But you can... OK. The nurse said...

Irvine stopped, and looked away.

—Irv...

—Sorry. It's just... seeing you here. Y'know? It's like... just makes me...

Peter looked at him. Irvine had a fading bruise around one eye going up onto the bridge of his nose. One hand was wrapped in a plaster cast.

—Irv... Where's Claire?

—Don't... no. He waved his good hand. —No.

—Irvine, why did the police say she didn't exist?

Irvine looked at Peter. —The police have been?

—Well... yeah. Look at me. They came to have a bit of a laugh, didn't they?

—What did you tell them?

—Not a lot. Don't worry about it. Just tell me Claire is alright. Please?

—Fuck Claire! What did you actually tell the police?

He had edged forward on the chair.

—Don't worry! I said... I said I didn't really see anything. I gave them some vague hints and stuff, but... they'll never...

—Hints? What the fuck do you mean?

—I didn't give them any names, absolutely not. No.

Irvine stared, then got up and came and leant over the bed.

—So what the merry fuck did you tell them?

Peter stared up at him.

—Steve Robinson.

—What? Why the fuck did you do that!

—They were threatening me with obstruction if I didn't tell them what happened.

—Oh Jesus! Oh Jesus, Mary and Joseph! We are so fucking dead! Dead and fucking buried!

—I didn't fucking name him!

—Eh?

—I just, y'know, described his tattoo. On his neck. Y'know? 'He who dares, wins'.

—Christ on a bike! They'll know for sure! Fuck! He'll fucking crucify us!

—No he won't. They won't…

—How do you fucking know?

—How many dodgy cunts do you know with that exact same tattoo? Hmm? Now calm the fuck down!

Irvine stepped backwards, folding his arms, glancing around him.

—What happened to Claire? Please? The police said there was never any record of her. Anywhere. They did a search. Nothing. She doesn't exist.

He shook his head. —No, no… you don't… you really don't…

—Irv! For fuck's sake!

—Alright… sighed Irvine, leaning against the bed. And bending down. —It was all her idea.

Peter stared up at him. —What?

Irvine shrugged. —She came up with it. She organised it. Ben. The drugs. Couple of goons to beat you up. And now she's gone. Disappeared.

—No…

—Why do you think she over-reacted so much when she was told Ben was dead? Eh? She was lying, the whole time.

—Bullshit. Utter, fucking…

Irvine shrugged. —Told you not to ask.

Peter looked down at Irvine's broken fist again.

—Did you see her? How do you...?

—Course I haven't fucking seen her! And neither will you! Ever! And you'll be better off for it! Won't you?

Peter nodded. —Do you think she's safe?

Irvine shrugged. —Sure. Bitch like that, always looking out for number one. Course she is.

Peter smiled. —Yeah.

Irvine looked around the ward, staring at the other patients.

—Good crowd of fucking nutjobs in here, eh?

Peter laughed. —It's the nutjob ward. Headcases. Head trauma. They say I'm going to have problems. They don't know what. They say I'm lucky to be walking and talking. Some of these guys never will.

Irvine looked down at him. —Yeah...

There was silence.

—I'm going to leave. Said Irvine. —Going to go to some other town. Might go back home. See the folks. Best get away before trouble starts brewing. Know what I mean? Don't want to end up in the bed next to you, do I?

Peter nodded.

—I suggest you do the same. Continued Irvine. —Get away. Lie low. Stay out of trouble.

—Not a lot left here for me.

—Yeah. Best way, isn't it?

Peter nodded. —Good seeing you, Irv.

—Fucking poof. Just don't go nutting anyone's cricket bat again, alright? He laughed, then stopped.

—Sure thing. Said Peter. —You look after yourself.

Irvine looked down at him, silent and serious. He leaned forward to say something, his mouth open. But he stopped, and merely nodded, turning away and leaving the ward.

Peter checked the headings on the spreadsheet, adjusted the cell formats and moved the graph to the opening page, creating a text box and copying through the concluding figures. He started typing up the outcomes and strategy, explaining the results and what they should do, and how much money they would save by doing it.

Nearly there, he thought. Keep busy. Get it done. Almost over. Right on the cusp of...

—What are you doing? She had murmured from the pillow.

He stopped.

—I just need a shirt. He whispered. —Sorry. Go back to sleep.

—Moving out, are we?

—Louise... don't start that again.

—Why not? Look at me. Jesus! Look at me!

He turned. She was thin, white. The faint remains of hair framed her head. Eyes bloodshot and sunken.

—How long do you think this can go on for? She panted.

—You'll... be fine. We'll see the specialist this afternoon at three. Wait till you hear what he has to say, please?

—Oh, we both know what he's going to say...

He sighed and opened the wardrobe.

—We don't. Stop trying to predict the...

—It's going to be bad.

—Louise, you're not a doctor. You don't know that, do you?

—It's my sodding body!

Peter pulled out a shirt and stared at the collar, shaking his head.

—We... we need to talk. She said. —About what will happen... About...

He took a deep breath, looking into the darkness of the wardrobe. —We'll go to the hospital this afternoon...

—Oh for Christ's sake! Face up to it, Peter!

He turned and stared. —I am!

—No! No... you're not! Look at me! I'm...

He shook his head, putting the white shirt over his arm. He looked over at empty bottles of fruit juice and water cluttering up the bedside table. He picked up the tray from the floor and started clearing them away.

—Do you want some more of those protein drinks? He asked.

—Why bother?

—You've got to eat…

—No… You. Why are you bothering?

—Come on now… Calm down. Don't be like that.

She pushed herself upright.

—Jesus… Don't you know?

—What?

—I thought you knew. She cleared her throat. —I've fucked a lot of men behind your back.

Tears welled up in her eyes. He stared at them, then down at an empty bottle of water, which had an outline of a mountain in thick, white line across its label.

—All those conferences I've been on? All those trips with work? All of them… I always fucked someone when I was away. I always found some big cock to please me.

He imagined the mountain, veiled in freezing snow, the air above it thin and cold. He was flying above it all, looking down, seeing all the ravines and rocky peaks, covered with the soft, white flakes, swept into deep drifts.

—Most of the time, I didn't really mind who they were. Didn't care. Grabbed them in the bar. Took them upstairs. Everyone was at it. All bored business people, out for a bit of fun.

He realised that the snow would once have been flowing through the oceans, gurgling and rushing along jet streams, until one day when it was lifted from a warming surface, floated high up into the sky, where it condensed into cloud and sailed majestically over land, looking down on fields and towns.

—At that conference in Copenhagen? That was… was Brian Hendricks, the manager from Foreign Sales. The Glasgow thing? I fucked Michael Race from Accounts Admin. And the public inquiry in London? I fucked John

Waters, Paul Kincade, Alistair Green and… and…

She stopped, her voice cracking.

He opened his mouth to say something.

—Do you understand? I fucked all those men because they were all better than you! Big, muscular men who could fuck all night! Could fuck me upside down! Fuck me with their big, fat cocks! Filling me! Pumping into me!

And the clouds gradually drifted until they came to the mountain, where they met cold air, the freezing winds that whistled through the range, and the water started to crystallize, to bunch together, swirling round, white and sharp.

—I loved it! Of course I did! Sex with you was always shit!

She spat the words.

—You never made me come! I never climaxed with you! I had to pretend! Make little 'oh, oh, oh' noises to try and speed you up! Stop you rutting away endlessly on top of me! Boring. Miserable. They made me come. They made me shudder with… They…

And the snow fell, gradually drifting down over the mountain, sailing in with the wind, twisting and turning, fluttering, swirling, round and round, down and down.

Tears were rolling down her face.

He shook his head.

—You…

But he could not say it.

When the snow settled on the frozen slopes, it quickly got buried beneath more snow, packing it down, hardening it into the rock, where it would stay for years, centuries.

He turned with the tray, going to the door.

—Do you remember Bob Krigelow? She said, her voice high, loud.

He stopped, not turning.

—I fucked him.

Her voice wobbled.

—He was better than you.

Peter opened the door and walked down the stairs, along the corridor to the kitchen, where he smashed the tray into the sink as hard as he could, knocking over the clean plates and cups. The empty bottle with the image of a mountain bounced out and rattled across the floor. He stared down at it before stamping as hard as he could, teeth bared, crushing it beneath his slipper.

Breathing hard, he slumped against the worktop and put his head in his hands.

—Must get to work. He said. —Work. Keep busy. That's what they told me. Keep my mind off it.

He finished the brief text summary and moved the title and the start of the evidence down. He scrolled through, checking it looked alright, then hit 'save as PDF'. The laptop blinked, and another window opened with the print-ready spreadsheet, title page showing, with the written conclusion and the graph. He looked up at the number of pages. Seventeen! He imagined Geoff's face when he opened it.

Always good to impress the boss. Keep them on your side.

He remembered the face of Bob Krigelow, walking through Credit Control, looking left and right at them all, stopping and chatting, putting his fingers on your shoulder, leaning in to whisper into your ear. —You know James won't be your team leader this time next week, don't you? And with a wink he would move on to the next person.

—He never tells everyone, said Andy. —Just enough to undermine the team leader.

—He's such a dick.

—It's because we're doing better than he is. Not much of a stretch, I'll grant you, but it's always the same. His team are doing badly, so he'll sabotage another team to make him look slightly better.

—He just fucking grins all the time…

—I'm just glad not to be female. He always, shall we

say, 'pushes the boundaries of the acceptable'.

—Yeah...

Peter stared at the door Bob had left through

—Oh... I'm sorry. I didn't mean... Said Andy.

—Why can't they just sack him?

—For what? He never oversteps the mark. Never fails so badly that they have reason to.

—He's a fucking creep! If they employ him they ought to be able to un-employ him too.

—You ought to know why not. Has she not told you?

—She? Who? Told me what?

Andy smiled. —If they sacked him without good reason he'd just take the company to an employment tribunal. Sue us for every penny.

Peter shook his head. —Yeah, I know. He's still an asshole.

—Don't worry. I know Louise. You really know Louise. She has a plan.

—Why...? Why would I know Louise? I mean...

—Yeah? Just good friends? One-time colleagues here in Credit Control? Nothing more? He leaned closer. —I've seen you two having lunch, seen you heading off together after work. And I also see... He nodded at Peter's monitor. —All the emails between you!

Peter quickly minimised the window, blushing.

—It's fine, Pete! Don't worry! You're allowed! I know she's moved up into Management, but this isn't school! She isn't one of the teachers! You two are allowed!

—Well... we were a bit worried about gossip.

Andy blew a raspberry. —What for? They're only jealous. He smiled. —She's nice. I like her. Did you...? When she left or was it when you were here?

Peter looked at him, then around. —No. Look... He shuffled over. —It was after... after she got the nod for the training. We knew we wouldn't be working together anymore. We never thought it was... 'wrong', just a bit weird: that we'd be together all day at work, and then what? Go to a restaurant, sit opposite each other, find something else to talk about other than computer systems and credit codes?

—Fair point. Andy smiled. —She's very practically-minded is Louise, isn't she?

—Yeah.

—So has she told you her plan?

Peter grinned. —I thought she'd told everyone her plan. Everyone except… and he pointed at the door Bob had left through.

Andy shook his head. —Well… I had my own ideas, of course, being aware of some the dark arts available to HR.

—What she's said, is that she's basically going to make him know he isn't liked, y'know? Pull the same shit on him that he does to everyone else: hold meetings with his staff without inviting him, tell them to ignore him, she'll reorganise his department without telling him, buy everyone cakes and presents, apart from him… Whisper in people's ears… Really, really undermine him at every possible level. She's going to make him want to leave.

—Or make him snap loudly enough to give them cause to fire him…

Peter paused, looking at the door. —Yeah, or that.

—Don't get me wrong, I think it sounds like a decent plan.

—Yeah. She knows what she's doing.

—Yeah…

—We've… we've already planned a holiday. For when… When he…

—Oh yeah?

—Well, she said she'd need a break. Just a weekend away in Rome.

—Very nice! Get used to staring at ruins. Going in the new year?

—Nope. Already booked for three weeks time.

—Wow! She's confidant.

—She knows what she's doing.

—Scary mind-manipulation shit. You sure you want to get into a relationship with this woman?

Peter laughed.

He hit 'send' and saw the On-Boarding email wink back into the folder.

Gone.

Sorted.

Hopefully… it'll work in my favour. Get Geoff to think twice.

He gently closed the laptop, and sat there, hands resting on top, breathing softly.

A finger tapped.

Bob Krigelow.

It tapped again.

He frowned. His fingers tapped.

Why is Bob Krigelow bothering me?

The fingers stopped tapping.

—Just promise me you won't… fuck about. Said Louise, walking beside him up the road, car headlights sweeping past them, the faint sound of music from the pub behind them.

He frowned, slightly. —What? You mean…? He laughed. —Sleep around? Or…

—Yeah. And whatever else. Just… don't, alright?

—Yeah, sure. I… I took that as understood. Basic rules of relationships.

She looked down at her feet. —I think we both know that there aren't any real rules: nothing stops people doing terrible things, not if they want to.

—Sorry. No. Of course. Are you alright?

—Yeah… Sorry. Didn't mean to get… It's just… She reached out and clasped his arm. —I wasn't expecting this. Getting into something… I wasn't looking for it.

He smiled. —Me neither. He lied.

She sighed. —No, seriously. I really wasn't.

—And then I came along!

—No. Someone else.

He felt himself go cold.

—They really... they wanted just a one-night thing... I didn't realise. It was...

—Do you... like him?

—What? God, no! This was... it was a few months ago. Before we... He was a colossal wanker. Met him in a pub. That was probably my first mistake: getting off with someone in a dimly-lit bar. But...

She looked at him. —You don't need to know the details, do you? We met a few times, then he stopped returning my calls. A friend of mine phoned and said she'd seen him with someone else. I went round, yelled at him. God... it was embarrassing. He said he hadn't. But he also said he was sorry. He said he thought we were just casual. He didn't think he needed to phone me.

They walked a bit further down the road.

—I hated the feeling that every time he wasn't with me, he was shagging someone else. Or that when he was with me, he didn't want to be. Who wants to live like that? Have it hanging over them? It just felt wrong. So I don't want that, not with this.

—I won't...

—I just wanted to be clear. To say it out loud. Make sure you understand.

They walked passed a bus stop. People were stood, staring down the road past them.

—If I'm honest, I'm not sure I can. Have you seen my face?

She turned to him, and smiled. —Your face is beautiful. Your face is better than his was.

—Was? What did you do to him?

She laughed.

—You're special, you know that? Really wonderful. I was ready to become a nun after that arsehole. And then I met you. You changed my mind.

He smiled, feeling his face warm.

—The nuns' loss.

She laughed again, throwing her head back.

Sat in the toilets, Peter remained still, hands clenched round each other, fingers clasped white.

He saw her face in the darkness, glowing in bed beneath him, teeth clenched as she juddered, gasping, eyes tight shut.

A tap dripped in the toilets.

—Do you ever want to get married? He had asked, sat beside her in bed, Sunday morning sunshine streaming in through the window.

—Hmm? She turned a page. —What?

—Married. Have you ever thought…?

—Are you asking?

She looked at him.

—No! Just… wondered.

She looked back down at the magazine. —Whoever I married, he'd have to be fucking wonderful. She smiled.

—Yeah… I just…

Their eyes met.

—I…

—What?

—I want to know! Seriously! What do you think?

—I think… She turned the page. —I think that my parents had a really bad marriage. They grew resentful to each other, became resentful of the institution. Jo and I were stuck in the middle. Their experience used to make me think that anyone who wanted their relationship to be legally binding is someone you don't want to be in a relationship with.

—Used to think?

—I… can see the… She stared out the window. She laughed. —I always said I didn't want to get married. But now… Now I can see that you don't simply become married: you just realise one day that you're going to spend the rest of your life with one person, and all you want is that person.

He looked up at her.

—Yeah. Yeah you do.

She grinned. —Despite all their flaws!

—I try to look past them, he said, running a finger along her thigh.

She laughed.

Sitting in the toilet, he stared at the door.

Slowly, eyes elsewhere, he picked up the laptop and slipped it into the case.

If I… If I go now… I could be home by…

I could be home in time for…

I could be home…

He put his face in his hands and took a deep breath.

I…

I've fucked up.

She…

She said…

And I believed her.

I should've known.

I should've thought!

Should've remembered…

Fuck.

Is it too late?

He flicked his wrist round and looked at his watch.

Three o'clock has been and gone… twelve, plus four, sixteen hours ago.

Did they ring?

She can't have gone on her own?

They would have rung. Called her and found out if she was alright. —Just tell me the results, please, she would have asked. The little voice spoke into her ear. —So sorry, it said, wittering on. And she would have nodded, listening, then pushed the button to end the call, tossing the handset down on the wrinkled duvet, beside the laptop and a book. And she would have lain there, staring up at the ceiling.

Peter stood, hands grabbing at his jacket and the laptop case.

I have to go...

Have to...

Be... there.

She had lain there, waiting, listening for the car in the drive, footsteps, a key in the lock. The sun slowly setting.

He slid open the bolt and walked out of the toilets, trembling hands grasping at metal handles, slippery coat getting in the way.

Outside, the corridor was bright with sunlight coming through the glass doors in Reception.

—Pete?

He turned. The man was still in his coat, hand on the push plate of the canteen door.

—Geoff?

—Ah! Glad I caught you, Pete: wanted to have a word.

—Can this wait? I've... I know what this is about. And... I can explain, but... right now... I have to... go.

—Go? But you just got in, right? Unless you've been here all night, eh? Pushing for promotion? After my job?

Peter frowned at him. —What? No...

—I just wanted to say, just very quickly... Geoff took his arm and gently lead him away from the canteen doors. ——how valuable you are to us, not only because how important your work is within the team, but how much we enjoy your company. You are a trusted and important member of the team and I hope that you will want to stick around for many years to come.

The evening had darkened and deepened, the bedside lamp would have been turned on, and still she would have looked to the window, waiting.

—I remember when I came here, when I was made manager, you made me feel welcome, you helped out as much as possible, showed me the ropes, so to speak. You didn't bitch about having a new boss recruited from outside the team, even though most of the others did. You got on with it and showed me that everyone could get along and do a good job. I always really respected you for that. And you could have been a real stick-in-the-mud, like the rest of them, about the new way of working. But you weren't. You've really picked it up and run with it. Sitting in the canteen: love it. Always there, so that people can bring ideas to you, access every level of the business, always available, that kind of thing. Love it. Brilliant, creative thinking. You realise half the guys just went home! Ridiculous, isn't it?

In the depth of the night, when all the world seemed silent and still, black and alien, it would have been very easy for her to imagine that she was the only human in the universe, alone in the endless inky ocean, hung about with scattered, glittering stars. And gradually the current will have pulled her deeper down, swallowing her up, shutting off those floating specs of light around her.

—I've always been impressed with your results, always clear, always concise, always well-presented. Good stuff, and I want it to continue.

And when the sun rose and shone down upon the land, it streamed in through glass, green-filtered by trees, pushing darkness into the nooks and corners around the room.

—But look, I've been trying to get hold of you, I think your mobile has been turned off, and the whole email system crashed yesterday…

—What? The emails… crashed?

—Yes! Everything lost! Been telling them for years the intranet system in this place desperately needs updating…. Whole system went down yesterday evening like the proverbial heavy-metal balloon. Nothing sent or received after six. IT had to dump everything that was pending. Didn't you know? Bloody hell, you have been focused on this project, haven't you! Anyway, now I've got you…

The bright morning sun would gaze down at a bald figure lying still and quiet in a room that smelt of soiled sheets and mildew.

—Look, I hope you know how much I like, and

respect, you. I want you to know that, because of that, you can talk to me any time you like. Say whatever you like and I'll just listen. I won't judge at all. Not my style, not in this case certainly. Do you think you can do that? Talk to me when things get rough?

The body was emaciated, flesh shrunken back to the bones. The skin was pulled tight over the skull, stretched thin, revealing veins and the cavities around the eyes.

—I know things aren't going well for your wife. Wife? Sorry! Partner. Louise. How is she? Last you said, she was going for the post-therapy scan. When do you get the results?

Peter looked suddenly at Geoff. —Oh... It was... It was yesterday.

Geoff stared back, an eyebrow raised.

—Really? Okay. Well what did they say?

Peter shook his head and shrugged. —I don't know. I... I was here...

Geoff took a deep breath. —OK. Look: I think you ought to take a bit of time off. We talked about this, didn't we? Everything will be OK here. That project you're working on? It's not due for another couple of weeks, so... But I think it's really important that you go home, isn't it? And stay there, with Louise.

Her skin was cracked and peeling, red-raw around the lips and eyes, pock-marked with sores and spots.

—My aunt had cervical cancer, and my uncle really struggled to cope. He was ex-forces. Falklands Veteran. Saw all sorts. Tough as the proverbial nail. But when his wife became terminally ill and there was nothing he could do, he went to pieces. Absolutely broke him.

Only a few, fine, curled hairs remained on her head, emerging between the scabs of blistered skin. A yellow crust lined her eyes, and mouth, where the lips were grey, gums red-raw, teeth loose. Her tongue was swollen and dotted with white ulcers.

—Look, Pete, why don't I give you a lift home? Hmm?

You... you can barely stand upright. Come on.

Geoff took Peter's arm again and started towing him down towards the bright, sunlit glass doors in reception. Peter looked out, just as a red car drove slowly past, the wet tarmac reflecting the red in a shimmering mirage. Peter gasped and looked again, searching for Ben's face among the puddles.

Geoff searched through his pockets as they walked along.

—It's for the best. Take a couple of weeks. Try and relax. Give yourself some time to... to get to grips with things.

His hand flapped about his pockets. —Where did I put my bloody pass...? ...Had it a second ago. He grinned at Peter. —Got in with it, didn't I?

He continued to fumble about from pocket to pocket. Peter slowly reached out towards him. Geoff stopped and watched as Peter's hand moved slowly to the centre of Geoff's chest, where the pass dangled at the end of a lanyard.

Geoff laughed, and leaned forward to drag the card down through the slot. There was a buzz and a click as the door opened. Peter took an involuntary gulp as the cold, fresh breeze rushed in.

—Right, come on. I'm parked just across the way there. Best get a wriggle on before it starts raining again...

Peter looked at him for a second.

The hand laid on top of the duvet was cold and stiff. The chest did not rise. The heart was silent.

She had gone.

He knew it.

—Sorry... He spluttered, thumbing back down the hall. —I've just realised... left something in the... Just be a minute.

Peter turned, pulling away his arm, and walked quickly back down the corridor, towards the canteen door, turning at the last moment towards the toilets. Stopping at the corner, he looked back towards Geoff and the open door, sunlight streaming in. His heart pounded as he looked at the outside world. Geoff watched, frowning. He stepped towards him.

Peter lurched into the toilets, the door slowly swinging shut behind him.

Acknowledgements

I want to thank Phil Taylor, Don Verdin, Bob Murdoch, Ray Simes and Stuart Jones for their stories of life in the Merchant Navy. (For other firsthand accounts visit: iancoombe.tripod.com, or bbc.co.uk/history/[and search 'merchant navy'], or merchant-navy.net, or balmaha.net/mnavy/) Much of the sequences of war and army life came from: Encyclopaedia of Modern War by Roger Parkinson (Routledge and Kegan, 1977); Encyclopaedia of Modern British Army Regiments by P.D. Griffith (Sutton Publishing, 2006); Oxford Companion to Military History, ed. Richard Holmes (OUP, 2001); The Visitors Guide to the Normandy Beach Landings by Tonie and Valmai Holt (Moorland Publishing Co., 1989); and A Dictionary of Battles by David Eggenburger (George Allen and Unwin Ltd., 1967). And thank you to the good, good people of Wikipedia for almost everything else! Special thanks also have to go to Rosie Hunt, Tessa Keeble and Sarah Moore who read early drafts, and to Dave Stoker, who not only hammered the importance of pacing into me, but gave me the impetus to get writing. He is much missed.

About the Author

Richard McCarthy studied art and has an MA in English Literature from the University of Sheffield. He has written book reviews and numerous short stories. You can read a few of them at rchrdmccrthy.com. He is married and lives in Sheffield.

Printed in Great Britain
by Amazon.co.uk, Ltd.,
Marston Gate.